A WARM KIND OF WRECKAGE

A WARM KIND OF WRECKAGE

ALYS MYKELS

PART ONE:
UNDERTOW

1

CHAPTER ONE:
RETURNING CURRENTS

The rain was a relentless grey smear against the window of The Chiron Café, blurring the already muted hues of Ashcliffe-on-Sea. It was the kind of drizzle that seeped into your bones and settled there – a constant reminder of the town's damp soul. The soundscape was a familiar comfort: the mournful cries of gulls wheeling overhead, punctuated by the steady, rhythmic thump of waves against the cliffs, and now, the quiet hum of the café itself. Krissy moved with a practised grace, polishing mismatched teacups – chipped porcelain, faded floral patterns, a hefty pewter one – each bearing its own small story. She answered the phone without looking up, her voice low and slightly detached. "Hello?"

"It looks like we've got a boy!" Eve Thornton's voice burst through, bright and bubbling with happiness, laced with a touch of weariness. "He's perfect!" A hearty, Welsh howl of joy followed – Geraint, Eve's husband, was ever enthusiastic. Krissy paused her polishing, a flicker of surprise crossing her face. "Oh! That's lovely." A small smile touched her lips, fleeting and subtle as the rain on the glass.

Miles away, in Cardiff, Llewellyn Morgan was walking home, laden with bags of local Welsh cheeses and sourdough. He was planning on having the kind of ploughman's dinner that would make the gods weep. The phone rang – a familiar, insistent tone. He answered without hesitation. "We need you! We just found out – he's going to be a boy!" Geraint's voice crackled through the line. Llewellyn didn't bother to ask questions. His decision was made in that single moment, a quiet certainty settling over him. He started gathering his things – a crumpled scarf, a worn copy of the Mabinogion, and a half-empty mug – a little haphazardly, but with the focused energy of someone already halfway out the door. His flat, small and comfortably cluttered with books and student relics, felt suddenly empty. I'll call mum on the train, Llewellyn thought, and then maybe get Geraint to help me talk her round.

Hours later, the rain hadn't really stopped, not truly. It had softened to a persistent drizzle – the kind that clung to everything and settled in the creases of your skin. It suited Krissy, really. Like the town itself. She was perched on the edge of Rita's worn velvet armchair, sketching in her notebook – a habit she couldn't shake, even when she should have been busy fielding complaints about Earl Grey strength or recommending tarot spreads. It wasn't that she didn't like it here, in Ashcliffe-on-Sea. It was just a little fragile at times. Like one of those mismatched teacups – beautiful on its own, but a little wobbly when you looked at it too closely. Her life felt similarly constructed: a collection of borrowed spaces and fleeting connections. Rita and Tom's cottage was cosy and comforting, all floral wallpaper and the scent of sage; Eloise's flat above The Chiron Café was gloriously cluttered with crystals and astrological charts – smelling faintly of patchouli and something vaguely herbal. Chamomile? Krissy was a collector of temporary homes, it seemed. A nomad in her own way.

Her illustrations – that's what kept things somewhat stable. They were melancholy, mostly, tinged with a touch of the surreal. Ashcliffe demanded it, she supposed. They captured the light and shadow of the town – the grey skies reflected in the slate roofs, the ghosts of sailors lingering on the harbour, the feeling that something ancient and slightly mournful lay just beneath the surface. She'd done landscapes, portraits, even a rather unsettling series depicting Ashcliffe's local folklore, but lately she'd been getting weirder commissions. A deck of cards featuring werewolves arguing over a silver candlestick. A family portrait where everyone had tiny, iridescent wings. "Another one?" Rita grunted from behind the counter of The Chiron Café, stacking teacups. "Fancying yourself a demonologist now, are you?"

Krissy grinned and nodded, capturing Rita's grumpy expression in her sketchbook – a flash of shrewdness and quiet resilience. "Just trying to keep up with the local legends." A small detail caught her eye – a smudge of ink on the windowsill, reflecting the muted light. The bell above The Chiron rang, a cheerful chime that seemed slightly out of sync with the drumming rain. It pulled Krissy from the careful shading of Rita's eyebrow and deposited Llewellyn Morgan – Geraint's older brother – squarely into her peripheral vision.

Llewellyn was a solid shape against the grey outside, now softened by the warm glow of the café. Rain-damp, he looked like he'd just stepped out of a Welsh river – a little wild, a little ruggedly handsome. A worn leather jacket, faded navy with patches on the elbows, hung loosely over a dark green sweater, and his boots were scuffed but clearly well-loved. He carried himself with that same relaxed confidence he always did, like he'd just strolled in from wherever he pleased, as if distance and delayed trains were merely suggestions. He paused for a moment by the door, shaking off a spray of water that shimmered briefly in the light, before turning his head slightly. It was those eyes, really, that caught Krissy's attention – deep brown and flecked with gold, they held a kind of knowingness, like he'd seen a thing or two and wasn't entirely surprised by it. A hint of sun-kissed skin peeked from beneath his collar, evidence of the Welsh sunshine he'd undoubtedly been enjoying. He exuded warmth – not just the physical heat of a man who'd likely spent some time outdoors, but something deeper, more comforting, like a slow-burning hearth on a chilly evening.

It wasn't an obvious reaction, not at first. Krissy didn't jump or gasp. But as he moved further into the café and his eyes met hers, she felt it – a subtle widening of her eyes, a small intake of breath that caught in her throat. He smiled then, an easy, genuine smile that seemed to reach all the way to his eyes. Krissy found herself moving instinctively. She closed her sketchbook with a little thump and pushed it slightly aside on the table, rising quickly. Before she could over-think it, before her nerves could fully take hold, she was offering him a quick, slightly awkward hug. "Llewellyn? What are you doing here? Oh, but you're as handsome a devil as you were at Eve and Geraint's wedding!" He chuckled, returning the embrace with a warmth that chased away some of the dampness clinging to her.

"And you, Krissy," he murmured into her hair, his voice a low rumble. "Still sketching away, I see." He pulled back slightly, tilting his head to look at her sketchbook. "What is it this time? Another grumpy portrait?" Llewellyn settled at the counter with a quiet grace that somehow managed to look both casual and deliberate. He slid into the worn velvet armchair opposite Krissy, immediately pulling his jacket tighter around him as if trying to ward off not just the chill but also the lingering dampness. "Black coffee," he said to Rita, his voice warm and laced with a hint of Welsh lilt. "And make it strong."

"Ooh, I don't know about that," Rita said, "Here at The Chiron Cafe there aren't many rules, but one is that you get what you need, not necessarily what you want. And I," she pointed to her own smiling face "am the one who decides what you need. You'll need to remember that when you're behind the counter, Llewellyn." And with that, Rita went about mixing something alarmingly floral smelling.

"'When you're behind the counter'?" Krissy queried, ears ready for gossip.

"Ah, yes." Llewellyn pushed his hair from his damp forehead. "I'm to be a bit of a fixture here for a while... Rita and Geraint have sorted the whole thing out, apparently, all I had to do was turn up. And, well, here I am.

The café itself was a comforting embrace – a small, cosy space crammed with books stacked haphazardly on shelves that threatened to spill onto the tables, tarot cards spilling from overflowing boxes, and mismatched mugs clinging to hooks above the counter. The air smelled deliciously of tea blended with the comforting aroma of sage from Rita's gardening herbs and a touch of vanilla from the always-burning candle on the counter. It felt like stepping into a well-loved secret – a place where time slowed down and stories were readily offered. "Right then," Rita said, "here's your beverage, and is tonight too soon to start? Or do you want to clean up a bit first?" Rita's gaze lingered significantly on Llewellyn's muddy boots. Llewellyn grinned, taking in the café with a thoughtful gaze. "A slight exaggeration, I think. Though the coastal path was rather boggy."

"Those boots do have the general air of having been through a war or two." Krissy chimed in, unable to help herself.

"A fair point," he conceded, gesturing to his scuffed leather boots. "They've certainly seen some battles – mostly with sheep, although there were some pretty fair streams they've forded too." He offered with a small smile.

The conversation flowed easily from there, punctuated by the clinking of cups and Rita's occasional grunts of approval or mild complaint. They talked about the weather – a particularly grey and persistent drizzle that seemed determined to settle over Ashcliffe for the foreseeable future. "It's the kind of rain that seeps into your soul," Llewellyn commented, taking a sip of his coffee.

"Yes," Krissy agreed quietly. "Perfect for stories."

"Ashcliffe certainly has its fair share of those," Llewellyn said, leaning forward slightly. "Everyone here seems to have at least one good ghost story or local legend. Makes you wonder what secrets are buried beneath all that slate."

"Oh, yes, if living here has taught me anything, it's that Ashcliffe is a town built on secrets," Rita offered from behind the counter, polishing a mug with a practiced hand. "And a little bit of melancholy."

"You've clearly been here long enough to capture it," Llewellyn observed, turning his attention back to Krissy. "That's why I thought you were sketching – capturing the soul of Ashcliffe, one gloomy landscape at a time." He subtly tilted his head and noticed her sketchpad lying open on the table. "What have you got there?" He gestured casually towards it, and Krissy instinctively shifted slightly, pulling the sketchbook closer to her. It was a subtle movement, almost unconscious, but Llewellyn caught it. He didn't say anything further about the sketches, just continued to watch her for a moment, his dark eyes thoughtful, as if trying to decipher something within her.

The bell above The Chiron Cafe's door rang again, a little brighter this time, as Eve Thornton burst through, followed by a slightly rumpled but beaming Geraint. They were carrying a small black and white ultrasound photograph and looked, despite the obvious exhaustion around their eyes, like two people who'd just been given the world.

"We have photographic proof!" Eve announced, holding up the scan with a flourish. "Our little man!" The image showed a tiny, slightly blurry face – it was undeniably adorable, but Krissy didn't know what else to say about the little soon-to-be person. Llewellyn leaned forward, his own expression softening as he studied the photo. He let out a low whistle. "He's got your nose," he said, nodding towards Geraint.

"And your stubbornness!" Eve laughed, squeezing his arm. Geraint, always the more demonstrative of the pair, enveloped Llewellyn in a hearty hug. "Good to see you, Llew! You're just in time. We were starting to think you'd escaped to Patagonia."

Llewellyn returned the embrace with genuine warmth, his grip firm and reassuring. A small smile played on his lips – a flash of something deeper than simple politeness. He felt it then, that familiar pull, a quiet warmth spreading through him at the sight of them. He choked up slightly, a tiny prickle of emotion he quickly pushed down. "You both look... wonderful," he managed, his voice a little hoarser than usual. "Tired," Eve corrected, tilting her head and giving him a playful nudge. "But wonderful."

"I'm going to help out," Llewellyn declared, his gaze steadying. "Make sure it gets a bit of the Morgan spirit even with a Thornton name." He nodded towards Geraint, who took the hint – and the name – with a grin. A comfortable silence settled over them for a moment, punctuated by the steady drumming of rain against the windows. Krissy watched Llewellyn, his hand resting protectively on Eve's arm, and felt a small pang – not quite jealousy, but something close. He seemed to know exactly how to make her smile, how to ease her into conversation with just a touch or a glance. It was a subtle thing, but it struck Krissy all the same.

Rita, who'd been meticulously stacking teacups behind the counter, observed them both with her characteristic shrewdness. "He's good with her," she said, finally turning to Krissy. "Like he's always known her." Krissy shifted slightly in her chair, unsure how to answer. It was true, wasn't it? There was something about Llewellyn, a quiet certainty that made you feel like you'd known him for years, even if you'd just met. "I think," she said finally, choosing her words carefully, "that he just has a good eye for people."

"Well yes, there's certainly that," Rita agreed, returning to her teacup-stacking with determination. "And a good heart. Don't let him fool you with that rugged exterior."

Krissy caught Llewellyn looking at her, then, his eyes holding a hint of something she couldn't quite decipher – perhaps a shared understanding of what it meant to seek out little pockets of comfort in a sometimes-grey world. Just then, Geraint shuffled over and placed a second steaming mug in front of Llewellyn. "Black coffee," he said, grinning. "Extra strong. You'll need it." Llewellyn took a grateful sip, his eyes meeting Krissy's again for just a fraction of a second before returning to Geraint. It was enough. Rita noticed, friendly as ever and used to Krissy's emotional currents. "He'll be here a while," she said, watching Llewellyn with a knowing smile. "And I think he's exactly where he needs to be."

The last of the customers had shuffled out, leaving behind the lingering scent of conversation and cake. The rain continued its steady drumbeat against the windows, now punctuated by the soft glow of the café's single hanging lamp. It was one of those satisfyingly quiet moments that followed closing – a small pocket of stillness before the next rush. Krissy stacked the last few teacups onto a shelf, while Llewellyn methodically wiped down the counter, his movements economical and precise. "So," he said, leaning on the counter with his mug, "werewolf erotica? Seriously?"

Krissy chuckled, a little self-consciously. "Apparently. Eloise hooked me up with one of her astrology friends: she wanted a series depicting her werewolf husband serenading her with a silver candlestick. Said it was 'to spice things up.'"

"And you sketched it?" Llewellyn raised an eyebrow, a hint of amusement in his voice.

"Of course," she replied, drying her hands on a tea towel. "Look, it wasn't bad... but she was very specific about the candlestick." She paused, then added with a shrug, "I once did a map for a breakup party. Complete with little illustrated arrows pointing out all the best places to stage passive-aggressive arguments."

Llewellyn grinned. "That's brilliant. You capture the weirdness of life perfectly."

"It's mostly just... odd commissions," she admitted, her gaze drifting towards the window. "I don't know what I am – a professional observer of people's strange desires." He walked over and started to clear away some stray napkins. "You're more than that. You see things. That's why Rita keeps asking you about what's buried beneath all those slate roofs."

"She's got a point," Krissy said quietly. "Ashcliffe does have a way of... collecting secrets. You know that from Eve and Geraint, though."

"It's like it remembers everything," Llewellyn agreed, nodding. "That's probably why I'm here." He took a sip from his mug.

"It's funny, isn't it?" Llewellyn continued, turning to face her. "My brother is always chasing something – folklore, legends, old places. He'll be off in the Orkneys one week, tracking down a Pictish ruin's hidden truths, and then somewhere like here in Ashcliffe the next, looking for the ghost of a man obsessed by songs on the tides. For years, he was constantly moving."

"And you were...?" Krissy prompted gently. He hesitated, a flicker of something – vulnerability? – crossing his face. "When I was feeling most vulnerable, after... after Violet left, Geraint was in the Orkneys. Completely unreachable. It wasn't his fault, really, just the nature of his work – chasing shadows and old stories. But it... itched. It felt like being adrift. Like losing another piece of something you thought you knew."

Krissy shifted slightly in her chair, sensing a shift in tone. She'd noticed it before - the way he held himself sometimes, that quiet sadness lurking beneath the surface. "I get that," she said softly. "Moving around... it can feel like you're always just on the edge of something. I was always moving before I set up some roots of my own here in Ashcliffe. My walking group, the Ashcliffe Afternooners, is basically the reason that Stella, Eloise, and Albert got together. And now they're so much a part of The Saltwater Siren that everyone just accepts them. As they are." There was a silence between them, broken only by the rain and the hum of the refrigerator. Then, Llewellyn leaned forward slightly, his voice barely above a whisper. "I thought I was doing that, back in Cardiff. With Violet, you know? But then... well, that didn't work out."

Krissy was burning to lean into the story she just knew was lurking there. She nodded slowly, her gaze fixed on his."Yeah," she said. "Sometimes it's just way easier to be a little bit lonely than to risk getting completely destroyed."

Llewellyn looked at Krissy for a longer moment this time – a shared look, unspoken but laden with understanding. It was as if they were acknowledging something deep within each other – a shared history of loss and the quiet effort it took to trust again. A hint that they'd both experienced the ache of being adrift, of feeling like you're waiting for someone to pull you back in. "Well," Llewellyn said finally, breaking the silence with a small smile. "Looks like we've got a lot of cleaning up to do before anyone else shows up." He gestured towards a pile of upturned chairs. "And maybe," he added, his eyes twinkling, "you should do the mopping. These muddy boots aren't going to help matters, are they?" Krissy smiled back – a genuine smile this time, warmer and less fleeting than before. "Maybe," she said, rising to her feet. "Maybe we should get on with it. Together."

"I'll be here when you're done dodging," Llewellyn said simply, his voice a low rumble against the quiet of the café. He watched her gather her things – sketchbook, pencils, a half-empty mug of luke-warm coffee – the movement comforting, if not yet entirely familiar. Krissy turned – a small smile playing on her lips. "You're good at that," she murmured, tilting her head slightly. It was more than just obser-vation; there was a warmth in her voice now, a subtle shift from shy observer to something more receptive. As she headed for the door, Llewellyn caught her eye – a lingering look that said, "Soon." Not a de-manding promise, but a quiet certainty, like he'd already anticipated her departure and was patiently waiting for her return. It held a touch of amusement, too, as if he knew exactly how to draw out her hesita-tions.

He nodded, turning back to the counter. "Just needed someone to help with the mud. And maybe a little company." He started wiping down the surface again, his movements deliberate and efficient. Krissy stepped out into the rain, pulling her cardigan tighter around her. The drizzle felt softer now, less relentless, as if mirroring the shift within her. Looking back at Llewellyn, she saw him watching her – a small smile playing on his lips. Then, she was gone, swallowed by the grey of the evening. The sea was visible in the distance, restless and vast, its dark surface mirroring the sky. A single light from the café spilled onto the pavement, illuminating a puddle that reflected Krissy herself – slightly blurred, perhaps, but with a touch more warmth now. A sense of both anticipation and unease lingered, but mixed with it was the quiet promise of something new. Something rooted in the rain-soaked streets of Ashcliffe and the lingering gaze of a man who knew exactly how to pull a person back from their tendency to wander

2

CHAPTER TWO: A TROUBLE THAT SMILES BACK

The rain in Ashcliffe-on-Sea had settled into a proper grey, cling-ing to everything like a particularly attentive lover. It was one of those mornings where the light struggled to pierce through, painting the narrow streets in shades of pewter and slate. The air smelled thick with salt – a familiar, bracing tang – layered beneath the comforting scent of damp wool from the few locals pulling up their coats. Mid-morning now, almost noon, and the town felt comfortably settled after the night's downpour. Llewellyn took a slow sip of his coffee, the warmth spreading through him like a small comfort. Ashcliffe was... quiet. Not necessarily bad, just quieter than Cardiff. He liked it, in a way, this gentle rhythm of things. It felt good to be useful, to have a job – even if it was simply coming up with orders at the Chiron Café. A flicker of nostalgia for the bustle of his old life in Cardiff brushed against him – the sharper smells, the louder music – but he pushed it down. He'd come here on duty, and so far, it felt right. A little bit like coming home, though he hadn't lived here before.

The café was already stirring. Mrs. Prior was meticulously arranging her display of locally-made jams, a small mountain of raspberry and blackberry vying for attention. Old Mr. Jones, with his perpetually damp tweed cap, was nursing a black coffee and reading the paper – probably complaining about something, Llewellyn thought with a smile. A young couple, clutching steaming mugs, were debating over which table to claim. It was the same comforting hum of activity that had greeted him yesterday, and the day before. He took another order - "Flat white, please" – and his hands moved with an ingrained efficiency, grinding beans, frothing milk. Small tasks, simple pleasures, grounding him in this new place, this temporary role. He glanced out at the rain-slicked street, a small smile playing on his lips. Ashcliffe was proving to be a good kind of grey.

The bell above the door of The Chiron Café announced her arrival with a cheerful jingle – a little louder than necessary, perhaps, considering the rain. Krissy burst in, a small gust of wind and damp wool, leaving a trail of droplets on the worn floorboards. She wasn't dishevelled, not exactly, just... collected, as if she'd been somewhere interesting and hadn't quite managed to shake it off. Before anyone had a chance to offer a 'good morning,' or even properly greet her, Krissy was launching into a quick bit of café gossip. "Did you see Tom trying to wrestle the delivery van this morning? He nearly took out poor Mrs. Lucas's rhododendrons! Said he needed his Earl Grey urgently. Honestly, that man and his tea." She punctuated the statement with a small, delighted giggle. "And then the driver nearly slipped in the puddle outside: he was covered in mud!"

Llewellyn, wiping down the counter, raised an eyebrow. "Sounds like you've had a busy morning."

"Just keeping up with Ashcliffe," she replied, sliding onto a stool at the counter. "It's surprisingly eventful, you know." A quick glance confirmed he recognised her – a fleeting smile as she remembered their previous encounter. It was funny how quickly familiarity could bloom. Before he'd moved to Ashcliffe, Llewellyn had rarely ventured out of

Wales. But Eve and Geraint's wedding had stirred something in him, something that changed what home meant to him.

"Llewellyn," Krissy began, but he cut her off before she could finish her thought.

"Llew's fine," he said, a hint of amusement in his voice. "Please call me Llew." It wasn't just formality; there was something particular about it – a small step towards intimacy, a desire to chip away at the polite distance. Krissy tilted her head, considering him. "Llew, you say? Alright then. You're Llew." A touch of amusement danced in her eyes. "It's... shorter."

"It is," he agreed, smiling.

"What was Rita thinking, Llew," she continued, already surveying the space around them, "I think she could have chosen a better selection for the music. Little bit dreary, don't you think? And that forlornly chipped teacup over there – a tragedy! Needs replacing." She gestured vaguely with her hand, adding a final, observant detail. "It's all very... Ashcliffe, of course."

Llew chuckled, deep and low. He raised an eyebrow and turned to Krissy, who was meticulously arranging sugar packets in a neat little row. "How do you like my footwear today," he asked, nodding towards his newly-cleaned boots.

"Did you do them yourself? Especially for me?" Krissy asked, her eyes twinkling as she took in their pristine state. It wasn't really a question; more of an observation delivered with a playful lilt. It was enough to spark the beginning of a new day's verbal dance. "Well," Llewellyn said, leaning against the counter, "they were rather dusty. And I did happen to have a bit of time."

"Oh, you clean them that much?" Krissy tilted her head, studying him with a keen gaze. "Must be a sign of a good heart. Or maybe just a very tidy soul."

"Perhaps both," he replied, a small smile playing on his lips. "What about you? You look like you've been through a wind tunnel."

"Just returning from a spirited debate with Councillor Davies about the merits of blackberry versus raspberry," she declared dramatically. "He was very insistent that blackberry is clearly superior. It's all about the tartness, you know."

"Tartness," Llewellyn repeated, nodding thoughtfully. "Good to have someone who appreciates the finer things in life."

"Like perfectly polished boots?" Krissy shot back, raising an eyebrow. "Or a good cup of coffee?"

"Those are all certainly admirable qualities," he conceded. "You're quite observant, you know."

"It's a necessary skill in Ashcliffe," she said with a shrug. "Otherwise, you'll miss everything."

"So, you've been keeping up with the gossip," he observed, amused.

"Naturally," she said. "It's a full-time job." She paused, considering him. "You're from Cardiff, aren't you? What did you do there?"

Llew gestured around himself. "I worked in a coffee shop," he replied simply. "But it was much more... usual than this place!" Krissy laughed, a full-throated, head-thrown-back, guffaw at that. "Yeah," she agreed, "Cardiff probably doesn't have anything quite like The Chiron Cafe." Krissy said, her voice softening slightly. "So you're used to slinging tea across a counter for thirsty locals!" She grinned. "What else did you do?"

"I... played rugby," he admitted, a hint of self-deprecation in his voice.

"Really?!" Krissy exclaimed. "Do they still have all those lovely rugby lads in Cardiff?"

"A few," he said with a smile. "Though I haven't played seriously for years." He'd noticed she was quick-witted and observant, and there was something... genuine about her curiosity. Something that reached beyond the pleasantries. And just like that, it started again – the rapid-fire questions, the witty observations, the gentle teasing... a comfortable rhythm settling between them, fuelled by coffee and a shared appreciation for the small, quirky details of Ashcliffe.

The rain hadn't entirely relented, it was a persistent drizzle, clinging to the panes of The Chiron Café like a shy guest. Eve stepped in, a little out of breath and laden with bags – a crumpled paper bag from the local market, containing plump purple plums and a loaf of crusty sourdough, jostled against a brightly patterned tote filled with baby socks and a ridiculously soft cashmere blanket. She navigated the familiar space with a quiet grace, her worn boots making a gentle sound on the worn floorboards, a soundtrack to Ashcliffe's steady rhythm. Llew, polishing the counter with a practiced hand, looked up as she entered. It wasn't an enthusiastic greeting – no wide smile or boisterous "Morning!" just a subtle lift of his eyebrows and a flicker of something deep behind them, like recognizing a familiar current in the tide. There was a warmth to him now, not overt, but undeniably present – a feeling that settled around Eve like the café's comforting heat. It wasn't surprising; he always seemed to notice things others missed, absorbing the small details of a room and the people within it.

"Evening," he said simply, his Welsh accent deepening slightly as he spoke. "Didn't think you'd be back this early." Eve offered a brief smile, placing the bags on a stool by the counter. "I couldn't resist buying this for the little one," she replied, nodding towards the blanket. "And Geraint insisted I needed plums. Says they're good for pregnant ladies."

He raised an eyebrow, a ghost of amusement playing around his lips. "Pregnant ladies always appreciate a bit of luxury. Did he approve of the socks too?"

"Absolutely," Eve chuckled, rummaging in the tote. "Said they looked like tiny, fluffy clouds." She pulled out a pair – a pale blue with little silver sheep embroidered on them – and held them up. "He's bound to be obsessed with sheep." A beat of comfortable silence settled between them, punctuated by the gentle hiss of the espresso machine. Then, Llew said, his voice carrying just a hint of surprise, "You know, you still manage to make me feel like I've acquired a new hobby every time you walk in here."

Eve's lips curved into a genuine smile this time, a touch more expansive. "That's because you are, Llew. You're always acquiring something new with me."

It was a small thing, really – a shared acknowledgement of their history. It wasn't a grand declaration of affection, but it held the weight of casual familiarity and unspoken understanding. "Remember that time we got stuck in that torrential downpour after the mine and Geraint's wedding? You practically dragged me to the shelter, convinced I'd turned into an icicle."

Llewellyn's eyes softened slightly. "How could I forget? Your shoes were soaked through, and you were complaining about everything." He paused, a small smile playing on his lips. "You looked like a drowned little mouse."

"Well, you're the one who insisted on taking the scenic route," she retorted, playfully pushing him with her elbow. "And I was freezing." A fleeting memory – not hers alone – flickered in the air between them: Llewellyn shielding a shivering, mud-splattered Eve from a sudden burst of rain on the way home from Louisa's Cove. A small, unguarded moment of protectiveness, months ago.

He smoothly transitioned back into service mode, efficiently grinding beans and frothing milk for another customer, but there was no losing that underlying warmth now – it felt deeper, like the café itself had settled around her, welcoming her back to its familiar embrace. "Here you go," he said, handing a flat white to an elderly woman, his gaze drifting back to Eve for a moment. "And don't forget to look out for the rain."

"I will," Eve replied, already scanning the shelves for a bottle of lavender oil – Geraint had been particularly insistent on a calming scent in the nursery. She felt it then – that subtle tug of connection, that feeling of being seen and known, not just as Eve Thornton, the postwoman and archivist, or the wife of Geraint, but simply... as herself. As she moved to collect her plums, Llewellyn added quietly, "You're a good kind of complicated, you know that?" And in the quiet of The Chiron Café, surrounded by the scent of coffee and rain, Eve knew he was right. She always had been.

The rain was still doing its thing – a persistent, grey drizzle that clung to everything in Ashcliffe like it wanted to stay. It wasn't the dramatic, booming kind you got up on the cliffs, but a quiet, insistent one, seeping into your bones and settling there with a gentle dampness. It smelled of salt and wet slate, a familiar combination that always felt... comforting, in its own way. The rain had muted the colours of the street outside – turning the already-grey buildings into shades of pewter – and it softened the sounds too. The usual clatter of Ashcliffe was muffled, absorbed by the dampness. Llew started his morning like he always did nowadays: wiping down the tables at The Chiron Cafe. It was a small ritual, keeping things presentable, but it grounded him. Mrs. Prior was already fussing over her jam display – raspberry and blackberry battling for dominance on her little tiered shelves. "Morning, Llew," she chirped, adjusting a particularly plump blackberry with an expert hand. "You're looking like you've wrestled with the weather itself."

He chuckled and continued his work, glancing at the regulars settling in for their morning coffee. Old Mr. Linden was already buried in his paper, probably complaining about something – Ashcliffe residents of his particular vintage were rarely without a grievance, Llew was realising. And then there was Tom – always quiet, always observing – nursing a black coffee and reading what looked like ancient nautical charts. It was good. Quietly good. A little predictable, perhaps, but... good. It felt nice to have a routine after... well, after everything. This job – helping out at The Chiron Cafe, being near the sea – it wasn't glamorous, not by a long shot, but it was solid. And right now, solid felt pretty damn good. He took a slow sip of his own coffee, letting the warmth spread through him. Another cup? Maybe. Before his mind was fully made up, though, the bell above the door announced Krissy's arrival.

Krissy burst into The Chiron Cafe like a small gust of wind, shaking off rain and a little bit of Ashcliffe's gloom. She was a touch more dishevelled than yesterday – a stray strand of hair (shades of green and purple this week, like the Aurora Borealis she'd insisted) clung to her cheek, and her denim jacket looked as if it had just survived a minor skirmish with the elements. It was a small detail, but it felt like she'd left in a bit of a hurry. "Morning," she offered, her voice a little breathless.

"Morning, yourself," Llew replied, already turning to grind beans for another customer. The exchange was quick, familiar, but there was a subtle current beneath it, something a little warmer than yesterday's polite greetings. The banter began almost immediately. "Those boots are still muddy," she observed, tilting her head and taking in his scuffed leather footwear.

"They're reliable," Llew countered, a slight smile playing on his lips. "And they'll keep me warm."

"At the cost of looking like you wrestled with a particularly grumpy sheep," Krissy shot back, a dry amusement in her voice. "Least they look good on you!"

He chuckled. "You're determined to make me feel self-conscious this morning, aren't you?"

"Just stating facts," she said, leaning against the counter and surveying the café with a critical eye. "Did you see how many crumbs Mr. Linden left? A disgrace."

As he made her coffee, Llew tried to steer the conversation towards something more substantial. "So, what's keeping you busy today?"

"Just sketching," she replied, her tone vague. "Mostly landscapes. And occasionally, portraits."

"Anything interesting in your world?" He asked, handing her the mug.

She paused for a moment, taking a sip of the coffee and letting it warm her hands. "Nothing much," she said finally, though it didn't quite ring true. "Just... trying to capture the light."

He noticed she was quieter than usual, almost guarded. It wasn't a dramatic shift – she always had a touch of that Ashcliffe melancholy about her – but there was a stillness to her, a slight reluctance to fully engage. He caught himself noticing little details: did she avoid eye contact? Did she linger on the space between them for just a fraction longer than usual?

"You seem thoughtful," he observed gently.

She shrugged, returning his gaze briefly before quickly looking down at her coffee. "Just thinking about rain," she said simply. He noticed then – a small detail, easily missed - that her fingernails were painted a deep shade of indigo, flecked with tiny silver stars. It was a subtle thing, but it caught in his attention. He wondered if he'd seen them before.

"You've got a good eye for people," she said, a small smile playing on her lips as she finally met his gaze again. "It's why you're always getting into trouble."

He raised an eyebrow, amused. "And what makes you so observant?"

"Well," she replied, tilting her head slightly, "I have to be. Otherwise, I don't notice how much everyone else is trying to hide."

The conversation drifted, settling into a comfortable rhythm of small observations and gentle teasing. Then, Krissy piped up with, "Oh, how's it going with the meringues? Rita says you've been battling them for weeks."

"They're proving to be... resistant," Llew admitted, a touch of self-deprecation in his voice. "I swear they have a personal vendetta against me."

She laughed – a genuine, bright sound that seemed to momentarily lift the grey from the café. And then, almost as an afterthought, she said, "Well, I did a deck of tarot cards for someone last week. A whole series. It's called 'Werewolf Erotica.'" It was a small thing, but it sparked something in Llew. He studied her face for a moment – a flicker of amusement mixed with... well, was that a hint of vulnerability? "Really?" he asked, genuinely intrigued. "Was it the same person as the werewolf and silver candlestick?"

Krissy laughed, a sudden shock of sound. "I love that you remembered that! Yes, it was her! Eloise's contacts are full of ideas... they keep me quite busy, in their ways." The laughter faded from her eyes, and she took a slow sip of her coffee. "Sometimes you get commissioned to do the strangest things."

And then, it started. A brief flash of memory, triggered by her words. Llew found himself transported back to a rainy evening – a grey drizzle falling on Cardiff, clinging to the streets like wet wool. It was late, and the street-lights cast long shadows. He remembered being at Violet's flat, talking... but she hadn't been listening. She'd been lost in her own world, sketching in her notebook. She'd been a tattoo artist, and she really believed in the 'art' part of her life: she'd rather have been seen without her clothes than without her sketchbook. He saw himself – a little younger, a little more intense – arguing with Violet about something small, insignificant. But beneath the surface of their conversation was a current of unspoken tension, a feeling that they were drifting apart. He remembered the way she looked at him – a mixture of affection and... sadness. She'd been so vibrant, so full of life, but then... suddenly, she wasn't. Or she was, but not with him.

He saw her hand – reaching for his, then pulling back just slightly. A small gesture, easily missed, but it held a weight of unspoken emotion. He remembered the feeling of loss – sharp and sudden – when she'd simply gone. No explanation, no goodbye – just... gone. The scene was muted, almost dreamlike, filtered through the rain and the soft glow of the street-lights. The quiet sadness, the lingering feeling of being adrift after Violet left. He remembered the hollow space she'd left in his life, a space that hadn't quite filled itself with anything else. Then, as quickly as it had begun, the flashback faded. Llew blinked, drawing back into the present. He looked slightly dazed, as if he'd just woken from a dream. Krissy was watching him intently, her expression thoughtful. "You alright?" she asked softly. "You were... lost for a moment." Llew nodded, still mildly reeling from his memory. "Take a minute, Llew, I'll finish this."

Krissy was halfway through wiping down the counter when Rita, with a deliberate movement, called her over. "You," she said simply, gesturing with a tea towel, a slight smirk playing on her lips. "Come here for a moment."

"What is it?" Krissy asked, a little impatiently.

"You're always bolting," Rita observed, not unkindly – but definitely with an experienced eye. "When things start to feel... real. You bolt when things get warm. That's not freedom, that's fear." Rita shot a quick glance at Tom, who was polishing mugs behind the counter and offered a subtle nod of agreement.

Krissy paused, considering her words. "Maybe," she admitted quietly. It wasn't a denial; it was an acceptance – a small acknowledgement of the truth in Rita's observation.

"Don't mistake running for being brave," Rita continued, her gaze steady. "Sometimes you just need to stand still for a bit. And sometimes... you need someone to catch you when you do." She paused, then added with a touch of gruffness, "It's not easy, is it? Especially when he's around."

Krissy's cheeks flushed slightly. Tom let out a low chuckle from behind the counter. "Well," Rita said, returning to her task of stacking teacups, "don't let him scare you off. Just... don't bolt too quickly." There was a definite edge to her words this time – an invitation, perhaps, or a warning.

"Noted," Krissy said softly. "Duly noted."

Llew watched them for a moment - a quiet observation of the two women who seemed to know each other effortlessly. Then, he turned back to his work, but as Krissy headed out into the rain, he said quietly: "You're a good kind of complicated, too."

Krissy paused at the door, turning slightly. "It's a double-edged sword," she replied, a small smile playing on her lips. She caught Llew's eye – and for just a moment, their gazes held – a shared understanding that wasn't spoken but felt deeply nonetheless. "You already know that." As she stepped out into the drizzle, Llew noticed something: she was looking back at him, a subtle lift of her chin suggesting a challenge, or perhaps... an invitation. He caught her eye again just as the door closed behind her – a lingering look, filled with warmth and a hint of something more... demanding.

3

CHAPTER THREE: NIGHTSHIFT CONFESSIONS

The rain began to fall with that characteristic Ashcliffe insistence – not a downpour, more of a persistent, clinging drizzle that seemed determined to soak you to the bone. It was just after eleven, maybe twelve, at night and the last of Rita's and Tom's cheerful chatter had faded into the comforting hum of the refrigerator behind the counter. The rain intensified for a moment, drumming a soft rhythm against the windows of The Chiron Café – like an old-fashioned metronome. It wasn't exactly messy, not in a chaotic way. Just... lived-in. A stack of slightly chipped coffee cups leaned precariously on the counter, casualties of a busy afternoon. A scattering of napkins, speckled with the ghosts of Earl Grey and sesame, lay crumpled beneath the tables. A thin film of dust kissed the brass counter.

The soft glow of the hanging lamps cast everything in a warm, honeyed light, chasing away some of the grey from the outside world. It was one of those moments where the rain and the interior combined to make it feel perfectly cosy – like you could happily spend an evening nursing a lukewarm cup of tea and losing yourself in thought.

But there was also a subtle feeling of loneliness. Not unpleasant, just...present. A quiet acknowledgement that, despite the friendly faces and familiar routines, Krissy and Llew were both, in their own ways, a little adrift. It was the kind of solitude that settled into you after a long day – comfortable enough to be content with, but perhaps a touch yearning for something more. The scent of roasted coffee beans mingled with the damp wool of the rain outside, creating a uniquely Ashcliffe aroma – a blend of melancholy and promise.

Right," Krissy announced, leaning against the counter with a dramatic sigh as if she were unveiling a particularly difficult masterpiece. "Let's just get this over with. My job situation is...well, it's like a small, slightly chaotic circus." Llewellyn raised an eyebrow, wiping down the counter with more enthusiasm than seemed necessary. "A circus? Did you juggle flaming pastries?"

"Worse," Krissy grinned, launching into her list. "First up: werewolf erotica. Tarot deck. Seriously. A very passionate divorce lawyer with an interest in the mystical needed a deck to help clients visualize their post-furry fury."

Llewellyn chuckled, a genuine sound that warmed the room. "Divorce lawyers and werewolves? Ashcliffe is certainly... varied."

"You have no idea," Krissy said, warming to her subject. "Then there was the breakup kingdom map. A detailed topographical survey – valleys, rivers, treacherous peaks... you know, typical breakup stuff."

"Did it have dragons?" Llewellyn asked, a hint of amusement in his voice.

"Maybe! I didn't ask. And then there was...oh, and let's not forget the miniature portraits of grumpy cats for a collector obsessed with Victorian literature." Krissy rattled off, her hand gesturing wildly.

Llewellyn shook his head. "You have some interesting clients."

"Interesting is one word for it," she agreed. "I think it says something about my life – a bit of everything, a little bit random. Like... like a collection of forgotten trinkets, slightly tarnished perhaps, but still colourful."

Llewellyn paused, considering this. He leaned against the counter himself, mirroring her pose. "Like a well-worn armchair. Comfortable, but with a few interesting patches."

"Exactly!" Krissy exclaimed, pleased. "Or maybe like a slightly mismatched jigsaw puzzle – each piece is unique, and you've got to find the right spot for it."

"And you're just wandering around looking for those pieces," Llewellyn observed quietly.

Krissy shrugged, a touch of melancholy in her eyes. "Something like that." She took a sip of lukewarm tea. "The werewolf deck was for a very... passionate divorce lawyer."

Llewellyn grinned. "I bet she had a good laugh. You know," he said after a moment, "you remind me of one of those old Welsh tales – all bright and colourful, but with a bit of mystery to it."

"Oh yeah?" Krissy asked, tilting her head. "Like what?"

"Like... well, remind me to lend you a translation of the Mabinogion to pore over, maybe it'll give you some new ideas for those magical clients of yours?"

"Are there werewolves?"

"Actually yes, there kind of are." Llew chuckled, thinking of the strange magical laws in old Welsh tales.

The rain seemed to soften a little then, falling in gentler sheets as they continued to chat about Ashcliffe – its eccentric residents and even more eccentric traditions. Krissy, after another sip of tea, turned the conversation towards Llew. "It's funny," she said, leaning slightly against the counter, "you always seemed... rooted somewhere. Like you'd been in Cardiff forever. You know? What made you just... wander?"

Llew shifted, his hand instinctively going to rest on the counter. For a moment, he looked almost uncomfortable. "Just... moved around," he said simply, avoiding her gaze. "Needed some changes."

"'Needed' is a good word," Krissy pressed gently. "Like you were being pulled in one direction and had to find out where you really wanted to land."

He took a small sip of his own tea. "I don't run now," he said, finally meeting her eyes. "I just...wander toward who needs me."

There was something in that – a quiet sadness, a hint of regret – that made Krissy pause. It wasn't a grand declaration, just a simple statement, but it felt laden with meaning. She noticed the slight tightening around his mouth, the way he seemed to be holding himself back. "That's... nice," she said softly, and then, almost without thinking, her hand brushed lightly against his on the counter – a brief, fleeting touch. "It's probably a good way to travel. Bit exhausting though, maybe."

He didn't pull away, just held her gaze for a moment longer than was strictly necessary. "It has its moments," he admitted quietly.

Krissy let the silence hang between them for a beat, then asked, "Was it hard? Leaving Cardiff?"

He looked out the rain-streaked window, lost in thought. "It was... sudden. Like someone turned off the lights and you were left standing in the dark." He paused again. "Violet... she just...left, you know."

The shift in his tone was palpable. It wasn't a dramatic retelling of events, but it was clear that Violet had been significant. "She was... special," he said finally, almost to himself. "A tattooist. Always sketching. Bright colours, messy hair. She just... walked out one day." Krissy didn't push for details. She simply nodded, letting him carry on. "I don't know what happened," he continued, a touch of bitterness in his voice. "Maybe I was too much. Too intense." He ran a hand through his hair – a gesture that always seemed to make him look younger, more vulnerable. "I didn't run then."

"It wasn't your fault," Krissy said softly, pulling her thoughts back to the present. "People do what they need to do."

He nodded slowly, his eyes distant. "I don't run now," he repeated, a small smile playing on his lips. "I just... wander toward who needs me."

This time, when their eyes met, it lingered. It wasn't an awkward glance, or a shy one – it was something deeper. A recognition of shared experience, perhaps. A suggestion that there might be more to this quiet connection than just friendly banter. The rain continued to fall, blurring the edges of the café and drawing them both inward, toward each other.

The lingering look broke suddenly, as if someone had gently switched off a light. Llew blinked, pulling himself back to the present with a slight shrug. "Sorry," he said, a touch of awkwardness colouring his voice. "Just thinking about the weather." Krissy mirrored his movement, turning her attention back to wiping down the counter. The smallness of the moment – the simple act of cleaning – felt significant in the quiet that followed. The rain intensified for a moment, drumming a steady rhythm against the slate roof above – a hypnotic sound. Krissy glanced up, noticing Llew's hand instinctively reaching for his worn coat, pulling it around him as if to ward off the chill. He hadn't even realized he'd done it. The silence returned, but this time it felt different – not lonely, exactly, but filled with a subtle hum of possibility. It was as if a small door had been opened between them, and they were both considering whether to step through. Krissy leaned against the counter again, picking up a stray napkin and folding it deliberately. "Well," she said finally, breaking the quiet. "I should probably get upstairs. I'm sleeping here... well, upstairs in Eloise's old flat, anyway, it's Rita and Tom's time tonight."

"Right," Llew replied, turning towards the door. "See you around."

As he stepped out into the rain, Krissy couldn't shake the feeling that she was seeing him differently now. Not just as a friendly face in the café, or as Eve's charming Welsh brother-in-law, but as something entirely more confusing. A person, one as thoroughly weathered by life as she was. She watched him disappear down the street, swallowed by the drizzle and the shadows.

For a moment, she stood there, arms crossed over her chest, fingertips absently brushing the fabric of her cardigan as though trying to remember the shape of that moment – the warmth of his hand beside hers, the rain-warped timbre of his voice, the way his eyes had softened like dusk at sea. Then the door closed with a soft click behind him, and the café was hers again. Alone. Krissy exhaled, long and steady. The silence that followed wasn't oppressive, but it was a little louder than she would've liked. It crept up the walls and into the beams, circled the tea-stained napkins and whispered across the glass of the windows like a finger trailing condensation. She reached for a cloth and idly wiped down the counter, though there was nothing left to clean. Her fingers moved on autopilot. Her brain did not. It was still back in that space between silences – the shared ache that had passed like a low note between them. The kind that didn't need to be named. He didn't run now, he'd said. He wandered toward who needed him. It had lodged itself somewhere just under her ribs. She stopped wiping. "Bloody hell," she muttered, chucking the cloth into the sink with more force than necessary.

This wasn't supposed to be happening. She was supposed to be floating above all this. Llew was just visiting. Spending a season in Ashcliffe. Staying only for one sketchbook's worth of mood and mist, a few late nights, a few warm bodies, a temporary fix. Krissy wasn't supposed to be watching rain fall with someone and wondering what his grief looked like in colour. She turned off the overhead lights one by one until the café was bathed in soft shadow and the residual glow from the streetlamps. It looked smaller like this. Softer, somehow. Like the inside of a memory. She slipped upstairs, into Eloise's old flat – still marked by star charts on the wall and the scent of chamomile clinging to the corners. The flat wasn't quite hers, of course. Just another borrowed stop. A place to perch. She passed by the half-finished sketch of the café that sat on the windowsill – rain-streaked glass smudging the pencil lines she'd started yesterday. But tonight, her hands didn't want pencils. They wanted warmth. She made herself tea with a touch too much honey, tucked herself into the nest of blankets on the sofa, and tried – failed – to not think about Llew's voice when he talked about Violet. Or the way he'd looked out into the rain like he expected her to come walking back.

And she tried – also failed – not to think about how familiar that posture felt. She knew something about vanishing. About becoming a shape that didn't fit in someone else's story. Krissy curled tighter into the blankets. It wasn't about Llew, she told herself. Not really. It was about how easy it had been. The way her words had landed with him like stones skipping water – playful, then deep. How he hadn't flinched when she was messy or ridiculous. How he looked like someone who knew how to hold fragile things and not flinch when they cracked. She fell asleep before she meant to, the rain soft as a lullaby on the windowpane.

The next morning brought fog. Ashcliffe disappeared into itself – wrapped in mist like a tortilla-shaped secret. Krissy woke up late, blinking against the unfamiliar softness of the morning light in this borrowed flat. The kettle hissed before she even stood up – a kindness from Rita, no doubt. A Post-it stuck to the fridge in all-caps read: USE THE GOOD TEA, YOU'RE WORTH IT. She snorted and peeled it off, sticking it to the corner of her sketchbook like a talisman. Downstairs, the café was in full swing. Rita was running it like a captain steering through a storm, Tom was ferrying trays of toast and mackerel, and Krissy... tried not to look for Llew. He wasn't there. Not that she cared. She didn't care. Obviously. She spent the morning drawing in the corner between deliveries — a trio of talking gulls arguing over sandwich crusts, then a dramatic seagull with an eyepatch she titled Sir Peckicles the Sassy. Anything, really, to keep her fingers busy. "Cute," Tom said, glancing at her sketchbook while passing by with a tray of peppermint scones.

"Don't patronise me," Krissy said dryly.

"Wouldn't dream of it," Tom grinned. "Though that one looks a bit like Councillor Davies."

She snorted. "It's the beady eyes."

He arched an eyebrow. "You all right, then?"

She blinked, caught. "What do you mean?"

Tom shrugged, not looking at her now, just arranging scones. "Last night. Looked like something shifted."

Krissy froze.

Rita appeared, sliding into the scene like a knife through silk. "If you're thinking about sleeping with Llew, just don't do it to prove you're still untouchable."

"I wasn't—!" Krissy started.

Rita raised a single eyebrow. "Okay."

Krissy sighed, pulling her knees up onto the café bench. "He's... different."

"He's present," Rita said. "That'll throw you off."

Krissy nodded, not sure what to say. Tom came back, slid her a tea she hadn't asked for, and gave her a wink that meant we've got you.

That evening, the sky turned strange – a dusky violet, bruised and streaked with sea-salt wind. Ashcliffe looked dreamlike again, the way it always did just before something new blew in. Krissy found herself walking down the shoreline, sketchbook in hand, boots crunching against wet stones. The tide was half-out, the sea murmuring secrets she didn't quite catch. She didn't really know where she was going until she saw the flicker of a cigarette in the distance, near the benches that overlooked the water. Llew. She almost turned back. Almost. Instead, she walked quietly toward him and sat without asking. He didn't flinch. Just offered the smoke without looking at her. She took it. "Didn't peg you as a smokey shoreline brooder," she said after a beat.

"Didn't peg you as someone who lets fog ruin their curls," he replied, glancing at her damp hair with something like fondness.

Krissy made a dramatic noise of offence. "I'll have you know this is a deliberate aesthetic."

"Oh, is that what we're calling frizz now?"

She elbowed him. "Watch it, Morgan."

He grinned. The wind tugged at his coat, at her scarf, at the invisible thread stretched between them. The silence that fell now wasn't heavy — it was like settling into a long exhale.

"I used to go to the water all the time back home," he said eventually. "The sea made more sense than people."

Krissy nodded. "The sea's honest. Brutal, but honest."

He looked at her, really looked. "You're a bit like that."

"What, honest or brutal?"

"Both. But not in a bad way."

She let that settle.

"I'm always honest in my art," she said eventually. "That's where I put all the stuff I can't say without running away."

"And does it help?"

"Sometimes. Other times, I just end up with ten versions of the same unfinished sketch and a headache."

He smiled, eyes still on the horizon. "You ever think about staying put?"

Krissy's chest tightened. "In Ashcliffe? Sure. This town suits me." she said. "But then I remember I don't really know how."

"Maybe you just haven't had a reason yet." The words weren't pointed. They weren't a question, either. Just a soft truth, placed carefully between them like a stone in the tide.

They sat like that for a long while – the sea breathing in and out, the smoke curling skyward, their knees almost touching. Eventually, Krissy leaned her head briefly against his shoulder. "You're not just wandering toward who needs you," she murmured. "You're finding who sees you."

He didn't answer. But he didn't move away. And when they rose to walk back toward the golden lights of the town, it wasn't just two people walking the same path. It was something that almost felt like choosing.

Back at the café, Rita was waiting. She didn't say a word, just passed Krissy a folded-up scrap of napkin. On it, in surprisingly delicate handwriting, was a single phrase: "You can't keep pretending you don't want something just because you're afraid it won't last. And you shouldn't keep pretending you want something if you don't any more." Krissy stared at it for a long moment, then tucked it into her sketchbook. Tomorrow could be anything. But tonight, she felt seen.

4

CHAPTER FOUR: FAULT LINES

The rain continued its steady argument with Ashcliffe. This morning, it felt particularly heavy, pressing down on the town and settling into the bones of its buildings. Krissy was hunched over her sketchbook at a small table near the window of The Chiron Café, capturing the grey wash of the sea on paper. The charcoal smudged slightly under her thumb as she worked, lost in a tangle of lines and shadows. Across the room, Llew meticulously cleaned a teapot shaped like a seaside cottage – a charmingly weathered piece that always seemed to be attracting dampness. It was a quietude that wasn't necessarily happy, just present. The kind of stillness that settled after a good storm, holding both the promise of sunshine and the lingering scent of rain.

"You're staring," Rita said, emerging from the kitchen with a tray of steaming mugs. Her voice cut through Krissy's concentration. "And you haven't blinked in five minutes."

Llew didn't look up from his teapot. "Just admiring your craftsmanship, Rita."

"Well, it's not as good as yours," she grumbled. "You're big and strong enough to make a better job of fixing my shelf than I am."

He finally glanced up, a flicker of amusement in his dark eyes. "It's just a shelf, Rita." He returned to his work, carefully polishing the spout with a soft cloth. Krissy hadn't realized she'd been watching him for so long – sleeves rolled up to his elbows, dark hair damp with sweat, jaw tight as if wrestling with something stubborn. It wasn't just that he was handsome – though he certainly was – it was the way he moved, the focus in his face, the quiet strength that seemed to radiate from him. It felt unexpected, almost jarring, like a note played slightly out of tune in a familiar melody. It was an unfamiliar pull, one she hadn't anticipated.

The rain hammered against the windows, blurring the grey of the sea. Krissy shifted slightly in her chair, pulling her sketchbook closer. The charcoal felt rough beneath her fingers. She'd been sketching the cottage teapot – trying to capture its sturdy charm – but now it seemed almost foolish, a frivolous distraction. Her gaze drifted back to Llew. She noticed then the calluses on his hands— small ridges of grey and white, evidence of hard work and touch. The way his brow furrowed in concentration as he worked, pulling slightly at the corners of his eyes. And that slight dip of his jaw when he was thinking – a subtle detail that seemed to hold a whole universe of unspoken things. It felt overwhelming, this sudden awareness. She hadn't realized how often she noticed him, or how little time had passed since they'd last been together. It was as if the quietness of Ashcliffe itself was holding its breath, waiting for something to happen. And Krissy suddenly suspected it might be about to crack.

Llew noticed Krissy watching him, then – a subtle shift happened in his expression, a small smile that barely touched the corners of his eyes. It wasn't an obvious acknowledgement, just a flicker of awareness that made her feel like she'd stepped out from under a spell. He didn't seem annoyed, though, more curious. "You're staring," he said, turning the teapot slightly in his hands. Krissy flushed, instinctively pulling her sketchbook closer. "Was I? Sorry. Just…you looked like you were wrestling with something."

He tilted his head, a small smile playing on his lips. "You look like you're trying to capture the soul of the storm," he said, tilting his head. "Or maybe just its dampness."

"Trying," Krissy replied, her voice a little breathless. "It's proving more stubborn than usual."

"Storms can be," he agreed, returning to his work. "They tend to hide things."

The exchange was simple, but it felt charged with something unspoken. It wasn't exactly flirtatious – not yet – but there was a warmth to it, a comfortable familiarity that eased the initial surprise of being noticed. "I'm working on a new tarot deck – not werewolves this time, but forest creatures. With hats." Krissy offered, gesturing vaguely towards her sketchbook. "I'm trying to capture their whimsical intensity."

He chuckled, a low rumble in his chest. "A fitting subject for Ashcliffe."

"That's exactly it," she said, feeling herself relax slightly. "Like you need to watch out or something will bite you." She grinned, a little self-consciously.

They fell into a comfortable rhythm of shared observations – about the perpetually grey sky, the grumpy Mr. Jones complaining about the price of fish, the eccentric Mrs. Prior and her endless supply of jams. He commented on the way she sketched, noting how quickly her hand moved across the paper, capturing the essence of things with a few deft strokes. "You have a good eye," he observed quietly. "Most people just see the rain. You see more."

Krissy felt a warmth spread through her chest. "Thanks," she mumbled, suddenly self-conscious about staring again.

He paused in his work, studying her for a moment. "It's nothing to be embarrassed about," he said softly, almost to himself. Then, turning back to the teapot, he added, "I used to think I was good at seeing things."

A small reveal – subtle and fleeting, but enough to pique her interest. "What were you looking for?" she asked, unable to resist the question. He hesitated, his fingers tracing the rim of the teapot. "Just a tattooist," he said finally, his voice quieter than before. "A woman with ink on her fingertips and a habit of disappearing." Krissy noticed then the slight tightening around his eyes – a brief flash of something that looked like pain. Violet. It was a small thing, but it felt significant, a tiny crack in Llew's carefully constructed facade. "Did she leave you for a storm?" she teased gently, trying to lighten the mood. He gave her a wry smile. "Something like that."

Krissy, feeling a little self-conscious after Llew's flirtation – and the way he seemed to notice her watching – bumped into Rita at the counter, sending a cascade of sugar cubes tumbling onto the worn wooden surface. "Sorry!" she exclaimed, quickly gathering them up. Rita didn't bother with apologies or pleasantries. She simply observed Krissy for a moment, her gaze sharp and assessing. "He's not scared of your fire," she said finally, handing Krissy a damp cloth. "That might be new for you." The comment hung in the air between them – brief, but loaded with meaning. Krissy paused, considering it. Rita always had a way of cutting to the heart of things, with little fuss or fanfare. It wasn't always comforting, but it was usually right.

Krissy glanced over at Llew, who was wiping down the counter, meticulously polishing each surface. He hadn't said anything, hadn't even looked her way – or had he? She caught him for a fraction of a second, his dark eyes holding hers for just a moment longer than necessary. It was subtle, almost imperceptible, but it felt like a confirmation. "Maybe," Krissy murmured to herself, tucking a stray strand of hair behind her ear. "Or maybe he's just getting used to then rain." Before she could dwell on it too long, Tom appeared, carrying a stack of empty mugs. He rumbled a greeting and deposited them by the sink. "Just don't let him set fire to you," he offered, his voice gruff as always. "You tend to burn with whoever catches your eye." The contrast between Rita's quiet wisdom and Tom's blunt practicality was always striking. Rita delivered a carefully measured observation; Tom offered a straightforward warning.

"He's not scared of my fire," Krissy repeated quietly, turning back to the spilled sugar cubes. "Maybe he just thinks it's annoying." She began to gather the last of the sugar, her fingers moving almost automatically. The rain continued its steady argument with Ashcliffe, and for a moment, she felt like she was caught in a small, contained storm herself – a mixture of curiosity, a little bit of nervousness, and something that felt a lot like hope. Rita watched her for another moment, a faint smile playing on her lips. Then, she turned to Llew, who was now meticulously arranging the tea towels by the door. "He's enjoying himself," she observed, stating the obvious.

"I am," Llew replied simply, his gaze meeting hers briefly over the rim of the teapot. And for a moment, Krissy felt like that small, contained storm within her might just – might – begin to grow.

Inside the Chiron Café, a different kind of warmth was beginning to spread – the comforting chaos of Eve and Geraint's arrival. They burst through the door, dripping slightly and radiating a palpable excitement that immediately brightened the room. "Morning!" Eve chirped, pulling off her coat. Geraint followed close behind, carrying a bag overflowing with knitted blankets and toys. "He's growing like a weed," he said, beaming at Eve. "Definitely a boy. And the sonographer thinks he's right on track." The usual morning routine kicked in – a flurry of mugs to be made, scones to be offered, and endless questions about the baby. Krissy found herself smiling easily, happy to provide a welcome distraction from her own thoughts. Llew, as always, was quietly efficient, wiping down counters and refilling sugar bowls with practised ease.

"We had another scan today," Eve announced, pulling out her phone and scrolling through pictures. "And it's even better news! He's definitely a boy, and he's growing really well."

She showed them the ultrasound picture – a blurry but undeniably cute image of a tiny, developing boy. Geraint gasped with delight. "He looks like a miniature version of me!" Llew took the phone from her, studying the image intently. And then, something shifted. A subtle tightening around his eyes, a slight intake of breath, and suddenly he was choking up – a small, almost imperceptible tremor running through him. It wasn't an obvious display of emotion; just a brief flicker of vulnerability that caught Krissy completely off guard. She'd seen him smile, she'd heard his quiet laughter, but this felt deeper. It was as if a memory, long held and carefully guarded, had been gently unearthed. Krissy noticed then – for the first time, truly saw – the depth beneath Llew's quiet exterior. He wasn't just a friendly face with a comfortable silence; there was a history there, a tenderness that hinted at something more.

"Are you –?" she started to ask, but he quickly brushed it off, dabbing at his eyes with the back of his hand. "Just...a bit tired," he mumbled, returning the phone to Eve. But Krissy wasn't convinced. She'd been watching him for so long, and in that brief moment, she sensed something deeper than just friendly affection. It was as if he might have missed out on something significant – a shared experience, a milestone. "He seems a little lost today," Eve observed quietly, noticing Llew's subdued state. "A bit distant."

Geraint nodded in agreement. "Yeah, he's been quieter than usual." The words hung in the air, unspoken but understood. Llew hadn't spoken about his own past with Violet – not really – but Krissy felt like she was glimpsing a piece of that story now. The thought struck her that he might've always wanted to be a father, and perhaps hadn't quite gotten there when he expected. It added another layer to his quiet intensity.

Krissy watched as Llew busied himself with polishing the counter again, effectively retreating back into his shell. She wondered what it was like – what it felt like – to have that yearning, that almost aching desire for a family. She glanced at Eve, who offered her a sympathetic smile. "He's a good man," she said softly. "Just a little guarded." Krissy nodded slowly, turning back to Llew. He looked so solid, so reliable, yet somehow fragile. She felt an unexpected pang of sympathy for him – and perhaps, just maybe, a hint of something else too. As she returned to her sketching, a new kind of tension had settled – a quiet, unresolved feeling that something was about to crack, revealing something beneath the surface. And Krissy, for the first time in a long while, found herself wondering what exactly she might discover.

The rain had eased slightly, transforming from a relentless argument into a gentle patter against the windows ands roof of The Chiron Café. It smelled of wet earth and something faintly salty – a familiar scent for Ashcliffe. The room felt quieter now, imbued with a comfortable stillness after the flurry of activity. Llew and Krissy were alone. They occupied the same space – leaning against the counter near the window overlooking the grey sea, their shoulders brushing occasionally – a small, almost imperceptible contact that sent a tiny shiver down Krissy's spine. The flirtation continued, but with a little more heat now – a longer glance, a lingering touch on her arm as he passed by, a shared smile that seemed to linger just a moment too long. Krissy found herself watching him, studying the way the light caught in his dark hair, the lines around his eyes when he concentrated. She wanted to reach out, to break through the quiet reserve that always seemed to surround him, but there was also a flicker of fear – uncertainty about what she might find if she did.

"You seem rooted here, despite it all," Llew said quietly, breaking the comfortable silence. "What keeps you?"

Krissy shifted slightly, pulling her sketchbook closer. Her fingers nervously traced the charcoal on the page. "Ashcliffe," she said finally, her voice a little hesitant. "It's complicated."

"Complicated how?" He didn't push, simply allowing her to find her own words.

She hesitated for a moment, considering how much – or how little – she wanted to reveal. "I don't know," she said finally. "Like I'm trying on different skins. Fitting in, then not quite fitting. It's like a puzzle with missing pieces."

"And you haven't found the right fit yet?"

"Not really," she admitted quietly. "I used to think maybe if I just moved around enough here, never putting my name on a lease or anything, somewhere new would feel like home. But it hasn't really worked." She glanced down at her hands, nervously twisting her fingers together. "It's hard to build something when you don't know where you belong."

The scent of Earl Grey tea mingled with the dampness of the rain and the faint, comforting aroma of old books – a perfect blend of Ashcliffe. Outside, the fog was beginning to roll in, thick and grey, swallowing the sea and the coastline in its embrace. Llew's gaze followed hers. He shifted slightly, bringing his arm a little closer to her side. Krissy looked up at him then, meeting his dark eyes. There was a mixture of curiosity and apprehension in her gaze – as if she were trying to decipher something hidden beneath the surface. She saw a flicker of vulnerability there, a hint of the pain he usually kept so carefully concealed.

"Maybe," she said finally, her voice barely above a whisper. "Maybe I'm starting to." As if on cue, the rain intensified again, drumming against the windows with renewed vigor. The fog thickened, swirling around the café and blurring the edges of the room. Outside, the sea was now just a grey expanse – a vastness that seemed to mirror the feeling in Krissy's chest. She looked at Llew – at his thoughtful expression, his dark eyes searching hers – and for a moment, she felt like she might actually understand something. Like maybe, just maybe, this wasn't just another fleeting connection. But then, as quickly as it had appeared, the feeling faded, replaced by that familiar sense of uncertainty. She was still not quite sure what to make of him – or of herself. Llew didn't say anything more, simply continuing to watch her with those intense dark eyes. And Krissy found herself wondering if, beneath all the quiet and the rain and the layers of shared glances, they were both on the verge of something significant. Something that might just crack open the walls around their hearts – for better or for worse.

The next morning broke with a pale, reluctant light. The kind that didn't so much arrive as seep in through the gaps – around shutters, beneath doors, along the jagged edges of the coastal town. Krissy was already awake, the ghost of a half-remembered dream tugging at the corners of her thoughts. She sat in bed in Eloise's old flat for a long time, wrapped in a cardigan that still smelled faintly of sea salt and paint, sketchbook balanced on her knees. Her fingers moved almost without thought, capturing fragments – a silhouette in the fog, the arc of a wave crashing against Ashcliffe's stubborn shoreline, a pair of callused hands holding a teacup. Her pencil paused, hovering just above the page. She drew a line, then erased it. Downstairs, The Chiron Café was waking up in its usual quiet way. The clatter of teacups, the low hum of the boiler, Rita humming some half-forgotten folk song under her breath. Krissy could hear it all from her attic flat above the café, and for once, it didn't feel like background noise. It felt like an invitation.

By the time she wandered downstairs, the place was already half full – familiar faces hunched over newspapers, fishermen shaking off the sea, young mothers balancing infants on hips while juggling coffees and croissants. Llew was at the counter, sleeves already rolled up, a smear of flour dusting one forearm. He looked up as she entered, and there it was again – that flicker of something warm and unreadable in his eyes. Not quite a smile, not quite nothing. "Morning," he said, nodding toward the seat near the window.

"Morning," she replied, brushing hair from her face. Her fingers tingled slightly from the sudden change in temperature, or maybe it was just him. She couldn't be sure anymore. "Rita's made you your usual," he said, sliding a mug toward her. The steam curled lazily into the air, carrying the comforting scent of cinnamon and cloves. "She says you've looked like a ghost lately. Her words, not mine."

Krissy raised an eyebrow. "Charming."

He gave a small, amused shrug. "She meant it with affection. I think."

Krissy took the seat near the window, letting her sketchbook fall open to a fresh page. "I've just been thinking a lot."

He leaned on the counter. "Dangerous habit."

She offered a wry smile, but didn't reply. Instead, she focused on the sea beyond the glass – calm this morning, strangely still, like a held breath. Llew followed her gaze.

"Too quiet," he said. "Makes me nervous."

"You think it's lulling us into a false sense of security?"

"I think Ashcliffe doesn't stay still for long. Not really." There was a pause then, filled only by the low thrum of conversation and the soft clink of spoons against ceramic. Krissy looked down at her mug, then up at Llew again.

"Can I ask you something?" she said.

He glanced at her, curious. "You can try."

"That woman you mentioned. The one with ink on her fingers." She hesitated. "Was she someone you loved?" Llew didn't respond right away. Instead, he busied himself with straightening the stack of napkins beside the till. When he finally spoke, his voice was quieter. "She was someone I thought I did," he said. "But looking back now, I don't know. Maybe I loved the idea of her more than the person she actually was."

Krissy nodded slowly. "That can happen."

"She was like a firework," he continued. "Bright. Loud. Beautiful, in a way that made your chest hurt. But she was always moving, always vanishing just when you thought you had her." He paused, then looked at Krissy. "I think I tried to hold on too tightly."

"And she didn't want to be held?"

"Not in the way I thought."

The honesty in his voice made her throat tighten. She looked down at her sketchbook, drawing without thinking. This time it was a moth – delicate wings outstretched, caught in flight. She wasn't sure why.

"She sounds like someone I used to know," Krissy said, after a moment. "Or maybe like a version of myself I've tried to leave behind."

Llew looked at her, his eyes steady. "You're not her."

"No," Krissy agreed softly. "But sometimes I think I still don't know who I am instead."

Rita appeared then, as if summoned by the weight of the conversation. She placed a plate of toast on the table without a word, then raised one eyebrow at the two of them. "It's early for existential crises," she said.

Krissy smiled faintly. "You ever feel like everyone here's trying not to drown, but we're all pretending it's fine because the tea's hot and the scones are fresh?"

Rita didn't miss a beat. "That's what community is, darling." Then she was gone, disappearing behind the swing door with the clatter of dishes.

Llew chuckled. "She's not wrong."

"No," Krissy said. "She rarely is."

They fell into silence again, but this time it felt companionable. Outside, the fog was beginning to thin, revealing patches of sea and sky in soft, hesitant hues. Krissy continued to sketch, and Llew continued to work, but something had shifted between them – a subtle new current, quieter than before, but steadier. By mid-morning, the café had emptied somewhat. The lull between breakfast and lunch. Llew was stacking chairs in the back, and Krissy had moved to the long wooden counter, a spread of drawings laid out before her. Little creatures – forest spirits, mischievous foxes in scarves, owls with monocles – stared up at her in various states of completion. She felt Llew's presence before she heard him. "You're building a world," he said, looking down at the drawings.

She shrugged. "Just trying to find something that feels like mine."

He picked up one of the sketches – a bear with a teacup and tiny spectacles. "It's comforting."

"That's the goal."

There was a pause, and then, quieter: "Maybe you already belong here more than you think."

Krissy looked at him, surprised. "You think?"

"I've seen the way people look at you," he said. "Rita, Tom, Eve. Even Mr. Jones – he only complains about people he secretly likes."

Krissy smiled at that. "He called me a 'charcoal goblin' last week."

"Exactly," Llew said. "That's affection."

She laughed, and something inside her loosened. Maybe it was the familiarity in his voice, or the quiet certainty with which he said it. Maybe it was just that she was tired of pretending not to care.

"You ever feel like you're standing on the edge of something," she said, "but you don't know if it's a cliff or a doorway?"

Llew considered this. "All the time.""And what do you do?"

"I usually wait. Let the fog clear."

"And if it doesn't?"

"Then I jump anyway."

The words hung between them, heavier than they had any right to be. Krissy looked at him, really looked. There was something in his expression that made her breath catch – a steadiness, a gentleness, but also a hint of fear. She felt it mirror in her own chest. Before she could respond, the door swung open with a gust of sea wind and the jangling of the bell. A newcomer stepped in – tall, soaked to the bone, dragging a suitcase that squeaked faintly on the tiles. Her coat was tattered, her face half-hidden beneath a scarf, but her eyes were sharp and bright. Llew's entire body went still. Krissy turned to him instinctively. "Do you know her?" He didn't answer right away, but she saw it – in the tightening of his jaw, the way his hands curled slightly at his sides. The woman moved toward the counter, peeling back her scarf. Ink-stained fingers. A crescent moon tattoo on her wrist. "Hello, Llewellyn," she said softly, her Welsh accent a gentle lilt. Krissy's heart lurched. It was her. The firework. The woman with ink on her fingertips. Llew's voice, when it came, was quiet but steady. "Violet."

5

⚬⚬⚬

CHAPTER FIVE: FIRST TOUCH

The rain outside continued its muted drumming, as if trying to decide whether to stay or go. Violet, seemingly unfazed by the sudden reunion, turned and glanced at Krissy, a brief flash of recognition in her eyes. "You're sketching," she observed, her gaze lingering for just a moment longer than necessary. "Trying," Krissy replied, feeling suddenly self-conscious about her charcoal sketch – a half-formed outline. "I keep feeling as if I'm breaking into the day's stillness," Krissy offered.

"Too much stillness can be boring. Keeps you on your toes." She took a slow sip. "Besides, I rather enjoy a bit of chaos."

Llew remained silent for a moment, simply observing the two women. Krissy felt a strange pull – a desire to ask him a million questions, to dissect every detail of this encounter, but she held back. It was as if he were already halfway out of the room, lost in his own thoughts. "So," Violet said, breaking the silence. "You've been keeping yourself busy? Good. Llewelyn here seems to enjoy a good conversation." She gave him a small, almost challenging smile.

He finally shifted, offering a slight nod. "Just cleaning up."

47

"Cleaning is important," Violet agreed. "But so are the messes you make while doing it." She gestured vaguely towards Krissy with her mug. "Like her."

Krissy felt a blush creep up her neck. It was... perceptive. And slightly unsettling.

"She's good," Llew said quietly, his gaze returning to Violet. "Very good."

"Indeed," Violet replied, her eyes twinkling. "A bit of a puzzle herself, no doubt." She paused, letting the statement hang in the air. "So, I'm here for a week. Thought I'd spread myself around a little, travel around, do some guest spots. Do you have anything interesting happening in Ashcliffe?"

Llew shrugged. "Just the usual."

"'Just the usual'," Violet repeated, raising an eyebrow. "That's what they always say." She turned to Krissy, offering another brief smile. "Well, I suppose that's me. Just asking for a bit of local colour. And maybe some coffee. Do you take oat milk?"

Krissy nodded, feeling her mind already racing. "Definitely."

Violet turned back to Llew, and he finally managed a small, almost hesitant smile in return. "Do you know," he said, his voice low, "it's been a while since I've seen you."

"And it's been a while since you've expected to," Violet replied, her gaze holding his for just a beat longer than was comfortable. "Just long enough to make things interesting, wouldn't you say?" She turned and moved towards the door again, the bell jingling merrily as she stepped back out into the rain. This time, Krissy didn't need to watch her go. She could feel her presence – a lingering warmth on the air, like the memory of a fire. Llew took a deep breath, turning his attention back to the counter. "She's persistent," he said quietly, almost to himself. Krissy turned to him then, and for a moment, she felt as if she were looking at two different people – a man carrying the weight of an unspoken past, and a man who was perhaps, just maybe, about to step into something new.

Later, the wind continued its insistent push along Ashcliffe's coast, carrying with it the scent of salt and seaweed. It was late – Llew and Krissy were on the way back from dinner at Eve and Geraint's cottage, leaving behind the comforting glow of their warm kitchen and the echoes of happy chatter. Krissy and Llew were walking back to The Chiron Café, both soaked through – a testament to their somewhat haphazard escape from the storm. It wasn't an uncomfortable wetness, not exactly. It was more familiar. Like coming home after being out in the rain for too long. A comfortable dampness that seemed to cling to everything – their clothes, their hair, even the air around them. Initially, there was a slight awkwardness hanging between them – remnants of Violet's sudden appearance and Llew's muted reaction. It felt like walking on eggshells, each step carefully measured but still gently crunching nevertheless. The steady rhythm of their footsteps on the wet pavement and the rustling of leaves in the wind a quiet soundtrack to Ashcliffe's evening.

Krissy still found herself noticing details about Llew – the way his worn coat hung loosely on his frame, hinting at a life spent outdoors; the small, almost imperceptible line etched between his eyebrows when he concentrated; the way he instinctively pulled his hat lower over his forehead, shielding his eyes from the last of the rain. She was usually so quick to catalogue and analyse – to dissect everything she saw – but tonight, it felt different. Less about observation and more about simply being in his presence. "It's like a good jam," Llew said suddenly, breaking the silence.

Krissy raised an eyebrow. "What is?"

"Mrs. Prior's blackberry jam," he replied, nodding towards the houses they were passing. "She says it's best when there's been a bit of rain. Makes the berries burst."

"So, the storm is good for the blackberries?" Krissy asked, tilting her head.

"Sometimes," Llew said, his voice quiet. "Sometimes, you need a little bit of disruption to really appreciate things."

They continued walking in silence for a few moments, then he broke it again, commenting on the sea. "The tide's going out. It's been low for days."

"It always seems to be," Krissy agreed. "Like Ashcliffe is slowly surrendering to the water."

"Maybe," Llew said, considering. "Or maybe it's just remembering." They fell into a comfortable flow of small talk – about the rain's effect on the sea, about Mrs. Prior's jam-making process, about Mr. Jones complaining about the paper being damp again. Each comment was simple, unremarkable, but Krissy noticed that beneath the surface, there were glimpses of Llewelyn's quiet observations – his knowledge of local details, his appreciation for the small things. And she, in turn, found herself offering more than just a casual response – her answers felt considered, almost reflective.

"It's funny," Krissy said, after a while, "how quickly you get used to things. Even the strange ones."

Llewelyn paused, looking out at the sea. "That's true," he agreed. And then, it started – the subtle circling back to Violet. It began with a casual remark from Llewelyn about tattoo artists – "They're interesting people. Lots of stories in their ink." Krissy noticed a slight tightening around his eyes, a brief flicker of something – was it sadness? – before he quickly dismissed it with a shrug. "Violet has a good eye," he said, almost to himself.

"Does she?" Krissy asked, her curiosity piqued. "What does she do with it?"

He hesitated for a moment, then simply said, "She travels."

Krissy noticed the way his hand instinctively tightened on the strap of his suitcase. "Like a lot?"

"Enough," he replied, his gaze fixed on the horizon.

"Hopefully, she'll be gone by next week," Krissy offered, trying to sound casual.

Llewelyn didn't answer immediately. "She doesn't like being tied down," he said finally, his voice low.

Krissy felt a prickle of something – a mixture of curiosity and perhaps a little bit of irritation? – that she couldn't quite place. It was as if Violet were still hanging between them, an unspoken presence in the air. As they walked on, the tension between them increased – it wasn't overt, not exactly. It wasn't like shouting or arguing. It was more subtle, almost imperceptible – a tightening of muscles, a slight shift in posture, a lingering glance. There was an undeniable chemistry between them, fuelled by shared history and unspoken emotions. They'd known each other for a while now, but tonight, it felt different. Like the surface of the sea between them was beginning to ripple. Krissy found herself wondering what he was thinking, what he was remembering. Was he still haunted by Violet? Did she, in some small way, shape his perception of things? Suddenly, Llewelyn stopped. He turned and looked at her, a slight smile playing on his lips. "You know," he said quietly, "for someone who's always sketching the world, you're surprisingly good at keeping secrets."

And then, as if on cue, the rain picked up again – an insistent shower that seemed to wash over them both, blurring the edges of the street lights and deepening the shadows. They stood there for a moment, caught in the downpour, the silence between them thick with unspoken words. It was then, under the flickering light of the street-lamp, that it happened – slow, surprising, real. The rain intensified for a brief, exhilarating moment – a burst of wind and rain that forced them to huddle under the small overhang of Mrs. Prior's cottage, sharing a quick, soggy shelter. It was just enough to heighten the feeling between them – the dampness clinging to their clothes, the warmth of his shoulder against hers as they leaned into each other for balance. When they stepped out from under the overhang, the rain had eased to a drizzle again, but the wind continued its insistent push along Ashcliffe's coast, carrying with it the scent of salt and seaweed.

And then, it happened – as if guided by an unseen force. As they continued walking, they found themselves beneath a flickering street-lamp – the only source of light in that section of town. It cast a warm, slightly hazy glow on their faces, highlighting the rain dampness in her hair and the lines around his eyes. They were close now – maybe just a few feet apart – the wind tugging at their coats, bringing with it the harsh scent of the sea. There was a palpable shift – eye contact lingered longer, a shared breath. It felt charged. Llew took a step closer, and Krissy didn't pull back. It wasn't rushed or passionate – instead it was slow, tentative, almost surprised. Like he hadn't expected it, or maybe like she hadn't. It was a brief touch – his lips brushing against hers, soft and gentle – but it held everything. A recognition of something that's been building between them. The scent of rain and sea mingled with the faint aroma of tobacco clinging to his coat. Krissy initially pulled back slightly – a flicker of surprise and perhaps hesitation in her eyes. It wasn't a rejection, not exactly, but it was uncertainty. She tilted her head up, regarding him, as if trying to decipher what just happened.

"This is a bad idea," she said quietly, almost to herself. Her voice was low, barely audible above the sound of the wind. He didn't immediately pull away, though. Instead, he gently cupped her face with his hands, tilting her head up slightly so he could look directly into her eyes. His thumbs stroked the corners of her mouth – a simple gesture that sent a shiver down her spine. "Or," he said softly, his voice low and laced with a hint of amusement, "a really good one." He leaned in just a fraction, brushing his lips against hers again for a heartbeat – longer this time – before releasing her. Krissy looked away, focusing on the flickering light of the streetlamp. Her cheeks were flushed, and she felt a strange mix of excitement and nervousness bubbling within her. It was unexpected. Wonderful. And terrifying all at once.

The rain had stopped, and a sliver of moonlight broke through the clouds, casting an ethereal glow on Ashcliffe's rain-slicked streets. It was as if the storm itself were retreating, leaving behind a sense of quiet expectancy. They stood for a moment longer, gazing at each other – suspended in that shared space between then and now. Krissy didn't immediately pull away this time. She looked at him, considering

– a small smile playing on her lips, a hint of surprise mingled with something else, something that felt undeniably like hope. "Why now?" she asked quietly, the question hanging in the air between them.

Llew's gaze didn't leave hers. "Sometimes you just have to," he said simply, his voice low and laced with a hint of melancholy. "Like the tide. You don't always know when it's going to turn, but you just wait anyway, knowing that it will." He gestured towards the sea, where the last of the rain was disappearing into the waves.

"And what if," she countered, tilting her head slightly, "the tide turns and you're not ready?" He reached out then, his fingers brushing lightly against hers – a small, tentative gesture that sent another shiver down her spine. "Then you just hold on a little longer," he said, his thumb gently stroking the back of her hand.

"It's... unexpected," she murmured. "And nice."

"Nice is good," Llew replied, a small smile playing on his lips.

Krissy felt a blush creep up her neck again. She was trying to make sense of it all – this sudden shift, this unexpected connection. It felt like stepping onto unfamiliar ground – exciting and a little bit daunting. He shifted slightly then, bringing himself up to his full height – and for a moment, she felt as if he could reach out and brush a stray strand of hair from her face. "It's been a while since I've seen you," he said quietly, his voice barely above the sound of the wind.

"And it's been a while since I'd expected anything like this," Krissy replied, returning his gaze. She noticed then – a flicker of sadness in his eyes, quickly masked by a trace of something else...perhaps anticipation? She was still grappling with her own feelings – the warmth of his kiss, the comfort of his presence, and the lingering question of what it all meant. Was this just a momentary spark, fuelled by rain and nostalgia? Or was it something more – the beginning of a connection that could actually last?

The memory of Violet hung in the air between them – a not so subtle reminder of past loves and unspoken emotions. Llewelyn's reaction to her arrival had been so immediate, yet now it felt as if he'd forgotten about her for just a moment. Krissy took a deep breath, trying to steady herself. She didn't want to overthink it, to analyse every detail until she missed something or worse, convinced herself that it wasn't real. She turned then, and without saying anything, began walking towards The Chiron Café. It was a simple gesture – a small step in the direction of home, of routine, of familiar faces. Llew watched her go, his hand lingering for a moment on her back – a gentle reminder of their brief encounter. He shifted again, turning to face the streetlamp, and then – just as she was about to disappear into the doorway – he offered one last look. It wasn't a frantic search, or a desperate plea. It was simply acknowledgement. Or maybe just a simple wish that she would be alright.

Krissy stepped inside The Chiron Café, the bell above the door jingling merrily as she entered. The warm glow of the café lights enveloped her, and for a moment, it felt like she was returning to something familiar and safe. But as she turned to face him – one last glance over her shoulder – she saw that he hadn't moved. He was still standing beneath the flickering streetlamp, his silhouette outlined against the moonlight, looking – waiting – for her. And for a brief moment, she felt like Ashcliffe itself – with all its secrets and stories – was holding its breath with them. A sense of both hope and uncertainty hung in the air – as tangible as the scent of rain and coffee – a promise of something new and, perhaps, beautiful.

Meanwhile, inside Eve and Geraint's cottage, a warm glow spilled out onto the rain-slicked path – a haven of warmth and conversation against Ashcliffe's moody backdrop. The fire crackled merrily in the hearth, casting dancing shadows on the walls, and the scent of chamomile tea hung heavy in the air. They were discussing Violet. "She always gave the impression of being remarkable," Eve said quietly, stirring her tea with a thoughtful expression. "The way he spoke about her, like she burned like Ashcliffe's sunshine – all bright and fleeting."

Geraint nodded, his gaze fixed on the flickering flames. "Years flying too close to her heat," he murmured, a hint of wistfulness in his voice. "He always did have that way about him – drawn to the beautiful and restless things."

"It's funny," Eve continued, "how easily we forget those who leave us feeling like we've caught a glimpse of something extraordinary. And then suddenly... years later, they turn up again."

"Violet," Geraint said softly, as if repeating his own thoughts. "He spent years chasing that spark, didn't he? Like she was some elusive treasure."

"Apparently," Eve replied, taking a sip of her tea. "A brilliant tattooist... Always sketching, always capturing the light."

"And she left him," Geraint said quietly, his fingers tracing patterns in the condensation on his mug. "Just walked out."

"Without so much as a note," Eve added, a touch of sympathy in her voice. "Just vanished. Like smoke."

Geraint sighed, leaning back in his armchair. "It's strange, isn't it? How one person can hold up your entire world for years, and then, with no explanation, they simply disappear." He paused, considering. "It's like a fault line, really – a little tremor that can set off a chain reaction." Eve nodded in agreement. "And Llewelyn, he always did have that tendency to get lost in the beauty of things," she said with a small smile. "Like a moth drawn to a flame."

"He's good company, though," Geraint countered, his voice softening. "Even if he is prone to getting swept away." He looked up, as if searching for something. "Do you think this time will be different?"

Eve took his hand and squeezed it gently. "Maybe," she said uncertainly. "Maybe this time, he's ready to hold onto the warmth he's found. Stoke the flames, instead of just letting them run riot over him."

The guesthouse clung to the hillside like an afterthought, its shingles warped from decades of salt and wind, its windows blurred with the gentle smear of rain and time. It had once been a handsome place, maybe, before the sea air softened its edges. Now it was all leaning eaves and rusted hinges, less a business than a stubborn relic. Violet liked it immediately. She stood, towel-drying her hair in slow, absent-minded circles. The scent of old books and lemon polish clung to the floorboards. A crooked mirror hung above a narrow dresser, reflecting a version of her she didn't quite recognise: tired around the eyes, perhaps, or simply older. Not the kind of older that shows in lines or grey, but something underneath – the kind of wear that only silence leaves. She tossed the towel onto the end of the iron-framed bed and opened the small window. The sea was a bruised stretch of slate, flecked with white where waves broke along the rocks. Gulls wheeled above the beach, their cries thin and distant.

The knock came lightly, followed by the unmistakable creak of Mrs. Prior's knees on the landing. "Tea's on," she called, voice muffled through the door. "Brought some jam for your toast, too. Blackberry. Best batch this year."

Violet smiled despite herself. "I'll be down in a bit," she said, her voice just loud enough to carry. She took a moment longer by the window before pulling on a worn jumper and descending the narrow staircase. The hallway smelled of salt and dust, a little like childhood if you squinted hard enough. In the kitchen, the kettle whistled merrily, and Mrs. Prior was already laying out mismatched china on the table. "I always forget how loud that old kettle is," she said, removing it from the heat. "Startles me every time."

Violet slid into the chair nearest the window. "I like it," she said. "Feels alive."

Mrs. Prior gave her a shrewd look over the rim of her glasses. "Not many your age would say that."

Violet raised an eyebrow, reaching for the jar of jam. "I'm not sure what age I'm meant to be, honestly." There was a pause as toast was buttered, tea poured.

"You didn't come here for the scenery," Mrs. Prior said finally, not as a question. Violet spread the jam carefully, deliberately, the dark smear glistening in the late afternoon light. "No," she admitted. "I didn't."

Mrs. Prior watched her for a long moment. "People come to Ashcliffe for two reasons. They're either running from something, or running toward it."

Violet took a bite of toast, chewing slowly. "What if it's both?"

The older woman nodded as if that made perfect sense. "Well, then I suppose you'll need to figure out which one's chasing harder."

Later, Violet returned to her room, setting her sketchbook on the sill and thumbing through its pages. Most of the drawings were impressions – shapes half-caught, lines that suggested more than they revealed. There were tattoos, of course. Ideas for pieces she'd never inked. A phoenix with kelp for feathers, flying up from the sea. A weeping stag. A sun that bled into a compass. But there were others, too. A narrow street she hadn't seen in years. A man, always drawn in fragments – his eyes, a thumb smudging charcoal where the cheekbone should've been. She never finished him. She never could. She didn't need to ask herself why she'd come. She already knew. It hadn't been a decision, not really. Just a moment – a single glance at the calendar, a cancelled appointment in Brighton, the sudden weight of everything she'd been pretending not to carry. Ashcliffe had been a pin on a mental map ever since Llewellyn's mother had complained to her that both of her sons had been stolen by it. A small town with a tide that never seemed to stay out, and a man she'd left like a letter without a signature.

Llewellyn. His name alone felt like salt on her tongue – bracing, grounding, a little bitter. Violet had told herself it was time to stop pretending he hadn't mattered. That she hadn't thought of him every time she passed a coast or caught the scent of wet tobacco. She'd told herself the time had passed, that it was curiosity, not regret. A week in Ashcliffe. Guest spots. Closure. She hadn't expected to see him that fast. Or to find him changed in all the quiet, devastating ways that mattered. He hadn't chased her when she left. She'd half-hoped he would. Half-feared it, too. Now, years later, he hadn't asked why she'd come back. Not yet. The sketchbook lay open on the sill, pages lifting slightly in the evening breeze. She pulled a pen from her bag – her favourite, weighted just right – and began to draw. Not Llewellyn this time. Not directly. But the coastline. The way Ashcliffe curved like a question mark. The small cottage roofs like teeth biting into the wind. The Chiron Café, with its warm windows and that steady little bell. She let her hand move without overthinking it, without trying to define the why. She just sketched. That had always been her way – capturing feeling before fact. There was something shifting in the air tonight. She could feel it in her bones.

Downstairs, the kettle sang again, and Mrs. Prior muttered something about forgetting it was even on. The scent of jam still lingered. Rain tapped gently at the windowpanes. In Room Three, Violet shaded the outline of the café door and thought about what she would say if Llewellyn knocked. If he came here, tonight, asking for something more than small talk. She didn't know if she'd be ready. But she knew why she'd come. Not to rekindle something. Not really. She just needed to see if the version of herself she'd left in his keeping – full of fear, full of fire – was still waiting beneath the surface. If she could hold it again, even for a moment. Because maybe it wasn't about him. Maybe it never had been.

6

CHAPTER SIX: GHOSTS
AND GRAVEL

The rain in Ashcliffe-on-Sea wasn't a gentle affair; it was a determined assault, lashing against the windows of The Chiron Café
with the kind of stubbornness only found in this little corner of Kent.
Inside, amongst the chipped teacups and lingering scent of Earl Grey,
Krissy was sketching furiously. Her brow was furrowed, her hair plastered to her forehead, and a smudge of charcoal adorned her cheekbone. She wasn't capturing a vibrant seascape or a charming village
scene – not today. Instead, she was wrestling with the silhouette of a
marionette, its limbs slightly askew, its painted face holding an expression of profound sadness. It felt heavy. The café was quiet, save for
the rhythmic drumming of the rain and the occasional creak of the old
building settling in. A grey, damp beauty – fitting, she thought, for
Ashcliffe itself.

"Krissy, dear," Mrs. Prior's voice cut through the café's quietude,
a little likeon of those wind gusts that whipped off the sea. Mrs.
Prior, owner of The Seabreeze Guesthouse and Ashcliffe's resident
purveyor of fine jams (raspberry & blackberry were her specialities),
was perched on a stool at Krissy's table. "How are the designs for the
haunted marionettes coming, lovely?" Mrs. Prior nudged Krissy gently

back into reality. The charcoal felt gritty beneath her fingertips. Another marionette took shape – this one with outstretched arms, as if reaching for something just out of grasp. It was melancholy, Krissy realized, a little bit desperate. It fit. Everything lately fit that description. She chewed on the end of her pencil, staring at the sketch. Her own sense of self felt like a mismatched jigsaw piece in a box full of ornate, perfectly-cut shapes. Was she always this adrift? Likeable as it was, the feeling lingered. She glanced at the rain, streaking down the windowpane – did darkness have to be so bleak? Or could it simply be another colour, another texture? Maybe even beautiful. A small idea sparked – these illustrations would look incredible tattooed on her arm. Big, bold, and a little bit haunted. Like her. She traced the outline of one of the marionettes with her finger, almost unconsciously. It was a strange comfort – capturing other people's sadness, giving it form and permanence. Perhaps, she thought, it was a way to make her own impermanence feel a little less fleeting.

The rain hadn't let up, but something about it felt calmer than this morning. Llew was wiping down the counter with a practised hand, a smile playing on his lips. He wasn't rushing, not fussing – just quietly efficient, like always, but there was a little more ease to him today. A touch of relaxation that hadn't been quite as prevalent when he first arrived. He'd already served three customers, each with a brief word and a polite smile. Rita and Tom were engaged in one of their usual animated discussions by the window – this time about their upcoming anniversary trip. "London!" Rita exclaimed, gesturing wildly. "All those museums! And that Italian place Geraint's been raving about." Tom nodded enthusiastically. "We're going to need a serious caffeine fix." Llew chuckled quietly, polishing a mug with care. He felt a familiar contentment settling over him – the simple rhythm of The Chiron Café, the faces he knew, the comforting scent of coffee and toast. It was a welcome change from, well, from whatever he'd been thinking about.

The bell above the door chimed, announcing the arrival of Eve and Geraint – looking slightly rumpled but undeniably happy. They were laden with bags and a palpable sense of having just escaped a minor disaster. "Morning!" Eve called out, her voice laced with sleepiness. "We've survived another day of plaster dust." Geraint squeezed her shoulder affectionately. "Just one more wall to go," he groaned. "And then we can finally start painting!" They settled into a cosy corner and soon the café was filled with their easy chatter. The conversation quickly turned to nursery plans – a subject that always seemed to trigger a mix of excitement and anxiety. "I'm thinking pale blue," Eve said, gesturing vaguely. "Something calming."

Geraint considered this carefully. "Perhaps with a little grey – like Ashcliffe on a cloudy day."

"Definitely need some sturdy furniture," Krissy offered, almost automatically. "And lots of space for toys, and maybe... a dog."

"You've been thinking about that," Geraint observed, raising an eyebrow. "Do you want to be an auntie?" Krissy shrugged, avoiding his gaze. "Maybe. It's... complicated." She glanced at Llew, who was observing them with quiet interest from behind the counter. He offered a small, encouraging smile. "Don't worry about it," he said softly. "It'll be wonderful."

As Eve and Geraint were discussing the merits of wallpaper patterns, Rita and Tom's flurry of excited chatter brought them over to the counter. Llew, leaning there, watched them with a wry smile. "She's dangerous, that one," Tom said, nodding towards Krissy, who was sketching in her notebook at a table by herself. "She'll drag you into her undercurrent worse than any storm."

Rita chuckled. "He's not wrong. She tends to bolt when things get too real. Remember last month? We thought she'd be with us all weekend."

"Well, she bolted from us," Tom corrected, grinning. "But she was happy doing it."

Krissy shot them a quick, slightly irritated glance. "I wasn't 'bolting'," she muttered, though her voice lacked conviction. "I just needed some space."

Rita raised an eyebrow. "Space? You used to spend every night at the cottage! Now you barely say hello."

Tom added, "Yeah, she's changed. Like a tide going out."

Llew observed the exchange with interest. He'd noticed it too – Krissy's tendency to retreat lately. He wondered what was pulling her away.

The rain had slowed to a persistent drizzle, but it still carried Ashcliffe's melancholic scent – salt and damp earth. Krissy was sketching again, attempting to capture the grey light filtering through the café window, but her hand kept returning to her left arm. She hadn't consciously noticed it before, but now she felt aware of the space where a tattoo might sit. It wasn't just wanting a new drawing; there was a pull, a curiosity about permanence – something to hold onto in this place that always seemed to shift and change. A small irritation flickered: Violet was conspicuously absent. Was she deliberately avoiding her? Or was it simply Violet being, well, Violet? The thought sparked a brief, hazy memory of Violet's quick smile, the scent of ink and sandalwood, and the feeling of being utterly captivated by a single brushstroke. It felt both distant and incredibly vivid. Krissy added weight to her wondering, should she get one of her own illustrations tattooed on her arm – something bold, something that would last?

She started sketching ideas in her notebook: a tangled vine, a soaring bird, a single, watchful eye. Then, the thought hit her – Violet. Of course. It felt almost inevitable. Should she want Violet to do it? The memory of Violet's precise hand and artistic eye was so strong. She pictured Violet meticulously layering colours, creating something beautiful and lasting. A small anchor, maybe? Or perhaps a little wren – delicate and resilient, like Krissy herself sometimes felt. She chewed on the end of her pencil, lost in thought. It wasn't just about the design; it was about the process, the connection, the feeling of being truly seen by another artist. "You staring at your arm again," Llew said quietly, sliding into the chair opposite her. He'd been stacking mugs behind the counter, but he'd clearly noticed. "Something interesting?" Krissy quickly snapped shut her notebook, a little flustered. "Just...thinking." Llew raised an eyebrow, his gaze gentle and perceptive.

"About a tattoo?" He didn't press it, simply observing her for a moment. "Violet used to do lovely work," he said softly. Krissy felt a slight blush creep up her neck. "Yeah," she murmured.

Llew paused, taking in her expression. "It's funny, isn't it? Like she vanished with hardly a ripple, and now she turns up here."

Krissy returned to her sketching, the rain intensifying outside, blurring the edges of the streetlamp. The light cast long streaks across the table, illuminating the charcoal dust and the half-finished sketch of the marionette. She traced the outline of its hand with her finger, a small smile playing on her lips. It was a simple design, but somehow perfect. It felt like a ghost of something – a memory, a feeling, perhaps even a hope. The rain continued to fall, washing over Ashcliffe and carrying away the day and its distant worries. She glanced at Llew, who was watching her from across the counter. For a moment, their eyes met – and in that brief exchange, Krissy felt a flicker of something tender before he turned back to polishing mugs, lost once again in the quiet rhythm of the café.

Krissy's pencil danced across the page again, this time freer, more certain. The marionette was shifting – less broken, more whole. It was subtle: the tilt of the chin, the suggestion of breath where there should be none. A puppet, yes, but perhaps one remembering what it meant to be alive. She didn't hear the door open. Didn't hear the bell jingle, or the sudden hush that fell over the café as the warmth of familiarity shifted into something else. She felt it, though – like a chill up her spine, like someone brushing past her shoulder in a crowded room. She looked up, slowly, her heart already knowing. There she was. Violet. Hair darker than she remembered – almost black, save for a stubborn streak of ink-blue curling behind one ear. Dressed in a leather jacket splattered with what looked suspiciously like paint, Violet carried herself like someone who had returned from some place far and strange. Her boots were damp. Her eyes – sharp, stormy – were scanning the café with disinterest until they found Krissy. For a moment, nothing moved. Then Violet offered a brief, lopsided smile. "Hi," she said.

Krissy blinked, unsure whether she'd said the word aloud or just imagined it. Violet crossed the room like a wave – steady, impossible to stop. "I heard you were here" Krissy said finally.

Violet glanced around. "You make it sound like I left on purpose."

Krissy's lips thinned. "Didn't you?"

A shrug. Violet laughed softly, and the sound cracked something in Krissy's chest. "Still better than a voicemail." The café had returned to its hum – Rita was nudging Tom and whispering not subtle questions, while Llew appeared very interested in rearranging the sugar jars. Violet pulled out the chair opposite Krissy and sat, folding her hands neatly in front of her.

"You draw sad things," she said, eyes flicking down at the sketchbook.

Krissy bristled, then softened. "You still show up like a ghost."

"I am a ghost," Violet replied. "Didn't you get the memo?"

Krissy didn't know what to say to that. So she said nothing, just closed her notebook carefully, sealing the marionettes back inside.

Violet drummed her fingers on the table. "I came to ask something. A favour, maybe."

Krissy raised an eyebrow.

"I'm doing an installation whilst I'm here," Violet continued. "Out near the old train graveyard. You know the place?"

Krissy nodded. Everyone in Ashcliffe knew it – a place of rusting carriages and ivy-choked engines, long abandoned when the new tracks were built inland. It was a magnet for graffiti artists, teenagers with torches, and the occasional ghost story. "I need help with the lighting design," Violet said. "And maybe some figures. Painted shadows. You look like you do hands better than me."

Krissy considered her. "Why now?"

Violet shrugged. "Because it's time."

The words hit harder than they should have. Maybe because Krissy didn't know if she agreed. Maybe because Violet had a way of making things sound inevitable. Maybe because part of her – a small, raw part – wanted to say yes.

From behind the counter, Llew appeared. "Tea?" he asked, his voice light.

Violet grinned. "God, yes. Something smoky."

"Lapsang?" he offered.

"Perfect."

He moved off, and Krissy felt a strange gratitude that he hadn't inserted himself into the conversation more. He understood boundaries – even the invisible ones. Violet leaned back in the chair, watching Krissy. "You thinking about it?"

"I don't know," Krissy admitted.

"You should come see it," Violet said. "Before you decide."

The train graveyard was still soaked from the storm. Gravel crunched beneath their boots, and puddles mirrored the thick sky above. The wind carried with it the scent of rust and wet metal – and something else, something nostalgic. Childhood dares, perhaps. Secrets never meant to be spoken. They walked in silence, Krissy lagging slightly behind. Violet seemed at home here – ducking under rotting branches, pausing occasionally to examine the decay like it was sacred. The further in they went, the more the air shifted. There were remnants of past lives here: spray-painted initials, old shoes, even a cracked ceramic doll's head, half-buried in the moss. Krissy shivered. Finally, they reached the carriage. It was one of the largest ones – painted black now, its windows covered with translucent canvas. Inside, pale lights glowed like fireflies. Violet stepped aside, gesturing. "Go on." Krissy climbed the rusted steps, her hand grazing the cold metal rail. Inside, the carriage had been transformed. Figures made of gauze and wire hung suspended from the ceiling, some whole, others barely there – fractured limbs, paper faces, silhouettes stitched together from shadow and thread.

They weren't terrifying. They were mournful. Music played softly, a kind of ambient hum that reverberated in the ribcage. In the far corner, one of Krissy's old sketches – the marionette – had been projected onto the wall in flickering light. She turned slowly, drinking it in. Every piece of the installation felt like it was holding its breath. And suddenly, Krissy understood: this was grief, visualised. This was memory, stilled. She stepped back outside, blinking at the light. Violet was leaning against the frame, watching her carefully. "What do you think?"

Krissy swallowed. "It's..."

"You can say it."

"It's beautiful," she whispered. "And awful. And – it feels like being haunted."

"Exactly," Violet said softly. "We all are, aren't we? Haunted by choices, by people. By who we were before we knew better."

Krissy looked at her then, really looked at her. "Is this about Llew?"

"Of course it is," Violet replied. "It always was."

Back at the café, the air felt warmer, but Krissy couldn't quite shake the cold inside her bones. Llew passed her a blanket without comment, just the way he always did – kind and quiet and unflinchingly observant. She sat by the window again, sketchbook open. But instead of drawing, she wrote a single word at the top of the page: Anchor. And then another: Ghost. Llew approached with a refill. "She still gets to you."

Krissy looked up. "Yeah."

He nodded. "You going to help her?"

"I think I already am."

A pause.

"She hurt me," Llew said gently.

"She left you," Krissy corrected.

"Isn't that the same thing?"

Krissy considered that. "No," she said finally. "It's worse."

Later, after the café had closed and the last of the mugs had been washed and stacked, Krissy lingered at her table, staring at the marionette. She added a single detail – a small string, tied to the puppet's wrist, trailing off the page. Unseen. Untethered. She heard footsteps approach. "I thought you might still be here," Violet said, sliding into the seat opposite her once more. She had a tin of paint in one hand and a folded cloth in the other. Krissy didn't speak. She just handed Violet the sketchbook, letting her see. Violet turned it slowly, her fingers ghosting over the page. "Will you ink it?" Krissy asked quietly.

Violet's eyes lifted. "You want me to do it?"

Krissy nodded. "I want it to be permanent."

Violet exhaled, the kind of breath that carried a thousand things unsaid. "Then I will."

Their eyes met across the table, like a wire being tied between them. Fragile, perhaps. But real.

Krissy looked down at her arm, imagining the marionette resting just beneath the skin. Then at Violet's hands. "Alright," she said. "Let's haunt each other a little longer."

By the time Krissy left the café that night, the rain had stopped completely. Ashcliffe-on-Sea was blanketed in fog, the kind that blurred edges and softened noise. She walked along the beach, waves a distant murmur, her boots crunching on wet stones. The sea, ever-shifting, ever-persistent, whispered against the shore like a promise. From the hill, the faint glow of the train graveyard installation pulsed through the mist, like a heartbeat. Like something waiting to be born. She didn't know what tomorrow would bring. But for the first time in a long while, Krissy felt like she didn't need to. She had a sketch, a name, a ghost. And maybe, just maybe, that was enough.

7

❦

CHAPTER SEVEN: THE ARTIST'S GLARE

The studio where Violet had her guest spot smelled like antiseptic with something sharper underneath – ink, nerves, unfinished words. Violet moved through the space with the grace of ritual: latex gloves snapping on, clean metal clinking on trays, a sterile cloth unfolding over the chair like a shroud. Krissy sat still, her hoodie shrugged off and pooled beside her like a discarded skin. Her tank strap was tugged down to reveal the stretch of her shoulder blade – pale and marked with faint freckles, a canvas that seemed both vulnerable and defiant. Violet crouched to eye-level, needle still capped. "You sure?" Krissy didn't look at her. She was staring at the sketch pinned to the wall across from her – the marionette with hollow eyes and crooked stitches, one of her own. Fragile and furious. "Yeah," she said. "Just don't make it sentimental." Violet peeled off the cap, the buzz of the machine still silent. Her smile was small, dry. "I never do." But they both knew that was a lie.

The machine came to life with a shiver of sound – sharp, relentless, oddly intimate. Krissy stiffened on instinct, breath hitching as Violet pressed cloth to skin, wiped, then began. The first puncture wasn't the worst. It was the realization that it was going to hurt the whole way through. Krissy kept her jaw locked, trying to will herself into detachment. Focus on the wall. The hum. The small pool of light. But every pass of the needle was a question her body didn't want to answer. Her fingers curled around the edge of the seat. She blinked too often. Violet's voice broke the silence, low and steady, like a hand cupped around a candle. "You draw pain like you've held it in your teeth."

Krissy didn't move. "Maybe I have." Silence again. Just the whirr. The soft drag of cloth. The scent of something too clean for how personal this all felt. It had been Krissy's idea, but now – sitting half-clothed under the gaze and touch of someone who used to break hearts for sport – it felt too raw. Like she'd walked willingly into a confession booth. Violet didn't push. She just worked. Her hands never faltered.

"So," she said eventually, the needle still working. "You and Llewellyn. Is that a thing?"

Krissy exhaled slowly, a kind of laugh buried in the sound.

"No one calls him that but you."

Violet didn't look up. "He never corrected me."

Krissy's smile didn't reach her eyes. "He doesn't correct people. He just leaves."

That made Violet pause. Just for a second. The machine hovered in the air, its buzz suddenly louder without motion.

"That's not fair," Violet said.

Krissy turned her head slightly, cheek pressed to cool vinyl. "Neither is a lot of shit."

Another beat of quiet, this one heavy. Violet began again, slower now. The pain returned like breath, rhythmic and inevitable. Krissy let her eyes close.

Outside, the rain was light, almost polite against the windowpanes. The town was held in that late-afternoon hush when everything feels damp and suspended. Violet didn't speak again until the needle stopped. She dabbed at the inked skin with practised tenderness, not quite clinical, not quite personal. Just enough. She stepped back, peeled off her gloves with a snap. "Done." Krissy sat up gingerly, shoulder stiff. Violet held up a hand mirror, angled so Krissy could see the reflection of her own back in the studio's tall frame. The marionette was there – etched in ink now. One string severed. One hand raised. A figure unfinished but enduring. Krissy tilted her head. "It's good."

Violet's voice was quiet. "It's you." Something in Krissy's throat caught, but she said nothing. Just reached for her hoodie and shrugged it on like armour, slow and mechanical. She didn't meet Violet's gaze. The door creaked slightly when she opened it. Violet didn't stop her. Didn't ask for anything else. Krissy left without another word.

Krissy climbed the narrow stairwell to Eloise's old flat above The Chiron Cafe, keys already clenched tight in her hand. The door stuck slightly, as it always did, before giving way with a wooden groan. The room smelled like turpentine, old varnish, and the ghost of someone else's cooking. She stepped inside and kicked off her shoes, the thud echoing in the stillness. Rain whispered against the glass panes. From below came the faint hum of life from the street, distant and indifferent. Music murmured from the corner – low, ambient, the sort of melancholy that didn't insist on itself but threaded through a person like mist. Canvases leaned against the walls at odd angles, some half-finished, others abandoned. A palette lay drying on the desk, stiff brushes poking out of chipped mugs. The whole space had the feeling of a life caught mid-breath. Krissy dropped her hoodie onto a chair, then pressed a hand to her shoulder, just above the fresh ink. It throbbed with that hot, taut ache – familiar, but this one felt heavier. Not just physical. The kind of ache you get when someone sees something you didn't mean to show.

She stared at the blank wall for a long moment, then crossed the room and pulled a fresh canvas from behind a stack. She told herself she was just stretching. Just loosening up. But her fingers already knew what they were doing. She didn't sketch. Didn't plan. Just reached for the ochres, the greys, the muted palette of in-betweens. Her body moved like it was remembering something without permission – wrist flicking, elbow shifting, heart quietly unravelling. A face began to emerge. Soft brown eyes. Gentle, uncertain, ringed with weariness. A mouth caught mid-thought, the corners neither smiling nor frowning, just there, suspended. The curve of a jaw half-shadowed by stubble. A throat swallowed by a worn, oversized jumper — that blue one he always wore when it rained. Llewellyn. But not Llew as she'd flirted with at the café, not the man who made her laugh or flinch or kiss back in the rain. This was him when he thought no one was looking. When he dried mugs with too much care. When he watched Eve and Geraint with that tight-lipped affection that almost seemed to ache.

She painted without checking herself – every layer revealing something that made her feel too close, too honest. There was a clearness in his gaze, something that didn't demand but invited. The kind of look people gave when they meant it. Krissy leaned back on her heels, brush still in hand, heart racing like she'd confessed something out loud. He's too good for this place. Too good for me. She mixed a cooler grey for the shadows under his eyes. He stays. That's the worst part. She didn't know when she'd started crying, but she was aware of the tightness in her chest, the hiccup in her breath. Her shoulder burned where Violet had worked earlier, skin still raw. People don't get to look at me like that unless they're leaving. The brush slipped from her fingers, landing on the floor with a muted clink. She wiped her hands on her jeans and stared at what she'd done. The portrait looked like him. But more than that — it felt like him. And that was unbearable. Krissy stood slowly. Walked across the room. The canvas still glistened, paint not yet dry. She reached out as if to touch it, then thought better of it. Instead, she turned it to the wall. The gesture was sharp, almost angry. Ashamed of what she'd told on it. Of how much she'd seen him. Of how much it meant that he hadn't run. She stood there a long while, the rain ticking like a metronome against the windows, her own breath unsteady in the silence.

The Chiron Café had its own kind of quiet after hours. The kind that hummed, low and soft, beneath the creak of cooling pipes and the faint whistle of sea wind under the door. Golden light pooled around the mismatched furniture, chairs upturned on tables like sleepy dancers mid-bow. Krissy stood barefoot near the counter, mop in hand, sleeves rolled up. A smear of paint stained the back of one hand, half-washed away in a hasty rinse. Rita was stacking glasses behind the bar, whistling tunelessly, her good mood oddly intact for a long shift. "You know you don't have to do this," Rita said, gesturing at the wet floor.

"I know," Krissy replied, not looking up. "That's why I'm doing it."

Rita raised a brow. "You sound like a fortune cookie from a haunted diner." Krissy smirked, but her mind was elsewhere. Her shoulder still ached — not sharply, but with the dull pulse of something healing. The tattoo. The quiet exchange with Violet. The painting she shouldn't have painted. The bell above the door chimed. Llew stepped inside, soft-footed as always, with a canvas bag slung over one shoulder. He looked rain-damp and tired in the way he often did — not worn out, exactly, just well-used by the day. "Evening," he said, holding up the bag. "Left my tools after the shelves."

Rita gave him a long look. "Only man I know who shows up to a closed café with a bag of screwdrivers like it's foreplay."

Llew chuckled. "Well, you know me. Practical."

Rita wiped her hands on a towel and glanced between them – Krissy, who was suddenly overly focused on an invisible stain, and Llew, who was not hiding the small, crooked smile playing at the edge of his mouth. "I'll leave you two to your domestic tension," Rita said. "Goodnight, weirdos." She grabbed her coat and vanished through the back, keys jangling like wind chimes. The door clicked shut. The café exhaled. Krissy kept mopping. Llew didn't move. Just watched her for a moment. Then, lightly: "You've got war paint on again."

Krissy paused, blinked. "What?"

He pointed at her hand – the grey streak along her knuckle. "Who are you fighting this time?"

She considered. "Just ghosts."

He nodded, as if that made perfect sense. "Winning?"

"I don't think ghosts ever really lose," she muttered. Then, glancing at him: "Why are you here really?"

"I told you. Tools." He hoisted the bag. "And maybe I was hungry for one of Mrs. Prior's abandoned scones."

"She took them all. Said they were for 'her jam and her man.'" Krissy made finger quotes.

"Fair enough." He leaned against the counter, eyes flicking down to her arm. "So... you got it."

Krissy's stomach tightened. "Yeah."

"Does it look like the sketch?"

"More or less."

"Can I see?"

She shook her head too quickly. "Not tonight."

Llew didn't push. Just nodded, slow and easy.

"I saw your painting," he said after a pause.

Krissy stilled. "You... what?"

"You left the flat door open. I was dropping the bag off. Didn't mean to spy. Just... recognized myself. Sort of strange."

Krissy didn't look at him. "It wasn't finished."

"It didn't have to be."

The mop clunked into the bucket. Water sloshed.

"You see people," he said quietly. "Even when you pretend not to."

Her throat tightened. "It wasn't – I didn't mean – "

"You don't have to explain," he said, gentle again. "Just... thank you."

Krissy's mouth twisted. "Don't get all poetic. It's just paint."

He didn't argue. Just smiled faintly and looked down, picking at a crack in the counter.

She hated how warm her chest felt. How seen. How terrifying it was that he hadn't called it love, but she'd heard it all the same. Llew looked up again, studying her the way he sometimes did – not prying, just patient. "I'll be here," he said, softer now, "when you're done dodging." Krissy went still. It was the same line he'd thrown at her the day he'd turned up to work in The Chiron Cafe – a joke then, light and teasing. Now it landed differently. Like a tether. Like a promise. She didn't know what to say, so she didn't say anything. He didn't move toward her, didn't press, just reached out and gently squeezed her shoulder – the uninjured one. His hand was warm and steady, grounding. She didn't lean in, but she didn't flinch either. After a beat, he let go, turned, and left with a soft click of the door. Krissy stood there in the golden hush, heart thudding against the quiet. Her hand drifted to her upper arm, where the tattoo lay beneath fabric and skin — tender, healing. It burned a little. And comforted, all at once.

The flat smelled faintly of turpentine and the salt-brushed night. The heater clicked occasionally, slow and tired, while the sea wind pressed against the single-pane windows like a ghost trying to get in. Krissy stood barefoot, hoodie sleeves pushed to her elbows, staring at the painting she'd tried to forget. She'd turned it to face the wall two nights ago. Cowardice dressed as modesty. Now she shifted it back out. Set it in the corner where the light from the streetlamps would catch the ochres, the greys, the softness she hadn't meant to reveal. She stood back. Crossed her arms. Uncrossed them. He looked the way he always did when he wasn't watching anyone. Like he didn't know how kind his face was. How it made her ache in places she'd buried. She sat cross-legged on the rug. Lit a cigarette out of habit, not need. It burned too quickly, bitter on her tongue. She didn't finish it. Let it die in the glass tray beside her. The room was still. No music. Just the hush of the waves and the wind like breath through broken lips. Her tattoo itched under the fabric of her hoodie. It was healing. So was she, supposedly. Krissy looked at the portrait and thought, He doesn't ask for anything. That was the worst part.

People always wanted something – answers, apologies, attention. Even Violet, for all her clinical edges, wanted to be understood without ever having to explain herself. But Llew... Llew just waited. With his steady eyes and open silences. People who didn't push made it harder to keep the armour on. They didn't give you anything to fight against. Just held space until you stepped into it. If you did. Her phone was face down on the coffee table. She reached for it and typed quickly before she could second-guess, to the number she'd been given by Violet for aftercare questions: 'It looks better than it feels.' Three dots appeared almost immediately: 'Then it's honest.' Krissy exhaled through her nose, a laugh too small to be heard. Violet always cut to the vein.

She dropped the phone and leaned back until her shoulder blades hit the floorboards. Cold crept through the fabric of her hoodie, grounding and uncomfortable. It helped. She reached up, pulled the duvet off the unmade bed nearby, and dragged it down to the floor. Tucked it around her like a shield. Or a surrender flag. The painting loomed quietly across from her. Llew's soft expression. The slight curve at the corner of his mouth – not a smile, exactly. More like the idea of one. He watched her. Or he didn't. But it felt like he did. She whispered to the ceiling, voice frayed and quiet, "Don't wait too long, okay?" She didn't know if she meant him. Or herself.

The morning was an ache. Not just the one stitched into her shoulder – though that was a pulsing reminder of everything she'd done and said and not said the day before – but the deeper, duller ache that came from too much stillness. Krissy woke tangled in the duvet on the floor, hair matted, mouth dry. The light from the window was that watery grey that didn't promise anything: not sun, not rain, just a kind of atmospheric shrug. She sat up slowly, feeling like her body belonged to someone else. The painting still faced outward. It hadn't moved in the night. Neither had she. Krissy rubbed her eyes and padded barefoot to the tiny kitchen alcove. The kettle clicked on with a tired wheeze. The tile was cold against her feet, grounding. Familiar. She poured water over instant coffee, stared at the steam for a long minute, then added nothing. No sugar. No milk. Just bitterness, straight and unadorned. Like the rest of her week. She sipped, then checked her phone. No new messages.Not from Violet. Not from Llew. The last message was still there – Then it's honest. Violet didn't do follow-up. Krissy respected that. She thumbed it closed, shoved the phone into her pocket, and looked around the flat like she might find something to hold onto. A reason to stay. A reason to leave. All she saw were half-finished canvases and a dried-out palette, the mess of a person who never quite committed to anything whole. Except for that painting. And now it was looking back at her like it knew.

The Chiron Cafe was half full by mid-morning, enough to be noisy but not chaotic. Krissy took her usual place behind the counter, apron knotted loosely, her hair shoved into a messy bun that wasn't really trying to win the fight against her thick curls. Her shoulder was sore under the fabric, but she'd taken two painkillers and told herself to get on with it. That was how healing worked, right? You just... got on with it. Rita noticed the second she came in. "You look like you either murdered someone or fell in love."

Krissy raised an eyebrow. "Pretty sure that's the same look."

Rita snorted and handed her a tray. "You left this in the sink yesterday. Coffee sludge apocalypse."

"I was busy not having a breakdown on the floor," Krissy said flatly.

"Glad to hear it went well." Rita leaned closer, voice softening. "You okay?"

Krissy hesitated. "Not sure."

"Yeah. That sounds about right."

It was enough. She didn't need more than that from Rita. They worked in easy silence after that, falling into a rhythm of machines steaming, plates clinking. The café held them like it always did, like a favourite coat that still fit even if you'd grown in strange places. Around noon, the door chimed. Violet walked in. Krissy froze for a moment – not visibly, she hoped, but something in her spine locked. Violet looked exactly the same as always: sharp, unreadable, her black boots echoing slightly on the floorboards as she crossed the room. She wasn't here for coffee. She wasn't here for conversation. She was holding something. A small, flat box. Wrapped in brown butcher paper and tied with black thread. Krissy met her at the counter. "You left your aftercare balm," Violet said. Her voice was neutral, but her eyes lingered.

Krissy took the package, fingers brushing Violet's. "Thanks."

"You alright?" Violet asked. Not like Rita had asked. More like she was taking inventory.

Krissy nodded. "I will be."

Violet's lips curved – not a smile, just the ghost of one. "Let it peel. That's how you know it's working." Krissy watched her leave. The door swung shut behind her with a gust of sea wind. She unwrapped the parcel behind the counter. The balm was there, sure, but so was a folded piece of sketch paper. When she opened it, she found a quick, rough ink drawing — her own shoulder, rendered in lines that were softer than Violet usually allowed herself. The marionette was there. But this time, both arms were free.

Krissy didn't go home after her shift. She walked. Past the Post Office, the old cinema that still showed movies with reel projectors, the bookstore with its crooked windowpanes. Past the point where the pavement ended and the cliffs began. She walked on. The sea was restless – not angry, but unsettled. Gulls cawed above her, and the clouds hung low enough to scrape the horizon. She sat on the bench where Llew had once told her he liked the quiet. Back then, she hadn't believed him. Thought it was just something people said when they didn't know how to be interesting. But now... She pulled her hoodie tighter around her and let the wind rush through her like a rinse. Her phone buzzed. Llew: 'Still painting ghosts?' She stared at it for a long time before replying. Krissy: 'Thought I'd try painting the living for once.' The typing bubble appeared, paused, disappeared. Then: 'Let me know if I need to sit still.' She laughed. Alone, hair lashing her cheeks, throat tight. She didn't reply. Not yet. But she saved the message.

That night, she didn't smoke. She didn't paint. She just stood in the doorway of her flat, staring at the canvas she'd turned back around. The man in the picture still looked like Llew. Still looked kind. She crossed the room, crouched in front of it, and added one last stroke to the corner of his eye – a highlight. Just enough light to say yes, I see you too. And then she started something new.

A week passed. Then another. The studio that Violet had borrowed for her guest spot had already been packed up, her things boxed and gone like she was never there. Krissy hadn't gone back. She didn't need to. The tattoo itched and healed and settled. Sometimes she caught herself touching it without thinking – a reflex when she was unsure or lost in thought. The Chiron Cafe kept humming. So did the town. Eve showed up with a tray of leftover cupcakes. Geraint brought in an old guitar to hang on the café wall "for ambiance." Rita sneaked a bottle of whiskey behind the juice fridge and made a game out of trying to get Krissy to do shots after closing. Life didn't pause for anyone's un-ravelling. And maybe that was okay.

One night, Krissy stayed late. The café was empty, just her and the echo of the day. She set up an easel by the window and started paint-ing. Not Llew. Not ghosts. Just the scene outside – the cobbled street, the pub signs swaying, the sky bruised with indigo. She heard the bell ring but didn't turn.

"Still open?" Llew asked softly.

"For you," she replied, before she could second-guess it.

He stepped inside, quiet as always. No canvas bag this time. No ex-cuse. Just him.

"I've been thinking," he said after a pause.

Krissy lowered her brush. "Dangerous habit."

He smiled. "Probably. But I was wondering if maybe you'd want to come with me. Just... a drive. No talking unless you want. No plans."

Krissy looked at him. Looked and looked. Then nodded. "Okay." He didn't smile like he'd won. He smiled like someone who'd been wait-ing for a seed to sprout, and now that it had, he was just glad it hadn't died in the soil. She cleaned her brushes in silence. He waited.

The drive was quiet in Geraint's old runaround car. No music. Just the low rumble of tires on wet roads, and the occasional creak of the heater turning over. They didn't talk. Krissy watched the landscape blur past – trees and hedgerows, darkened fields, the occasional flash of a fox in the underbrush. Finally, Llew pulled over near a clearing. Got out. Didn't ask her to follow, just started walking toward the edge of a wooded path. Krissy hesitated only a second, then followed. They walked under the hush of trees, the night sky barely visible through the canopy. Finally, the woods opened into a clearing lit by moonlight. A rope swing hung from an old oak. Llew glanced at it. "Reminds me of pushing Geraint when he was young: he used to go high enough that he could kick the clouds, he'd say." Krissy looked up. "Want a turn?" He continued. She didn't answer. Just walked over, gripped the rope, and sat. Llew stepped behind her, hands gentle on her back. He pushed. Not hard. Just enough. Krissy let herself swing, the wind lifting her hair, the stars tilting slightly. She didn't laugh. Didn't cry. Just breathed. He caught her on the backstroke. Held her there.

Their silence stretched. A good silence. Then, very quietly, Krissy whispered, "I'm scared I'll ruin this."

Llew didn't let go. "Then don't," he said. Simple. Steady.

"I don't know how to keep something that doesn't need fixing."

"You don't have to keep it," he replied. "Just let it stay." She turned slightly, just enough to see his face. The kindness was still there. The patience. And the promise. She nodded. The swing creaked softly as it settled. And the night held them both.

PART TWO:
BREAKWATER

8

CHAPTER EIGHT:
COLLISION

The rain hadn't fully relinquished its hold on Ashcliffe, clinging to the cobblestones and blurring the edges of The Chiron Café like a watercolour left out in the sun. It was a good sort of grey – perfect for Krissy's mood. She pushed open the door, the familiar scent of coffee and burnt sugar doing little to lift her from whatever unsettled state she was currently inhabiting. It felt like she'd woken up in someone else's body – a slightly paler, more hesitant version of herself. The marionette tattoo on her shoulder pulsed with a dull ache, a tiny, insistent reminder of the way Llew's fingers had brushed hers. He was already there, perched on his stool behind the counter, polishing glasses with an expert hand. He looked contained. Like he'd been squeezed through a keyhole. It wasn't the usual quiet, comfortable Llew; this one was sharper, almost brittle.

"Morning," Krissy offered, attempting a cheerful tone that felt thin and forced.

"Yeah," he replied, his voice a little too clipped. "You." It wasn't exactly warm. Not like it used to be. Or maybe it was, but the warmth was layered with something else – a cautiousness, an awareness of the precariousness of their current state. The banter, usually a comfortable current between them, felt strained, like wading through treacle. "Sleep well?" Krissy ventured, instantly regretting it when he raised an eyebrow.

"Fine," he said simply, and returned to his glasses.

"Just...fine?" She prodded gently. "Did you have that dream about the lighthouse again? The one where you were chasing a seagull with a tiny umbrella?"

He didn't smile. "It was a vivid dream."

"Vividly unsettling," Krissy countered, and then immediately wished she hadn't said it. It landed sharper than intended. He just tightened his grip on the glass.

The morning progressed in this fashion – small, off-kilter moments. Llew corrected Mrs. Prior's pronunciation of "raspberry" (it was definitely 'raspery'), and Krissy teased him about it, but he didn't even glance her way. Rita, perched on a stool by the counter, observing with her usual sharp wit, commented dryly, "He's been like that all morning. Like someone stole his favourite spoon.

"Maybe he just needs to be fed," Krissy offered, earning a pointed look from Llew.

"Some things need to be measured carefully," Llewelyn replied, placing the coffee in front of him.

It was a loaded sentence. They were both carrying things – the portrait of Krissy hanging in her mind, Violet's sketch still tucked away, the lingering warmth of their kiss, and all those moments of comfortable silence that now felt thick with unspoken questions. "Did you see Eve and Geraint yesterday?" Krissy asked, trying to steer the conversation towards safer ground. "They were showing off the ultrasound again."

"Briefly," he said, stirring his coffee. "They seem delighted."

"Delighted," Krissy echoed, a little hollowly. It was a word that felt distant, like something she'd heard about other people's lives.

Suddenly, Mrs. Prior bustled over with a plate of jam scones. "Here you go, dearie! Fuel for the soul." She paused, studying them both.

"You two are acting like a pair of grumpy squirrels. What's got your tails in a twist?" They both offered a quick, slightly awkward smile, and Krissy felt a familiar pang – the feeling of being trapped, of needing to say something, anything, but not wanting to break the fragile surface. As she took a scone, she noticed Llew staring out the window, his gaze fixed on the rain-slicked street. He looked lost. And for just a moment, Krissy wondered if he was looking for her, or trying to remember where she'd gone.

The rain had softened to a persistent drizzle as they were left alone in the café back room, stacking chairs and wiping down the counter. It was one of those late afternoon moments where everything felt slightly muted, like the world was settling into its evening hues. A small, almost comforting routine – a shared task that usually eased the tension between them, but today, it only seemed to highlight it. "Did you put the 'Extra Strong' tea bags in with the Earl Grey?" Krissy asked, stacking chairs haphazardly.

Llewelyn paused, his hand hovering over a stack of napkins. "I thought you did."

"Well, you were the last one to make tea," she retorted, a little sharper than intended.

"Right," he said, returning to the napkins with deliberate efficiency. "So, who put them in?" It started small, almost ridiculously – over tea bags. But it was the kind of small thing that had been building for days, accumulating like dust motes in a sunbeam.

"You're always so calm," Krissy said, her voice laced with something approaching frustration. "Do you ever feel anything? Like, really feel?"

Llewelyn turned to face her, his expression unreadable. "What's that supposed to mean?"

"I don't know," she shrugged, stacking another chair a little too forcefully. "You just absorb everything. Like it doesn't bother you at all."

"And you?" he countered. "You disappear when things are real. You treat everyone like a temporary sketch." The words hung in the air, heavier than they had any right to be. Krissy felt her cheeks flush. "It's not that simple," she muttered, turning back to the chairs.

"Isn't it?" Llewelyn stepped closer, his voice low. "You always let yourself get so invested, and then you bolt. Maybe not physically, but emotionally for sure. "

"Because," she snapped, finally turning to face him, "because sometimes people just use you." She didn't elaborate, but he knew. He'd seen glimpses of it – the way she'd laughed at his jokes when she wasn't really listening, the quickness with which she'd packed up and moved on from previous relationships.

"You've been used before," Llewelyn accused, his gaze unwavering. "You haven't let anyone in properly."

"And you?" Krissy shot back. "You're always so guarded. Like you're terrified of being left again." The words tumbled out, raw and a little vulnerable. It was a direct hit – he'd been haunted by Violet, by her sudden departure, by the feeling that she hadn't truly valued him.

"It's not 'terrified,'" he said, his voice tight. "It's... remembering." The rain seemed to intensify for a moment, drumming against the windowpanes. Krissy felt herself getting smaller, as if shrinking under his gaze. "You make it sound like I chose to be lonely," she said quietly. "Like I wanted to be an inspiration. Like some muse you used up and discarded."

"That's not fair," he argued, but the defensiveness in his voice betrayed him.

"Isn't it?" She gestured vaguely. "You know, when you were talking about Violet, it felt like you were still trying to figure out how she could just walk. Like you weren't quite sure if she'd actually left or if you'd imagined the whole thing."

The tension in the room thickened, palpable and electric. Llewelyn took a step back, his hand instinctively moving towards the door frame.

"It was real," he said, his voice barely above a whisper. "She just... vanished."

"Maybe," Krissy replied, her own voice equally quiet. "Or maybe she simply chose to run."

He turned away, running a hand through his hair. The silence stretched between them, filled with the unspoken weight of their shared pasts and their hesitant hopes for the future. Suddenly, Llewelyn took another step back, bumping into the wall behind the counter with a soft thud. He didn't seem to notice, continuing to stare out at the rain. Krissy found herself instinctively taking a step towards him, wanting to bridge the small distance that had opened between them, but then hesitated – as if afraid of breaking something fragile. The air felt suddenly tight, constricted by the shared space and the unresolved emotions. It was like being trapped in a small room with a storm brewing – the feeling that anything could spark.

Krissy felt herself getting smaller, as if shrinking under his gaze. She turned and walked towards the door, stepping out into the drizzle. Llewelyn didn't hesitate, following close behind. They ended up under the old railway bridge, a grey sentinel overlooking the sea. The rain plastered Krissy's hair to her face and softened the edges of the village lights in the distance. It was quiet – just the sound of the rain and their breathing. "It's silly," she said finally, her voice barely audible above the water rushing beneath the bridge. "I always feel temporary. Like I'm squatting in other people's lives. Like I don't really belong anywhere." Llewelyn didn't say anything for a long moment. Then he spoke, his voice low and hesitant. "You know, Violet left. Just vanished. One day she was there, the next gone. It scared me, that a person could just do that."

"It's just," Krissy continued, looking out at the sea, "it's like... you always think I'll run."

"Maybe," he admitted, his gaze meeting hers. "Maybe I do. Krissy, you're not Violet. You don't just disappear." He paused. "It scares me that you might."

A small, painful understanding passed between them – a recognition of their shared fears, of the ghosts they carried with them. She thought he wanted everything from her, needed her to stay, to be anchored like him. He thought she was already planning her escape, seeking out the next interesting place to squat. "It's not that I don't want—" Krissy began, then trailed off, unsure of how to articulate her feelings.

"You just want to run," Llew finished for her, a little sadly.

She nodded, feeling a familiar pang of guilt. "Maybe," she said softly. "Maybe you're right." The silence returned, but this time it felt different – not as tight or brittle, but heavier, laden with the weight of unspoken fears and tentative hopes. He shifted slightly closer to her, seeking warmth in the rain and each other. Krissy instinctively leaned into him, finding a small measure of comfort in his presence. It was just then that she noticed he'd moved – a little too quickly, a little too deliberately – and found herself pressed against the rough stone wall of the bridge, her back brushing against his. It felt... intimate. And for a moment, she thought he wanted too much – to hold on, to keep her from running. But then again, wasn't that what she craved?

The rain hadn't quite given up its hold on Ashcliffe by the time they stepped out from under the railway bridge. A bruised purple was spreading across the sky, promising a brief respite – and perhaps, a little bit of heat. They stood there for a moment, simply listening to the rain's increasing intensity, as if afraid it would shatter the fragile quiet that had settled between them. Krissy found herself staring at Llewelyn's face – the way the light caught in his dark hair, the slight furrow of his brow, the vulnerability she hadn't expected to see. It was like looking into a half-remembered dream – familiar and yet profoundly distant. He shifted slightly closer, almost unconsciously, and suddenly they were inches apart. The air crackled with unspoken words, with years of missed opportunities and tentative hopes. Krissy felt a strange pull – a desperate need to bridge the gap that had always separated them, but also an instinctive fear of what might happen if she did.

It wasn't a planned thing, not really. It was more like a collision – a sudden, undeniable rush of emotion that swept over them both and propelled them forward. Llewelyn didn't hesitate. He leaned in, his hand moving almost to her cheek – a gesture so simple, yet so loaded with meaning – and then he kissed her. It wasn't neat. It was messy, a little awkward at first, as if they were both rediscovering each other after a long absence. It was breathless, filled with the taste of rain and something else – a hint of salt from her tears. It was too much – a chaotic blend of grief for what might have been, longing for what could be, and years of silence finally finding release. It felt like colliding with a familiar shore after being adrift at sea. He wasn't just seeking warmth; he was seeking to break through the layers she'd so carefully constructed around herself. She met his lips with a hesitant eagerness, her arms instinctively moving forward to cup his face. It was as if they were trying to capture something fleeting – a moment of connection before it slipped away again. But it wasn't just about lust, not entirely. It felt like intimacy trying to break through the panic – a desperate attempt to prove that maybe, just maybe, they weren't completely lost to each other. It was a collision of shared sadness and the fragile hope that perhaps, after all this time, they could finally find something real. Then, as suddenly as it began, it ended. Krissy pulled back sharply, her eyes wide with surprise and a little bit of fear. "I—I didn't mean—" she stammered, pulling her hand away as if burned. "This isn't—"

Llew didn't push. He simply held onto her gaze for a moment, his expression unreadable in the gathering gloom. Then, he tilted his head up and said softly, "You don't have to mean it yet." He paused, letting the words sink in. Then, with a gentle smile – a genuine, warm smile that Krissy hadn't seen on his face in years – he added, "But we did." It was an acknowledgement – a quiet affirmation of the connection they'd just shared. It wasn't a promise of forever, not yet, but it was enough to make her heart skip a beat.

They remained frozen for a moment, suspended between two worlds – the one they knew and the one that suddenly seemed possible. The rain picked up, drumming against their faces like a restless heartbeat. Then, almost as if by instinct, Krissy stepped back – not out of rejection, but out of fear. She didn't want to break the spell, didn't want to risk shattering the fragile connection they'd just forged. Llew mirrored her movement, stepping back too – leaving a small space between them, filled with unspoken questions and tentative possibilities. "It was... nice," she offered, trying for casualness, but her voice sounded a little shaky.

"It was," he agreed, his eyes still fixed on hers. The storm above them intensified, flashes of lightning illuminating their faces – revealing the vulnerability and longing that lay beneath. They stood there for a long moment, caught in the eye of the storm – both wanting to move forward, to take the next step, but also both hesitant to let go of the magic they'd just created. It was as if they were poised on the edge of something – a new beginning, or perhaps, simply another collision.

Krissy's use of Eloise's flat had turned it into a small haven of controlled chaos – a mismatched collection of furniture, half-finished canvases, and teetering stacks of books. It smelled faintly of turpentine and rain. She'd been sketching for almost an hour now, but the paper remained stubbornly blank. It wasn't that she couldn't draw; it was that everything felt... wrong. Like trying to capture a fleeting memory with a brush dipped in lukewarm water. She tried again – sketching the view from her window: the rain-slicked rooftops of Ashcliffe, the distant glimmer of the sea. But the lines were shaky, uncertain. It felt like she was fighting against something – a current pulling her back to whatever had just transpired under the railway bridge. Her fingers instinctively reached for the marionette tattoo on her shoulder. The ink pulsed faintly beneath her skin, a reminder of her own restless nature, of always feeling like a mismatched piece in someone else's puzzle.

She traced the lines with her thumb – thinking of Violet, of the idea of permanence, of Llew and his quiet strength. Was she even capable of wanting something that lasted? Or was she destined to be just another fleeting sketch, admired for a while and then discarded?

She wasn't sure what she wanted, just... stability, perhaps. Something solid to hold onto. But it felt like a selfish desire, given everything else going on. She feared letting herself feel – of truly opening up, of allowing someone to see the messy, uncertain parts of her soul. Meanwhile, across town, Llew was lost in his own quiet turmoil. He sat at his small kitchen table, nursing a cup of tea and scribbling in his journal – trying to make sense of the fight, of the kiss, of everything that had suddenly shifted between them. The words spilled onto the page – a mixture of frustration, relief, and a surprising amount of hope. It felt real – not like one of those fleeting moments that dissolved into nothingness.

He wasn't angry – just... relieved. Relieved that they hadn't brushed it off, that they hadn't retreated back to their usual guarded selves. The fight had unearthed something genuine – a connection that had been buried beneath layers of silence and fear. He stared out the window at the rain, watching the water cascade down the glass, carrying with it all the unspoken words and lingering emotions. As he finished his tea, he noticed Krissy's sketch lying on the table – the one she'd left for him after their walk. He picked it up – a simple drawing of a marionette, its arms outstretched as if reaching for something. He glanced over at her, and she caught his eye – both of them holding onto small tokens from each other: her sketch lay beside his chipped ceramic mug, which she'd given him last week. And on the side table sat Violet's little sketch – a reminder of everything that had been, and perhaps, everything that could be again. They were suspended – holding onto these fragments, wondering what just happened, and if it meant anything at all. Outside, the rain continued to fall – a steady, melancholic rhythm that seemed to echo within them both. Krissy was sketching again, this time by the window, capturing the grey light of late afternoon. A memory flickered in her mind – a brief moment from months ago: Llewelyn smiling, raindrops clinging to his eyelashes as he watched her paint. It was a simple image – but it felt significant, like a key unlocking something within her. She whispered to herself, almost without realizing it, "This shouldn't matter." But it did. It definitely mattered.

Krissy didn't sleep. Not really. She lay sprawled across Eloise's lumpy couch with one arm slung over her eyes, listening to the occasional tick of the radiator and the constant whisper of the rain outside. Her sketchbook lay open on the floor, pages fluttering every time the wind rattled the window. The marionette drawing stared up at her, its outstretched arms feeling less like a symbol and more like a plea. She finally sat up just before dawn, the light in the sky that uncertain shade of steel-blue. Her limbs ached with the kind of tiredness that came from emotional exhaustion, not lack of rest. She made tea. Let it steep too long. Drank it anyway. And then she stood by the window, forehead pressed against the cold glass, staring out at the street below. Ashcliffe looked like it was still sleeping. No cars. No movement. Just the occasional gust of wind sending a swirl of damp leaves tumbling down the alley. A decision pressed in on her chest. She felt it, heavy and unfinished. She didn't know what it was yet, only that it was coming. Maybe it had already arrived.

Across town, Llewelyn had fallen asleep in the chair beside his bed, still half-dressed. The journal had slipped from his lap onto the floor, pages open to a sketch he hadn't even realized he'd started. Not words this time, but lines: Krissy's back, standing in the rain, the outline of the railway bridge behind her like the ribs of some ancient creature. He woke to the sound of gulls. The rain had slowed to a mist. His first thought was of her. By mid-morning, Krissy found herself walking along the shoreline path, boots squelching in the mud, sketchbook tucked under one arm like a shield. The sea was low and sullen, exposing slick stretches of sand and the broken skeletons of forgotten boats. Driftwood littered the beach, tangled with seaweed and lost bits of rope. She thought she'd feel better out here, away from the weight of closed rooms and unspoken things. But the air felt just as heavy, just as uncertain.

She sat on a piece of driftwood and flipped open her sketchbook. Not to draw, just to look. Her fingers brushed the marionette again, and she frowned. It felt... wrong now. Or maybe incomplete. Behind her, footsteps. She didn't turn around. Llew sat beside her without speaking. The silence between them stretched, but didn't snap. It had changed. Become something quieter. Less brittle. "I thought you might come here," he said finally.

Krissy offered a weak smile. "It's the one place that doesn't ask questions."

He looked out at the tide, rolling in slow and reluctant. "Everything else does."

She was quiet for a moment. Then, "Do you ever think about leaving? Just... starting over somewhere?"

Llewelyn nodded, slowly. "Sometimes. But I think I'm too rooted. Even if I left, part of me would stay."

She exhaled, nodding. "That's what scares me. That I'll leave and still carry it all with me."

He turned toward her then. "Krissy, you're not a ghost. You don't vanish just because you're afraid."

"I do, though," she admitted. "I evaporate. I become someone else. That's why I'm so good at sketching people – I never stay long enough to get stuck."

Llew looked down at his hands, as if they held the answer. "I never wanted you stuck," he said softly. "I just wanted you to stay long enough to believe you could choose not to leave." They sat in silence again, watching the tide creep in, each wave dragging more of the past out to sea. Finally, Krissy spoke. "Do you still have that sketch Violet gave you? The one with the birds?" He nodded. "It's on the mantel." "She drew me once, you know. Without asking. Said I looked like I was always in motion, like something about me hadn't landed yet."

He smiled faintly. "That sounds like her."

"I hated it," Krissy admitted. "Because it was true."

Llewelyn reached for her hand, tentative. "And now?"

She looked down at their fingers – his calloused, hers stained faintly with charcoal. "Now I think maybe landing isn't the same as stopping." They held hands in the growing light, not as a solution, not as a promise – but as something. An anchor, perhaps. Or just a beginning. Far down the beach, a gull cried, lifting into the sky with a flap of sudden wings. The tide edged higher, and the mist began to thin.

CHAPTER NINE:
INK-STAINED SHEETS

The rain hadn't truly stopped in Ashcliffe: it was more of a persistent drizzle, clinging to everything. It had been with Krissy since she'd woken – a grey, insistent presence that seemed determined to mirror the feeling in her chest. She'd spent most of the morning wrestling with sketches, each one dissolving into a tangle of lines before she could commit it to paper. They were all vaguely melancholic, haunted by violet and charcoal. The rain-streaked window of Eloise's flat offered a blurry view of The Chiron Café, now buzzing with the familiar rhythm of morning. Rita was already behind the counter, wiping down the surfaces with a practised efficiency, while Tom was stacking chairs near the door. It felt normal. And unsettlingly so. The knock on her door was tentative, almost hesitant – a small relief amidst the gathering tension. She hadn't expected him. Not yet.

"Come in," she managed, her voice sounding thinner than usual. Llew stood just inside, leaning against the door frame with an air of quiet observation. He wore a simple grey jumper and his jeans were slightly damp – a detail that, for some reason, felt significant. The scent of sea salt and something faintly woody – like polished wood or old books – clung to him.

"Morning," he said simply, his voice a little rougher than she remembered.

"It's...fine," Krissy replied, turning back to her desk. She picked up a pencil, then immediately put it down again. "The rain."

He didn't move. "It is. Like yesterday. And the day before." He stepped further into the room, his gaze sweeping over the scattered pencils and charcoal sketches – remnants of her restless morning.

"You've been staring at my paintings," she observed dryly, not turning around.

"Just thinking," he said, a small smile playing on his lips. "They're good, Krissy. Really good. You see things."

She finally turned then, tilting her head slightly. "Do I?"

A beat of silence hung between them, punctuated only by the drumming rain. He moved closer, and she could feel the subtle warmth radiating from him – a welcome contrast to the chill in the room. "You capture the edges," he said quietly, gesturing towards her sketches with a hand that lingered for a moment on the edge of her desk. "The bits you don't always show."

She felt a blush creep up her neck. He was good at seeing things, Llew was. It was one of the things she found so unsettling about him – and yet, also somehow comforting.

"I'm a mess," she said finally, a little defensively. "A chaotic, messy illustrator."

"You're not a mess," he countered, his eyes holding hers for a moment longer than necessary.

"You're complicated. And interesting." He paused. "Like the sea." He reached out and gently straightened the crumpled sheet of paper on her desk – the sketch she'd been working on just before he arrived. It was a study of him – not a portrait in the traditional sense, but a capture of his profile as he leaned over the counter at the café, a half-smile playing on his lips.

"You saw me," she said softly, tracing the line of his jaw with her finger. "You actually saw me."

"I'm getting better," he replied, his voice low. "At seeing things." He hesitated, then added: "I wanted to ask about Violet's tattoo. The one you're doing." He stepped closer still, his eyes searching hers. "Do you think...do you think it needs more than just ink? Do you think it needs... a story?" She looked down at her hands, suddenly aware of the faint blue stain from Violet's ink that lingered beneath her fingernails – a tangible reminder of their last encounter. "Maybe," she whispered. "Maybe it does."

He gently took her hand in his, his thumb stroking the back of her hand. The touch was light, tentative - yet electric. "Well," he said, his voice barely audible above the rain, "I think I'm going to help you tell it." And then, without another word, he leaned in and kissed her – a brief, hesitant brush of lips that sent a shiver down her spine. It wasn't particularly passionate or dramatic; it was simple - a quiet acknowledgement of the tangled threads connecting them. As they pulled apart, she noticed something on his sleeve: A tiny, almost invisible smudge of violet ink. She looked at him – and for the first time in days, Krissy didn't feel quite so adrift.

The rain continued its steady drumbeat against the windowpanes of Eloise's old flat, now casting long, shifting shadows across Krissy's desk and the sketches scattered around. It felt like a contained storm – warm and cosy inside, yet still hinting at something brewing outside. Llew stood near the window, his back to her for a moment, as if absorbing the grey light. The dampness of his jeans seemed to have settled into a comfortable softness.

"About earlier..." Krissy began, her voice a little huskier than she intended.

He turned then, turning towards her with an almost gentle curiosity. "It wasn't... awkward."

"Maybe not," she conceded, fiddling with the pencil in her hand. "But it was...surprising."

"I thought maybe you were deliberately brushing me off," he observed quietly.

"Maybe I am," she replied, a small smile playing on her lips. "Maybe I'm just good at dodging."

He stepped closer, his gaze settling on the sketch of him – the one with the half-smile. "You did it."

Krissy followed his line of sight. The drawing felt sharper now, somehow - more defined than she remembered. "It's not just ink," she said, gesturing towards the portrait. "It's... you."

He reached out and lightly brushed a stray strand of hair from her cheek – a simple gesture that sent a jolt through her. "I know." His fingers lingered for a beat longer than necessary. Silence descended again, heavier this time, filled with the unspoken possibilities of their tentative connection. You could almost feel the static in the air – the sense that they were standing on the edge of something, poised to either step forward or retreat back into their respective corners.

"It's a little... intense," he said finally, his voice low and thoughtful.

"Maybe," she agreed. "But it's also...real." She glanced down at her arm – at the delicate blue tracery of Violet's ink, still visible. "I don't know if I'm ready for real."

He tilted his head slightly, studying her face. "Maybe you just need to find someone who doesn't scare you away so easily."

Another beat of silence – this time charged with a different kind of tension. It felt like they could either break the spell and retreat back into their comfort zones - or risk letting themselves be caught. "Don't apologise," he said softly, stepping closer still until they were close enough that she could smell the faint scent of sea and wood on his sweater. "It was real."

She met his gaze – searching for something in those familiar, yet somehow distant, eyes. "I didn't... I don't want to apologise. Just... surprised."

He reached out again, this time taking her hand in his. His thumb gently rubbed the back of her hand – a simple, grounding touch. "It's okay to be surprised," he murmured. "It's okay to be afraid." Their fingers intertwined, and for a moment, Krissy felt like she could simply melt into him – lose herself in the quiet warmth of his presence. She didn't pull away. He leaned in slightly, his breath warm against her cheek. "This might be a mistake," he whispered, almost to himself.

"Maybe," she replied, letting herself be caught by – and by his gaze. "But it's worth the risk." And then, without another word, he kissed her – a little longer this time, a little deeper.

Llew didn't speak at first. He simply stood there, close enough that Krissy could feel the space between them pulse with quiet tension. The room had grown softer somehow—muted by the steady hush of rain, the shadows long and liquid around them. He glanced down at her hand, still held gently in his. Then, slowly, he reached for her shoulder, the one wrapped in a faint strip of gauze where Violet's ink had seeped through skin and meaning. "May I?" he asked, voice low – almost reverent. Krissy nodded, pulse thudding somewhere near her throat. He peeled the bandage back carefully, his fingers ghosting along her skin. The line of the tattoo peeked through: delicate, curling, with a feathered flourish at the edge. A mark of someone else's story, but part of her now. He brushed his thumb across it, barely touching. Her breath hitched at the sensation – cool and warm at once. "You trusted her with this," he murmured, not looking away. Krissy didn't answer. Couldn't, really. Not with the way her chest was tightening – not painfully, but expectantly, like waiting for a wave to break.

When his lips found hers again, it was slower this time. Less of a question, more of a response. Like he was answering something she hadn't said aloud. Their mouths moved with a tentative rhythm, unhurried. It wasn't smooth or cinematic – there was a soft bump of noses, a shared laugh, an awkward shifting of angles – but it was real. And full of want. A kind of aching curiosity that had been building since the café, since the first moment she'd really seen him. Llew's hands were warm on her waist. Steady. Not pulling her closer, just letting her decide. She did. Her fingers found the hem of his sweater and paused. "If you want to stop..." she whispered, unsure why the words felt so necessary in the moment. "I don't," he replied, immediate and quiet. Still, neither of them rushed. His jumper came off with a slight tug, the wool catching briefly on his shoulder. She traced her fingertips down his chest, along the faint line of a scar, then back up to the ink etched along his collarbone – a small, intricate compass. "North," she said softly.

"Not always," he replied, and smiled.

Her own shirt followed, sleeves sticking a little from the humidity. Their bare arms touched, skin brushing skin, and the simple friction of it sent a shock through her spine. She tried to make light of it, tried to ease the tension crowding her throat. "So… um, is this the part where I ask if you've got a tragic backstory to go with that tattoo?"

Llew chuckled, the sound low and rolling. "Only mildly tragic," he murmured. "Mostly just… directionally confused."

Krissy huffed a breath that was almost a laugh. "That makes two of us." He kissed her again, this time deeper. More certain. But never demanding. His hands framed her face like she was something fragile – but not in the way people break, in the way people matter. They moved together towards the bed, navigating each other like a new language – tentative, exploratory. Clothes slid off in stutters: the clumsy tug of jeans, the stretch and release of seams, the cotton sigh of shirts dropping to the floor. She touched the tattoo on his ribcage, fingers brushing the inked line of a wave curling into a spiral. He inhaled sharply. Not from pain – just from feeling. "You draw like this," he said against her skin. "You touch with detail."

Her breath caught. His words slid into her chest and settled there, warm and unwieldy. Then it was just breath and hands and warmth, the slow unravelling of thought into sensation. She traced the compass again, then lower, fingertips splaying across the line of his hip. He kissed the edge of her tattoo – right where Violet's ink met skin – like a promise, or maybe a question he didn't need answered. There was no script to it. Nothing choreographed. Just the creak of the bed frame, the hush of the rain, the occasional gasp or half-laughed murmur between them. His hand on her back, firm and grounding. Her fingers in his hair, tugging gently. The small, surprised sounds they made – like discovering tenderness for the first time. It wasn't perfect. But it was honest. When she shifted beneath him, he paused. "You okay?"

"Yeah," she said, a little breathless. "Just... surprised again."

He smiled, forehead resting against hers. "We're good at that." And when they moved together – slow and unsure and real – it felt less like something being conquered and more like something being offered. Not performance, not pressure. Just presence. Every brush of skin, every exhale, every caught breath felt charged – not with tension, but with meaning.

Later, wrapped in the tangle of sheets, she ran her thumb over the line of his collarbone. "You're warm," she murmured.

"You're shaking," he replied gently.

"I know." She exhaled. "I think I forgot how to just... be held."

He pulled her closer, his arms firm around her back. "Then we'll take our time. No rush."

Krissy blinked up at the ceiling. The rain had softened outside, falling in a lazy rhythm now. Inside the room, the only sounds were their breathing and the occasional rustle of fabric. She leaned in, resting her forehead against his shoulder. "You know what scares me the most?"

"What?"

"That I'll need this. That I'll... want it. And then it'll vanish."

Llew didn't answer right away. He reached down, lacing their fingers together. His touch was warm, slightly callused, grounding. "Then I'll just have to keep not-vanishing," he said quietly. "At least for as long as you want me here." Krissy turned to look at him – really look – and saw that he meant it. In the quiet that followed, nothing was resolved. The world outside was still grey, and complicated, and waiting. But here, for now, she was warm. And known. And whole. And when she closed her eyes, she didn't feel adrift. She felt anchored. Krissy lay awake, the sheets pulled up to her chin, tracing the delicate curve of Violet's tattoo on her shoulder with a fingertip. The room was darkish, just the grey light from the rain filtering through the curtains. It smelled faintly of him – sea and something else... wood polish, maybe? – a comforting blend that felt both new and strangely familiar. She'd been lying there for ages, listening to the steady drumming of the rain on the roof, wrestling with a tangle of thoughts and half-formed sentences.

"This is a bad habit," Llew murmured, his voice low and close to her ear. She smiled, turning her head slightly to look up at him. He was propped up against the pillows, one arm flung over across, his face turned down towards the mattress. "So's breathing." The only sound was the rain. Then: "I'd rather not give up either." They didn't say "what this is." Not out loud. But it hung in the air between them – a shared understanding of something shifting, something new and slightly unsettling. It wasn't explosive or dramatic; it was more like the quiet recognition that you've been doing something a little differently lately, and it feels... good.

"I've just been... staring," Krissy said finally, breaking the silence. "At your tattoo."

He chuckled softly, a low rumble in his chest. "It's rather interesting, isn't it? A tiny compass." He shifted slightly, bringing his arm up to rest on his stomach. "Lost direction, Violet suggested."

"She was brutally honest," Krissy said, a small smile playing on her lips. "Which is why she's herself."

"Indeed. She had a way of cutting through the noise." He paused. "You've got a lot of them, don't you? You and your habits."

Krissy considered that for a moment. "I'm good at collecting them," she admitted. "Like half-finished projects. Running away."

"And I'm good at spotting them," he replied quietly. "Before you do."

Another silence, this one filled with the comfortable quiet of shared history and unspoken feelings. She wanted to say it – Stay. Wanted to cling to that feeling of warmth and connection, to push back against the familiar pull of her own solitary drifting. But she didn't. Not yet. It felt too fragile, too precious to risk shattering. "It's funny," she murmured, turning back to trace the tattoo again. "How small things can feel... big."

"They usually are," he agreed softly. "Especially when they involve letting someone in." He shifted again, bringing his arm up higher so that his hand rested lightly on her hip. It was a casual gesture, but it sent a little shiver through her.

"I'm not very good at letting people in," she confessed quietly. "Not really."

"Neither am I," he said, his thumb gently stroking the line of her tattoo. "But maybe... maybe we can work on it." Krissy looked up at him then. She saw the quiet strength in his eyes, the hint of sadness lurking beneath his smile – and something else, too. A willingness. A hope. And suddenly, saying "Stay" didn't feel like such a daunting thing after all. "Maybe," she whispered, letting herself be held for just a moment longer – before the thought that maybe, just maybe, this time it was different truly settled in.

Dawn was just beginning to bleed into Ashcliffe-on-Sea, a pale grey light that seemed determined to make everything feel too real. It cast long shadows across the room, highlighting the dust motes dancing in the shafts of light and softening the edges of familiar objects – her sketchbooks, piled up on the desk; the chipped mug she'd used for last night's tea; the worn armchair where he'd been reading. It was a beautiful morning, undeniably so, but it also felt...exposed. Llew moved with a quiet grace, like he was underwater – familiar, yet somehow separate. He was dressed now, his sleeves rolled up slightly at the cuffs. Krissy watched him, mostly, contenting herself with watching him button his shirt, each movement deliberate and small. It felt like she was studying a photograph, trying to capture the precise moment when he seemed most... present.

He turned then, catching her gaze for a brief second – a flicker of something – before turning back to his reflection in the mirror. He leaned down, gently kissing the side of her temple. "I'll see you at the café," he murmured, his voice still carrying the trace of sleep. She nodded, offering a small, almost imperceptible movement of her head. Didn't say 'please don't go'. It felt too obvious, too desperate. She wanted to simply acknowledge his departure, as if it were an inevitable part of the morning – like the rain that always returned. He straightened up then, smoothing down his shirt with a quick hand. The simple gesture held a weight for her – a silent acknowledgement of the connection they'd shared, and perhaps, a hint of the vulnerability that had hewn it. As he reached the door, she exhaled – like she'd been holding her breath all night. A long, slow release of air that carried with it a mix of relief, sadness, and a touch of something akin to anticipation. It was a small sound, almost lost in the quiet of the room, but it felt significant – a tiny marker of the shift that had taken place. She watched him go, watching him disappear down the hallway, his footsteps muffled by the worn carpet. The door closed behind him with a soft click, and for a moment, the room seemed to shrink around her.

It wasn't a dramatic silence – not filled with unspoken words or lingering glances. It was the quiet of an empty space after a shared warmth – the comfortable hush that settles over things after they've been touched. She shifted slightly on the bed, pulling the covers up higher, as if trying to create a little more distance between herself and the memory of his presence. Krissy wandered over to her desk and picked up her pencil, turning it over in her fingers. She wanted to sketch him – capture that fleeting moment when he'd looked at her with such quiet understanding. But she couldn't quite bring herself to put pen to paper. It felt like trying to hold onto smoke – beautiful, but ultimately elusive. She glanced out the window again, watching as the light strengthened and the rain began to fade. The sky was starting to lighten, revealing patches of blue – a promise of a brighter day. But for now, she felt a little bit grey herself.

A small smile touched her lips – a bittersweet acknowledgment that evenings like last night, with their quiet intimacy and unspoken hopes, were often the hardest to bear. They were beautiful, yes, but they also came with a gentle ache – the reminder of something good that was temporary. She chewed on the end of her pencil for a moment, then returned to her sketchpad – a blank page waiting to be filled. She didn't know what she would draw yet, but somehow, she knew it would have something to do with capturing that feeling – that quiet pull back – and the knowledge that, even though he was gone, a little piece of him remained. The kettle whistled a cheerful tune, a little incongruous with the soft melancholy that clung to Krissy like morning mist. She made herself a pot of Earl Grey – strong, just how she liked it – and then, without much ceremony, poured a cup and settled at the window seat. Dawn was fully here now, painting the sky in shades of pale pink and lavender, casting a gentle glow across Eloise's flat. It felt good to be alone with it, with the quiet hum of creativity and the lingering scent of ink.

Her eyes drifted almost unconsciously to the corner of the room where she'd hidden the portrait – a simple act of defiance against the burgeoning awareness that it was, perhaps, too revealing. It had been there for hours now, a silent sentinel guarding a secret she wasn't quite sure how to unpack yet. Slowly, deliberately, she reached out and peeled back the sheet of brown paper that covered it. The light caught on the charcoal lines just as she'd remembered – capturing his profile perfectly, a quiet intensity in his expression, a hint of that familiar warmth around the corners of his mouth. He looked... thoughtful. Almost vulnerable. "He didn't even flinch when he saw it," she murmured to herself, turning the sketch over in her hands and examining it more closely. It was strange – how a simple portrait could feel like such a bold statement, a small but significant act of vulnerability.

She thought about Violet then – about letting her ink that design onto her skin, trusting the tattooist with a piece of herself. There was something undeniably comforting in that memory, a sense of shared intimacy and understanding. Violet hadn't just marked her; she'd listened to her. She'd seen beneath the surface. Krissy shifted slightly, bringing her hand up to rest on the arm of the chair, tilting it slightly so she could see clearly. Her gaze settled on her own shoulder – on the marionette that now dominated her skin. It was a simple design – a single figure gazing out at the world with an expression of quiet determination. "Arms free," she whispered, and suddenly it clicked. It was about not being tethered; it's about choosing where to be tethered. For so long, she'd felt like a mismatched puzzle piece – tossed around by the currents of her own life, never quite fitting in anywhere. She'd let others define her place, letting them dictate her direction. The metaphor hadn't resonated as strongly when she'd first chosen it – just another quirky detail to add to her collection of oddities. But now... now it felt like a key unlocking something within her.

She traced the line of the marionette's free arm with her finger, feeling the slight roughness of the charcoal beneath her skin. It was a reminder – a quiet affirmation – that she wasn't simply drifting any more. She was navigating – sometimes stumbling, sometimes falling – but always moving forward on her terms. "I wasn't untethered," she said softly to the room, as if speaking to Violet herself. "I was just choosing which strings to let go." She glanced back at the portrait of Llew – his gaze seemed a little less distant now, a little more knowing. He'd seen her, really seen her, and hadn't judged her for it. He'd simply acknowledged her – with that quiet understanding that she was beginning to crave so deeply.

The rain had stopped completely now, and a single ray of sunlight pierced through the clouds. It felt like a blessing – a tiny affirmation of hope after the quiet sorrow of the morning. Krissy took a sip of her tea, letting the warmth spread through her chest. The scent of Earl Grey mingled with the faintest trace of ink and wood polish – a perfect blend of memories and possibilities. She reached for her sketchbook again, a new idea already taking shape in her mind. Maybe she would draw it – the portrait. Maybe she'd finally commit it to paper, not as a secret, but as an acknowledgement of – well, maybe as an acknowledgement of him. For the first time that morning, Krissy didn't feel quite so adrift. She wasn't sure where she was going yet, or what she would find along the way – but she knew, with a quiet certainty, that it wouldn't be by accident. Impulsively, Krissy began to sketch. It wasn't planned, not really – just a need to capture something that had been swirling around in her mind since she'd woken. She worked quickly, almost frantically, the charcoal gliding across the paper with a satisfying scratch. It was a simple scene: a small fishing boat, bobbing gently on a grey sea. But it wasn't the boat itself that held her attention – it was how it was anchored. Not by a rope or a chain, but by a single, almost invisible thread – pale blue against the dark water.

She worked for ages, capturing the way the light caught on the weathered wood of the hull, the gentle curve of the sail, the subtle tension in the thread that held it steady. It was a quiet image – full of suggestion and unspoken meaning. Finally satisfied, she pinned it to the wall above her desk – not for anyone else, really. Just herself. A small, understated declaration of something – a feeling, perhaps. A reminder that even when tossed about by the currents, you could still be anchored. Just as she was about to return to her tea, a soft knock sounded on the door. It was subtle – a gentle tap rather than a forceful rap – and it made her pause. Could it be Llew? Or could it be Violet? She hadn't seen her since yesterday, but the image of her sharp eyes and knowing smile lingered in her mind. Krissy took a deep breath, holding onto the charcoal sketch in her hand. It was uncertain – and perhaps that's exactly what she wanted. The knock came again, slightly more insistent this time. Krissy smoothed down her hair, a small smile playing on her lips. She wasn't sure who was waiting for her outside, but she was determined to find out.

10

CHAPTER TEN: THE MORNING AFTERMATH

The rain hadn't truly quit its hold on Ashcliffe, though the morning was softening into a grey wash. It dripped steadily from the slate tiles above, a gentle percussion to the quiet hum of the town. Krissy opened the door to reveal Tom and Rita, standing awkwardly in the doorway like two well-worn photographs suddenly thrust into the light. The flat above The Chiron Café – Eloise's old space – was comfortably cluttered, a little bit of a mess. Sketches spilled from her desk onto a worn Persian rug, a tangle of charcoal and watercolour pencils. A half-finished cup of tea sat cooling on a small table, its milky surface reflecting the diffused light. The scent of Krissy and Llew's shared intimacy – a heady mix of sea air and something sweeter, something undeniably her – still lingered in the air, a fragile reminder of the previous evening. It felt exposed now, almost vulnerable, amidst the chaos of her creative life.

Rita swept in, radiating the familiar energy that usually made Krissy feel like she'd stumbled onto something exciting. This time, though, there was a sharpness to her gaze, a subtle note of impatience. "So," Rita began, dropping into the armchair opposite Krissy's desk. "Let's get to it. We were wondering where things are going with you."

Tom joined her, folding his arms and leaning forward. "You've been our unicorn for ages, Krissy. The sexy singleton who always pops up when we need a bit of excitement. You'd join us for anything – the pub quiz, the dodgy disco night...but lately...you've just been absent."

Krissy shifted uncomfortably. "I've been busy," she repeated, but this time it felt thinner, less convincing.

"Busy with Llew?" Rita pressed, her eyebrows arched. "Because he's suddenly the centre of your universe."

"It's just comfortable," Krissy mumbled, picking at a loose thread on her cardigan. "He's not demanding."

"That's exactly it," Tom said, his voice gaining a little edge. "You used to want things. You weren't content with being a comfortable option. Now you seem almost relieved to be back in the sidelines."

"Is it him?" Rita asked directly. "Do you feel like a third wheel? Like this thing with Llew is so captivating that it's just pulled all your enthusiasm from us?" Krissy felt a knot tighten in her stomach. It wasn't just them, was it? Was there something else she'd missed, some subtle shift in her own feelings?

"Maybe," Krissy admitted quietly, the word hanging in the air like a small, fragile thing. "Or maybe it's just that I don't want things to change too fast. I liked being comfortable. I like being invisible." Rita studied her for a moment, a knowing look in her eyes. "Well," she said finally, rising to her feet. "Don't get too invisible, alright? We miss the chaos."

Before Krissy could respond, Rita and Tom were gone, leaving behind only the lingering scent of their perfume and a slightly uncomfortable silence. The rain continued its gentle drumming outside, a soundtrack to the quiet discomfort that had settled over her. She picked up a charcoal pencil and began to draw – not a landscape, not a portrait, but a small, intricate sketch of a single raindrop clinging to a leaf, reflecting the grey light back at her. It felt like a good description of how she was feeling: present, yet distant, caught between wanting to be seen and wanting to disappear altogether

Later, after Krissy had wandered downstairs to The Chiron Cafe for food and company, Krissy found herself listening to the distinct click of heels on the pavement. And then she was there – Violet. Not a dramatic entrance, not a flurry of apologies or a cascade of perfume, just there. She slid into a chair at the counter, as if it were the most natural thing in the world. Her once-sharp features were softened around the edges, there was a slight weariness to her eyes, but she still carried an undeniable air of elegance – like a perfectly preserved vintage dress, slightly faded but undeniably beautiful. She was casual and almost detached, as if she'd simply stepped off a train from anywhere and everywhere. "Llewelyn," she said, her voice clipped, without warmth or fanfare. "It's been a while."

He didn't startle, didn't offer the usual flurry of questions. He simply raised an eyebrow, a flicker of something – surprise? Recognition? – passing over his face. "Has it?" he replied, his tone neutral.

"Feels like yesterday," Violet countered, taking a sip of her coffee. "And a lifetime ago."

The exchange was brief, measured, yet it immediately snapped Krissy out of her quiet contemplation. It wasn't an angry confrontation, not overtly, but there was a current running beneath the surface – years of unresolved tension, of unspoken words and lingering hurts. It felt like two pieces of a puzzle that had been painstakingly separated and now were being tentatively brought back together, only to find they didn't quite fit anymore.

"You're sketching," Llew observed Krissy, who hastily resumed the rhythm of her pencil on paper. "Just trying to capture the drizzle," she said vaguely, not looking up. "It suits Ashcliffe."

"You're capturing a lot of things you don't want to acknowledge," Violet offered, her gaze fixed on Krissy for a moment before turning back to Llew. Llew's hand instinctively went to his chest, as if bracing himself against an unseen wave. A small frown creased his forehead. "The rain," he murmured, almost to himself. "It always reminded me of...that."

Violet followed his gaze, a subtle shift in her expression – something like recognition mixed with a hint of melancholy. It was then that the flashback began, triggered by Violet and seemingly pulled from the depths of Llew's memory. It wasn't a dramatic, sweeping recollection. It started subtly, almost imperceptibly, as if he were simply re-experiencing a particular moment in time. He was standing on a platform at Cardiff Central Station – rain lashing, blurring the lights of the arriving and departing trains. The air smelled of wet wool and smoke. It was grey, relentlessly grey, like a painting by Turner. He'd been clutching his bag, still packed with essentials – a half-finished sketchbook, a worn copy of Yeats, a small collection of violet ribbons. He turned to look for her, scanning the throng of travellers rushing through the station. She should have been there, waiting for him, her head tilted back, laughing at one of his terrible jokes. But she wasn't. "Where are you?" he'd asked then, his voice barely a whisper above the din of the station.

He remembered the feeling of disbelief, of confusion, of something being ripped away – as if a vital part of him had been suddenly and irrevocably severed. The rain seemed to intensify then, soaking through his coat, mirroring the coldness that was spreading through him. It felt like the world was tilting on its axis, and he was desperately trying to hold onto something solid, but everything was slipping away. A quick visual – a suitcase rolling along the platform, swallowed by the rain; a blurred face in the crowd – then...nothing. Just the lingering scent of rain. The flashback faded as quickly as it had begun, leaving Llew blinking slightly, as if emerging from a dream. He looked momentarily lost, vulnerable, like a boy stripped bare.

"It was raining that day," he said quietly, his voice still carrying a trace of the past. "Always rained when she left." He took a sip of his coffee, avoiding Krissy's gaze. "She just...vanished." Krissy watched him, sensing that she had glimpsed something significant – a hidden corner of Llew's heart. She looked back at Violet, who was now studying her with an almost predatory interest.

"You're good," Violet said softly. "You've always seen things. It's why you pull people into your orbit."

"Is that what I do?" Krissy asked, a small smile playing on her lips. "Just suck everyone in?"

The rain, thankfully, had begun to ease its grip on Ashcliffe, leaving behind a damp and slightly shimmering air. But the feeling within the walls of The Chiron Café hadn't quite lifted – it was more like a muted hum now, a blend of lingering humidity and unspoken anxieties. It felt as if the café itself, with its chipped teacups and familiar scent of coffee and cinnamon, had become a sort of confessional for Krissy, absorbing everyone's quiet observations and offering a small measure of comfort. Mrs. Prior, ever attuned to the moods of the townsfolk, appeared at Krissy's side with a steaming mug of Earl Grey and a generous dollop of strawberry jam. "Just a little something to chase away the grey," she offered, her voice as warm and comforting as her homemade preserves. "Rita was saying you've been looking like you haven't slept in days. Is it him? That man of yours?" Krissy took a sip of tea, letting the warmth spread through her. "Just thinking," she mumbled, avoiding eye contact with Llew, who was nursing his coffee and observing her from across the counter.

Mr. Jones grumbled from his usual armchair, stirring his sugar into a generous amount of milk. "She's always thinking," he declared to no one in particular. "Like a trapped moth, fluttering about trying to find its way out."

"Nonsense, Mr. Jones," Mrs. Higgins chirped from the corner table, knitting furiously. "Krissy just needs a bit of stability. She's been like a ship without a rudder lately." A snippet of conversation from two elderly ladies at the window table caught Krissy's ear: "She looks...haunted. Like she's carrying around a secret."

It was those small details, those quiet observations from the people who frequented The Chiron Café – the ones who knew her routines, her quirks, her little anxieties – that truly underscored her state. The need for routine, for the familiar comfort of Mrs. Prior's tea and jam, felt particularly acute today. She craved the predictability of it all, a sharp contrast to the unsettling shift in her own life. Llew, seemingly oblivious to the commentary, continued to watch her, his gaze steady and perceptive. He'd asked about Violet – about the "why" behind her abrupt departure – and she was still struggling with that, even now. "It was...complicated," she offered vaguely, sketching absent-mindedly on a napkin. She drew a tangled knot of thread, mirroring the feeling in her own heart. Violet's return had been subtle, but Krissy felt it like a ripple spreading through the water. She'd overheard Mr. Jones muttering about "that flamboyant tattooist" as she slid into the counter, and later, Mrs. Higgins had remarked on how "vivacious" she looked – a word that felt pointedly out of place.

It wasn't just the words themselves, though; it was the way she carried herself, the effortless elegance, the way she seemed to simply belong. It was as if a spotlight had suddenly shone on her, highlighting her own quietness and reminding her of everything she'd left behind when Violet had vanished. "Krissy! We need your opinion," Rita announced, pulling her and Tom to one side. "We were discussing you, actually. You seem...distant. Like you've got something on your mind."

"I'm fine," Krissy said, trying to sound nonchalant, but her hand instinctively went to cover her sketchpad.

"Don't 'fine' us," Rita pressed. "You were our unicorn!" Krissy felt a familiar flush creep up her neck. They weren't wrong. What was she waiting for? Was it Llew? Or was it something even deeper? Llew finally spoke, his voice quiet but firm. "She's just processing," he said, offering a small smile. "Give her time."

Even as he offered reassurance, Krissy sensed a hint of vulnerability in his tone – a subtle acknowledgment that perhaps he wasn't entirely sure himself. The rain had stopped completely now, and for a moment, the light spilled in, illuminating the dust motes dancing in the air and highlighting the small details of The Chiron Café – the chipped teacups, the worn armchairs, the comforting scent of coffee and memories. Krissy looked down at her sketchpad, at the tangled knot of thread she'd been drawing. It wasn't just a tangled thread any more; it felt like a representation of herself – pulled in different directions, struggling to find her way. And as she looked up, she realized that Llew was still watching her, and for the first time since Violet had returned, she didn't try to hide from him.

The quiet settled back into The Chiron Café, thicker this time, imbued with a touch more melancholy. Krissy felt a familiar pang of something she couldn't quite name – perhaps longing, perhaps just the residual echo of their shared history. The scent of violet perfume, faint but undeniably present, hung in the air – a delicate reminder of her return. "Do you think...do you think she ever really finds herself?" Krissy asked, almost to herself. It was a question she'd been wrestling with all day, and it felt particularly poignant now, amidst the quiet routine of the café. Llew paused, looking at her for a long moment. "I think," he said slowly, "she finds different versions of herself. Different places to hide." He turned back to the window. Krissy watched him, feeling a strange mix of sadness and fascination. Violet wasn't simply there; she was actively reshaping everything – pulling at threads, stirring up memories, disrupting the comfortable equilibrium they'd begun to find.

Rita refilled their mugs of tea, her movements slow and deliberate. "You know," she said quietly, "sometimes, the quietest storms are the most turbulent." The words hung in the air, perfectly encapsulating the feeling that had settled over Krissy – a sense of contained energy, ready to burst at any moment. Krissy noticed something on the counter – a single violet ribbon, lying neatly folded beside a small saucer. She picked it up, turning it over in her fingers. It was identical to the ribbons Violet always wore – little splashes of purple that seemed to capture the light. She remembered – Llew had mentioned she'd often left them for him – tiny tokens of affection and remembrance. A small, almost insignificant detail, but it felt laden with meaning.

Outside, a single ray of sunshine finally pierced through the clouds, illuminating the rain-slicked pavement and casting a golden glow on The Chiron Café. It was a brief, fleeting moment – as if acknowledging their shared experience, before being swallowed up by the returning grey. Krissy looked at Llew, who was standing by the door now, watching her. She caught his eye, and for just a second, she thought she saw something – not quite certainty, but perhaps a willingness to face whatever tomorrow might bring. "I think I'll sketch tonight," she said, clutching the violet ribbon in her hand. "Maybe that knot." Llew nodded, offering a small smile. "Good," he said. "Sometimes, you have to tangle a little before you can find your way." As Krissy stepped out into the street, the scent of coffee and violet perfume lingered on the air – a subtle reminder of the day's events and the lingering questions that remained. The rain had stopped, but there was still a dampness to everything – a feeling that something had shifted, that the equilibrium had been irrevocably altered.

11

CHAPTER ELEVEN: SEA-SALT AND SELF-SABOTAGE

Late morning found Ashcliffe draped in the aftermath of the rain – a lingering melancholy softened by shafts of sunlight that filtered through, giving the coastal town a slightly bruised glow. Krissy sat sketching by the harbour, the scent of salt and diesel hanging in the air. Fishermen mended nets, tourists snapped photos of weathered boats, and seagulls wheeled overhead – a familiar scene, yet today it felt like looking at her own life from afar. She was restless, a gentle current pulling her this way and that, but she wasn't quite sure why she felt adrift. Then he appeared. A quiet, observant man stood watching her sketch, his face etched with the same weathered lines as the coastline. He was older than she'd initially thought – perhaps late fifties – with eyes the colour of sea glass and a stillness that suggested he'd seen a good deal in his time. "That's lovely," he said simply, gesturing to her drawing. "You've caught the light beautifully."

They exchanged pleasantries about Ashcliffe – its quirks, its history, its tendency to both charm and frustrate. He introduced himself as Ryan, a retired cartographer who'd taken up residence in a small cottage overlooking the bay. Then, with a gentle observation that struck Krissy true, he added, "You might be happier somewhere new. Somewhere where the grey doesn't quite cling so." It was a simple comment, yet it resonated with her impulse – the constant itch to pack her things and move on. She shrugged, offering a non-committal smile. "Maybe," she replied, already returning to her sketch, hoping to lose herself in charcoal and paper before he could offer another perceptive glance. Ryan simply nodded, as if he understood perfectly, then turned and walked away, disappearing into the gentle bustle of the harbour, leaving Krissy with his words – and a renewed sense that perhaps running wasn't the answer, not this time.

Krissy returned to the Chiron Café, energized by Ryan's comment. It wasn't a jolt of excitement, more like a gentle current pushing her forward. He was right; perhaps she was clinging too tightly. She started to actively consider packing a small bag – just for a few days, maybe? A quick escape to somewhere new, somewhere with less grey. The thought took hold quickly, a tiny seed of possibility in the quiet restlessness within her. "Running to something... or running away?" she murmured to herself, sketching furiously in her notebook – capturing the café's familiar chaos: Mrs. Prior fussing over a tray of scones, Llew sorting through mugs, the low hum of conversation. It was a good question, and she wasn't sure she had an answer. The memories of Llew and Violet began to swirl around, each like a miniature current pulling her in different directions. Llew's quiet strength versus Violet's fiery intensity – both capable of holding her attention, yet neither quite able to anchor her down. Was she running from the possibility of another connection, or from the fear of being truly known again? Or was it perhaps the fear that, once again, she'd end up feeling like a third wheel?

Eve's cheerful voice broke through her thoughts. She and Geraint were excitedly discussing the baby, bubbling with anticipation. Krissy offered a polite smile, nodding along to their happy chatter, but felt slightly distant – as if observing them from behind a pane of glass.

A minor pang of envy mixed with her own uncertainty. They seemed so sure of things, so ready for the next chapter. Mr. Jones grumbled about the weather— "Proper drizzle it is," he observed, shaking his head – offering a small, comforting observation that Krissy almost appreciated. It was simple, unassuming, and felt like a tiny anchor in her swirling thoughts. Driven by an impulse she couldn't quite explain, Krissy headed out of the café and towards Ashcliffe station. The rain had cleared completely now, leaving the pavement glistening under the late morning sun. She checked the train times – a last-minute trip somewhere, anywhere. A quick look at Bath perhaps? Or maybe even Gloucester. Just to get away for a little while. The station was mostly empty, save for a few locals and a young couple huddled over a map. Krissy approached the ticket window, her hand instinctively reaching into her bag for some change. She was about to buy a ticket when she hesitated – just for a moment. Was this really what she wanted? To bolt before she'd even had a chance to figure out why?

She glanced back at the café, imagining Llew looking up as she left. A small smile touched her lips. Maybe not yet. Maybe she needed one last sketch, one last conversation – just to settle the dust. She turned back to the window and purchased a ticket for a train leaving in forty-five minutes, destination: London. As she clutched the ticket in her hand, a sudden feeling of self-doubt crept in. Was she running to something, or simply running? And what if, when she got there, she realized she hadn't actually left anything behind?

Before she could come up with an answer, Krissy noticed Violet sitting on a bench overlooking the tracks, staring out at the restless sea. The grey was deepening now, casting long shadows across the platform, and there was an immediate, palpable tension between them – a mix of recognition, suspicion, and perhaps a touch of lingering resentment that hung in the air like the damp coastal mist. Violet hadn't changed; her dark hair still fell in loose waves around her face, and she wore a simple, charcoal-grey coat that seemed to blend into the surroundings. "Violet?" Krissy asked, her voice barely above a whisper.

Violet didn't turn immediately. She simply continued to gaze out at the sea, as if searching for an answer in its vastness. "Well, well," she finally said, her tone clipped and slightly amused. "If it isn't the artist."

"What are you doing here?" Krissy pressed, a little more forcefully this time.

"Just leaving" Violet replied, turning to face her for the briefest of moments. Her eyes, the same shade of sea glass as she remembered, held a hint of something unreadable. "Didn't expect to see you."

The dialogue was sparse and loaded – short exchanges, mostly glances and clipped phrases that revealed more than they let on. Krissy questioned Violet's departure – was it curiosity, or something more?– and Violet was evasive, offering only cryptic responses about needing 'a bit of space.' It felt like a familiar dance, one she'd done countless times before: a brief spark of recognition followed by a deliberate retreat. They both seemed to gravitate towards the same bench overlooking the tracks – worn wooden slats that had likely seen countless arrivals and departures. Krissy pulled out her sketchbook and began sketching again, capturing Violet's profile as she sat there, lost in thought. The rain had stopped completely now, and the late afternoon sun cast a golden glow on Violet's face, highlighting the subtle lines etched around her eyes – lines that spoke of years lived, of joys and sorrows, of departures and returns. The scene was charged with unspoken history and unresolved feelings. It felt like stepping back into a half-remembered dream—a dream filled with charcoal sketches, shared silences, and the lingering scent of turpentine. Krissy tried to lose herself in her drawing, but Violet's presence – so sudden, so unexpected – kept pulling her back.

As she sketched, she noticed a small detail: a faint smudge of violet paint on Violet's cuff. It was a tiny thing, yet it felt significant, like a secret message whispered across the years. She glanced up at Violet again, and for a moment, their eyes met – a silent acknowledgment of Llew, and the complicated history that bound them together. Violet shifted slightly on the bench, pulling her coat tighter around her as if to ward off the chill. Krissy continued to sketch, capturing not just Violet's physical appearance, but something deeper – a sense of quiet strength, of a woman who had clearly seen her share of storms. It was as if she were trying to capture the essence of Violet herself – a fleeting, beautiful, and slightly haunted figure. A small, almost imperceptible frown creased Krissy's brow. She wasn't sure why she felt this way – a mixture of curiosity, suspicion, and perhaps even a touch of resentment – but there was something about Violet that didn't quite sit right. It was as if the past hadn't truly let her go, and now, with Violet leaving Ashcliffe, it was threatening to reclaim them both.

Krissy, unable to shake Violet's presence like a persistent sea mist, began a slow, deliberate conversation. She wasn't going to force anything, she simply wanted to get beneath the surface of Violet's carefully constructed facade – the air of cool detachment, the subtle scent of sandalwood that always seemed to cling to her. "You seem settled," Krissy observed quietly, as they sat side-by-side on the bench, watching the trains rumble past. "Or maybe just... comfortable." Violet's lips curled into a slight smile, tinged with something that could have been amusement or irritation. "Comfortable is overrated," she replied, her voice low and measured. "I prefer to think of it as being 'well-established' wherever I turn up." Violet was guarded, offering clipped answers and subtle digs – a quiet defence mechanism that Krissy had come to recognize as one of her trademarks. A question about her art received a dismissive "Oh, just dabbling." The mention of travelling elicited a brief, almost bored, "It's good for the soul."The pivotal moment arrived unexpectedly, triggered by something small – Krissy mentioning Llew. Violet stiffened slightly, her hand instinctively tightening on her coat. "You still see him, then?" she asked, her voice a shade quieter than before.

"Sometimes," Krissy admitted. Violet was silent for a moment, and then, almost as if the words had been building up inside her for years, she said, "Running helped. For a while, it really helped. But running doesn't solve everything, does it? It just postpones the reckoning."

A brief, evocative visual flashed through Violet's mind – a rainy scene at Cardiff Central Station, captured in a fleeting impression. The rain hammered against the station roof, blurring the faces passing through. Violet, clutching her bag tightly, hurried past Llewelyn's stunned expression, a single tear tracing a path down her cheek. He reached for her, but she was already swallowed by the crowd, disappearing into the grey afternoon. "It started with Cardiff," Violet continued, her voice barely above a whisper. "I needed to disappear. To be someone else. I didn't want to be tied down." Krissy took a deep breath and shared her own feelings of wanting to escape, feeling like she'd always just been drifting. "I think," Krissy admitted, her gaze fixed on the horizon, "a part of me enjoys it. The uncertainty. It feels safer than being rooted somewhere."

"That's a good way of putting it," Violet said, turning to look at her. "Like you're floating – not quite lost, but not exactly found either."

The dialogue became more honest and vulnerable as they both revealed fragments of their pasts and present anxieties. "You always had this air about you," Krissy observed. "Like you've seen a lot. Like you were carrying something heavy."

"Perhaps I was," Violet replied, a hint of sadness in her eyes. "Running can do that to you – it leaves its own kind of baggage." She paused, then added quietly, "I thought if I just kept moving, the pain would fade away."

"Did it?" Krissy asked gently.

"Not entirely," Violet admitted. "It just... changed shape. Became something a little less sharp, but maybe a little more persistent."

Krissy found herself saying, "It's funny, isn't it? How we think running is the answer – when sometimes all you need is someone to just see you."

Krissy was just about to say something – something perhaps bolder, more decisive – when Ryan reappeared, a cheerful wave as he boarded the train pulling away from the station. He offered her a quick smile, a familiar warmth that momentarily tugged at her, and then he was gone, swallowed by the carriage. She hesitated for a moment – tempted to take the chance, to step onto that train and finally let go of Ashcliffe, but something held her back. A small decision, but one that felt significant – Krissy decided not to leave. It wasn't a dramatic revelation, no grand pronouncements or sudden realizations. She simply bid Violet farewell, turned away from the platform, and headed back towards the familiar warmth of The Chiron Café. As she walked, she caught sight of her reflection in the station window – a slightly blurry image of herself, a little less adrift than before. She glanced back at Violet, who had stood up to meet her train arriving, watching her. A small, almost imperceptible smile played on Violet's lips. Krissy wasn't sure if it was a smile of triumph or simply understanding – perhaps a little of both. The two women waved to each other, and Krissy realized that maybe 'self-sabotage' wasn't just a default setting; perhaps it was simply her way of keeping things interesting. Of ensuring there would always be another journey, another possibility, even if it led back to the same grey coastline.

Krissy wandered slowly back through the streets of Ashcliffe, the late afternoon sun catching in the puddles along the cobblestones like pieces of melted amber. The ticket still sat folded in her coat pocket – warm now from her hand, though she had no real intention of using it. The thought of London, once so compelling, now felt hollow. She'd come to crave movement, change, novelty – but here, in this town of drizzle and salt, something unexpected had anchored itself in her. She paused near a florist's stall set up in the market square, a burst of colour against the muted tones of the town. Buckets of sea-thrift and hydrangea stood like little explosions of life. Krissy ran her fingers lightly over a bloom, then purchased a single stem of forget-me-not on impulse. As the florist, Jenny, wrapped it in brown paper, she caught her own reflection again in a rain-smeared window. There she was – intact. Whole, if slightly frayed around the edges. The wind was beginning to pick up again, tugging at her hair and sending stray leaves skittering across the stones. It reminded her that this town never stayed still for long. Not really. Even when everything felt frozen, Ashcliffe shifted underfoot – quietly, insistently, like the tide reclaiming shore.

At The Chiron Café, the warm glow from inside welcomed her. She stepped in and was immediately greeted by the familiar scent of baked cinnamon, damp wool, and something citrusy from the floor cleaner Llew had taken to using after Eve's complaints. The world outside melted away a little. "Back so soon?" Llew asked from behind the counter, looking up from a tray of half-frosted lemon slices. His eyes caught hers, and Krissy felt something flutter and settle in her chest. She nodded. "Trains were delayed." It was only half a lie. "Or maybe I just decided the drizzle suits me." Llew smiled faintly, not pushing further, and returned to icing. There was comfort in his silence—steady, unspoken understanding. That was the thing with Llew. He never tried to interpret her restlessness, instead he simply accepted it like he might the weather. And today, that was exactly what she needed. Rita clucked her tongue at the window. "Storm coming again. My knees are never wrong." Krissy slid into her usual seat by the radiator.

Minutes passed in comforting rhythm – the clatter of dishes, the dull hum of the espresso machine, someone laughing gently in the corner. Krissy pulled out her sketchbook and turned to a blank page. But the moment she tried to draw, nothing came. Her fingers hovered, uncertain. Instead of pushing it, she shut the book again and simply watched. She noticed Violet hadn't returned. The station platform had felt final, like a goodbye that didn't need words. Krissy had meant to say more – something honest, maybe, or even kind. But the moment passed. And now, a part of her wondered if that small, unreadable smile had been a door closing for good. "Want to help close up?" Llew's voice broke gently into her thoughts. She nodded, grateful for the grounding task. Together they wiped down tables, stacked chairs, swept the corners. The silence between them was easy. Only when he unplugged the coffee machine and leaned his elbows on the counter did he speak again.

"She's gone, then?"

Krissy didn't ask how he knew who she meant. "Looks that way."

Llew didn't respond immediately. "Sometimes," he said finally, "people leave because they're scared of staying. And sometimes they stay for the same reason."

Krissy gave him a long look. "Which one are you?"

He shrugged. "Ask me tomorrow."

She smiled, tired and warm, and patted his arm on the way out. "Fair enough."

That night, Krissy couldn't sleep. The coastal wind howled softly through the streets, rattling shutters and chimneys. Her sketchbook lay on the floor beside her bed, pages fluttering like restless thoughts. Eventually, she pulled a blanket around her shoulders and padded over to the window, gazing out at the black expanse of sea. The moonlight caught on the water in thin silver threads. She opened the window slightly. The cold hit her skin, but she didn't retreat. Instead, she breathed it in – salt, smoke, stone. A thought flickered at the edges of her mind: I am still here. She wasn't sure who she was saying it to – herself, perhaps. Or to Violet. Or to the version of herself that had nearly stepped onto that train.

The following morning broke with a fine mist, the kind that clung to your clothes and hair like breath. Krissy found herself walking the shoreline before breakfast, sketchbook in one hand, the stem of forget-me-nots tucked carefully in the other. There were very few people out – just the occasional dog-walker, a solitary jogger, and a fisherman adjusting buoys near the tidal pools. She liked it this way. The tide was creeping in, licking the sand in slow, deliberate waves. She settled near the rocks, drawing without thinking. Her lines were quick, instinctive. She wasn't aiming for perfection – just honesty. The curve of a tide-pool rim. A half-submerged buoy. A boot print slowly being erased by the tide. But before she left, she drew Violet. Not from memory. Not quite. It was more a feeling – a shadow of her sitting on the bench, the angle of her shoulders, the weight in her gaze. She drew her small, and the sea vast around her. Not diminished, just solitary. It felt right.

When she returned to the café, she slipped the sketch into her coat pocket. Not to show anyone. Just to keep. A piece of something unresolved.

A week passed. Ashcliffe returned to its routines – half-hearted storm-warnings, intermittent sunshine, The Chiron Cafe bustling merrily. Krissy stayed. The train ticket remained folded in a drawer, now slightly faded along the creases. She began painting again. Not large canvases – just small studies, seascapes, portraits of locals she convinced to sit for her. Llew brought her tea without asking. Eve, in her maternal glow, insisted Krissy paint something for the baby's room – a whale, or a fleet of puffins. She agreed without hesitation. Evenings found her walking with no destination. She liked how the town changed at dusk – how it seemed softer, more forgiving. On one such walk, she found herself outside Ryan's cottage. The cartographer was sitting on a bench outside, polishing a compass. "Still here," he observed, smiling without surprise.

"I am."

"Good. Thought you might be the kind to vanish without a word."

"I nearly was."

Ryan nodded, patting the bench beside him. She sat, and for a while they said nothing. Then Krissy asked, "Do you regret not leaving somewhere you should have?"

Ryan didn't answer right away. "No. But I regret some of the places I left too soon. Sometimes the maps we make aren't for places. They're for people."

She nodded. "I think I'm starting to see that." Back in her flat, Krissy unfolded the sketch of Violet and laid it on her table. She looked at it for a long time, then picked up a fine brush and began to paint the sea around her. Not stormy this time. Calm. Still. Full of space.

The postcard arrived on a Thursday. It was unmarked, no return address. Just a few scrawled words in calm, workmanlike script: "You saw me, once. That mattered. —V" Krissy held it between her fingers for a long time. She didn't know where Violet had gone, or if she'd return. But she no longer felt the need to chase the answer. It was enough to know she had been part of the story – even just for a chapter. That night, Krissy painted until dawn. Not to escape. Not to forget. But to remember what it meant to stay.

12

CHAPTER TWELVE: ANCHOR POINTS

The rain in Ashcliffe was a familiar comfort, though today it held a touch of golden light as it sliced through the grey. Inside The Saltwater Siren, the air thrummed with contained energy – a comfortable chaos orchestrated by Stella. It was one of those evenings where everyone seemed to be there, ostensibly for the Ashcliffe Afternooners' 'walk' around the harbour, but really just for each other. Rita dispensed lukewarm tea with a critical eye, while Stella moved through the crowd, ensuring everyone had a spot – Albert meticulously adjusting a microphone stand, Eloise perched on a stool shuffling her tarot cards, and Krissy blending into the background with a quiet sketch. Tom leaned against the bar, nursing a pint, and Llew stood watching Krissy from across the room, his posture subtly tightened like a stretched string.

"She's a force," Albert said, turning to face him, his brow furrowed slightly. "Like a small storm." Llew nodded, taking a slow sip of his beer. "I'm not afraid of her fire. I'm afraid she won't let me stand in it."

The room seemed to quiet for a moment, the murmur of conversation receding as if responding to his observation. Krissy, oblivious, was capturing the scene on paper – the worn velvet of Stella's seat, Rita's perpetually raised eyebrows, the way the light caught on Eloise's hair. "Just trying to capture a little bit of Ashcliffe," she murmured, offering a small smile to Stella. "It's got a good pulse, you know?" Stella simply nodded, her gaze lingering for a beat longer than usual on Krissy before turning back to the sound system. The group continued their meandering conversation – the price of fish, Mrs. Prior's latest jam recipe, whether it would ever be worth rebuilding the pier – but beneath it all, a current of unspoken awareness flowed. Llew felt it too – that familiar pull between Krissy and him, a spark threatening to ignite amidst the comfortable routine. He took another sip of his beer, bracing himself for whatever storm was brewing.

Then, almost as if summoned by his thoughts, a memory washed over him – Cardiff Central Station. It had been raining, a proper Welsh downpour, blurring the lights into hazy halos. He and Violet were waiting for her train, standing beneath the grand archway of the station. She was sketching in a small notebook, oblivious to his anxious gaze, capturing the rain on the glass roof with delicate lines. He remembered the way her hair, always slightly windswept, framed her face – the way the light caught in it like fairies had placed it there. He remembered how she had been sketching – a swirling design for a tattoo, incorporating waves and seabirds – a perfect reflection of her restless spirit. She'd glanced up at him then, a fleeting smile on her lips, and said simply, "Don't wait." The train pulled in with a screech, the doors sliding open to reveal a carriage filled with rain-soaked travellers. She stepped aboard without another word, disappearing into the thronging crowd. He'd stood there for ages, feeling foolish and strangely empty, the rain plastering his hair to his forehead.

Back at The Saltwater Siren, Llew was still lost in thought when Stella noticed. "You look like you've seen a ghost," she observed gently, placing a warm mug of Earl Grey beside him. "Cardiff Central again?"

He nodded, taking a sip. "Just... Violet. She always seemed to leave things unfinished, didn't she? Like a half-drawn sketch."

"Exactly," Stella replied, her voice soft. "Always on the move. Beautifully chaotic." He turned to look at Krissy, who was now sketching furiously in her pad. She caught his eye for a moment, a small smile playing on her lips, and he felt that familiar pull – the feeling of being seen, understood, perhaps even a little bit known.

Krissy, absorbed in her sketching, hunched over a small table near the window. He could see she was capturing Violet – not a portrait, but an impression: a slightly tilted head, a hand poised above a notebook, a hint of that elusive expression. Llew watched as she added delicate lines, capturing a flicker of something elusive – both melancholy and fierce determination. Eloise approached, her eyes twinkling with insight. "She's a captivating subject," she said, peering at the sketch. "Like trying to capture smoke." She paused. "Roots aren't traps. They're scaffolding. You need them to grow, but you don't want them to hold you back."

Krissy looked up, surprised. "That's... that's a good way to look at it," she murmured, returning to her sketch. "Roots... I hate roots. But maybe... maybe you're right. I just keep moving, thinking that's the answer. But is it? Or am I just running from something?" She added a few more lines to Violet's sketch – a small detail, a tiny wave curling around her wrist – as if trying to anchor her to somewhere.

Later, she sat at the bar, nursing a glass of water and sketching – a chaotic tangle of lines depicting the interior of The Saltwater Siren: Stella's watchful gaze, Albert's meticulous adjustments, Tom's quiet observation. She sketched against he table, capturing the pattern of the wood grain – rough but sturdy. Rita offered a pragmatic observation. "You'll burn out if you keep running," she said bluntly. "Eventually, even your feet will complain."

Krissy shrugged, not looking up from her sketch. "Maybe. Or maybe I just like the view." When it was finally time for their walk, the group made its way towards the shoreline – a steady drizzle now turning into a proper rain. Llew asked, "What are you trying to erase, Krissy? With those sketches?" She shrugged, pulling her scarf tighter around herself. "Just... Violet," she said quietly. "I feel like I need to burn away all traces."

"Then let's do it," he offered, extending his hand. She hesitated for a moment, then took it – warm and dry – and they continued on together.

At the shoreline, the group had gathered – Stella with her ever-present optimism, Eloise murmuring about celestial alignments, Albert meticulously adjusting the lighting of some lanterns, Tom offering everyone mugs of hot chocolate, Rita dispensing sardonic observations, Eve and Geraint excitedly pointing out a fledgling seagull, and Llew and Krissy walking hand in hand. The rain had intensified, but the gathering felt warm and contained – a small island of warmth against the grey. Stella lit the first piece of paper – a fragment of one of Krissy's sketches – with a single lantern flame. As it curled and crackled, releasing a delicate scent of ash and damp paper, she explained, "She wants to let go. To burn away the past."

One by one, they added their own memories – crumpled notes, faded photographs, snippets of conversation – each piece representing a shared moment or a lingering emotion. As each sheet was lit, a tiny wisp of smoke rose into the rain-streaked sky, carrying with it a fragment of Ashcliffe's collective memory. Violet's absence was palpable – a quiet space in the group, a missing note in the sound of the waves. It felt as if she were watching from afar, a shimmering ghost on the edge of the gathering. A sudden gust of wind rustled through the reeds, carrying with it the faintest scent of Violet's favourite perfume. As the last piece of paper turned to ash, and the rain began to ease, Llew squeezed Krissy's hand – a small, simple gesture that spoke volumes. She looked at him, a flicker of something – hope? – in her eyes.

Krissy didn't speak for a long time after the final ember faded. She stood in the hush that followed the ritual, her soaked scarf clinging to her neck, hands trembling slightly from the cold – or maybe from something deeper, something loosening inside her. The others slowly began to drift back up the path toward The Saltwater Siren, but Krissy stayed rooted to the pebbled shoreline, her eyes on the ashes dissolving into the wet sand. Llew stayed beside her, quiet. He knew the weight of silence. He'd carried it himself for years. And sometimes, he knew, the best thing you could do for someone was simply to be there, to stay. Krissy finally spoke, so softly he almost missed it.

"Whilst I was getting my tattoo, she'd talk about fire as if it were a person. Like it had moods. Sometimes generous, sometimes cruel."

"She was always like that," Llew replied. "Made metaphors out of everything. Said she didn't trust things that were literal."

Krissy gave a faint, weary laugh. "That sounds right." She paused. "You know... I don't think I ever stopped competing with her."

"You weren't competing," Llew said. "You were trying to understand her. And, maybe, to better understand yourself along the way. There's a difference."

Krissy turned to look at him. The rain had eased into a mist, silvering the air. "Did you understand her?"

Llew hesitated. Then shook his head. "Not really. But I think... I stopped needing to." They walked back in silence, shoes squelching in the mud, the village lights glowing softly through the mist. Inside The Saltwater Siren, warmth bloomed like a hearth – damp coats steaming on hooks, mugs of cider cradled in hands, and the hum of voices weaving around the wood-panelled room. Stella met them at the door with towels and dry jumpers. "You'll catch your death," she chided, her voice maternal, but her eyes kind. "Maybe I needed to catch something," Krissy replied, and surprised herself with the honesty of it.

Later, upstairs in the flat above The Chiron Cafe that Krissy had been calling home for the last few weeks, she curled under a crocheted blanket and stared at her latest sketch. It was the scene from the shoreline – but stylized, abstracted. Flames leapt upward, not consuming paper, but transforming it – turning memory into wind and light. She had added Violet's outline near the edge, barely visible, like a trick of the eye. For the first time, it didn't feel like an exorcism. It felt like a tribute. There was a knock at the door. Llew. She let him in without speaking. He handed her a book – one of Violet's old sketchbooks, the one with the green leather cover and the little sea-glass bead tied to the spine. "I thought you'd want this," he said. "I've been carrying it around for too long. Probably should've given it back to her when she was here... but it didn't feel like hers any more. Not exactly, anyway." Krissy took it reverently, running her fingers over the spine. She opened it slowly. The pages were filled with fluid lines and half-finished thoughts, bursts of poetry in the margins, diagrams of tattoo ideas, maps of imaginary places. There were small doodles of a house.They sat like that for a while, letting the quiet fill the room. Outside, the rain had stopped entirely, and the sound of the sea drifted in through the cracked window – not a roar, but a steady breathing, like the town itself was settling into sleep.

The following morning, the sun rose clear over Ashcliffe for the first time in weeks. Light pooled on the cobblestones, catching in puddles and dappling the glass windows of The Saltwater Siren. The Ashcliffe Afternooners met again, as they always did, this time on the chairs outside with mugs of strong coffee and folded blankets. Rita wore her sunglasses even though it was barely bright, and Albert was trying to repair a speaker that had suffered in the rain. Krissy showed up with a small stack of prints – finished versions of her sketches, newly scanned and printed on thick textured paper. She laid them out on a table near the bar: the interior of the pub, the lantern-light ceremony, Eloise with her cards, Stella adjusting the lights, Tom mid-laugh, Llew at the shoreline. And one sketch of Violet, quiet and defiant, watching over it all. "These are for the community board," Krissy said, a little too quickly. "Thought maybe we should put something permanent up. Something to remind us."

Albert raised an eyebrow. "You're leaving, then?"

Krissy hesitated. The old instinct was there – pack, run, disappear before the roots get too deep. But something held her still.

"Maybe not yet," she said slowly. "Maybe I'll stay through the next tide."

A murmur of approval rippled through the group. Eloise nodded, flipping over a tarot card and smirking at what she saw. Stella stood, raising her mug. "To Violet," she said. "And to the storms that bring us home." They clinked mugs and glasses, and Krissy felt, for the first time in a long while, a gentle tug beneath her feet – not the itch to run, but the steady anchor of belonging.

That night, after The Chiron Cafe had closed and the last dish was dried, Krissy and Llew sat at the edge of the harbour, legs dangling over the sea wall. The tide was low, and the moon cast long shadows on the sand below. Krissy held Violet's sketchbook loosely in her lap, thumbing through the pages. "Looking at this, it feels like she always wanted to sail," she said. "Did you know that?"

Llew nodded. "She talked about it all the time. Said she'd find a boat with a hull like a belly laugh and a sail like a secret."

Krissy chuckled. "Gosh, that does sound appealing when you put it like that."

"She made a list," he said. "Of places she wanted to see. I kept it. Thought maybe one day I'd go."

"Take me," Krissy said. "When you're ready. When we're ready."

He looked at her, surprised. But then he smiled. "Alright. When we're ready." The wind picked up, rustling the edges of the sketchbook. Krissy closed it gently. "For now," she said, "I think this is where I'm supposed to be." And for once, the thought didn't feel like a compromise. It felt like truth. The Saltwater Siren glowed in the distance, a beacon of warm light in the dark. The tide whispered promises against the shore. And Krissy – with rain-damp curls, ink-stained fingers, and the memory of fire still fresh in her chest – finally let herself be still. Not because she had nowhere to go. But because, at last, she knew where she was.

The days that followed were gentler than Krissy expected. She had been bracing for that familiar crash – the one that came after every moment of stillness, when she would usually retreat, restless and un-satisfied. But instead of the urge to flee, she felt something quieter settle in. Not certainty, not yet – but a tolerance for the uncertainty, as if Ashcliffe had taught her that roots could be flexible, like seaweed, and still hold fast. It started in small ways. She helped Stella with the window display at The Saltwater Siren, arranging jars of sea glass and yellowed paperbacks beside hand-drawn signage. She surprised herself by showing up early to help Rita prep for breakfast rush at The Chiron Cafe, sleeves rolled up, taking direction without bristling. She even let Eloise pull a card for her one morning, though she rolled her eyes and pretended not to care what it said. "The Fool," Eloise had murmured with a sly grin. "Not about foolishness. It's about beginnings. Trust. A leap into something unknown." Krissy had laughed then, but the card had stayed with her – tucked behind her mirror, out of respect as much as of belief.

The sketchbook, Violet's sketchbook, remained on her night-stand. Sometimes Krissy would page through it like a journal, tracing the line-work with the pad of her finger, as if contact might conjure the voice again. Other times, it would lie closed for days. And that was okay too. It no longer felt like a wound. More like a scar with a story behind it. One morning, Llew showed up with two coffees and a tentative invitation. "There's this place up the coast. Old lighthouse. Bit of a walk. Thought maybe you'd want to come?"

Krissy looked at him, suspicious. "Is this some kind of metaphor?"

"Maybe," he admitted. "But mostly, it's just a lighthouse." They walked along the shore path, boots crunching against shell-strewn sand. The path wound up through the cliffs, where seabirds dipped and shrieked in the wind, and the grasses bowed under their own weight. The lighthouse stood like a finger pointing skyward, the paint peeling but the windows intact.

Inside, the stairs spiralled narrow and steep. Krissy climbed them without complaint, her breath steady. At the top, they looked out over the sea. The horizon was a perfect line between ocean and sky – no ships, no movement, just the hum of vastness. "Would Violet have liked coming up here?" Krissy asked, the words tumbling out before she could think better of them.

"She always looked for edges," Llew said. "Places where one thing became another." Krissy pulled a folded paper from her coat pocket. It was a new sketch – done quickly, with broad, impulsive strokes. A girl standing at a ledge, wind tugging at her clothes, one foot lifted as if about to step. She left it tucked between the wooden beams of the lighthouse wall. "She said fire was a person," Krissy murmured. "But I think maybe she was the fire." They stood in silence for a long time, just listening.

In town, word of Krissy's prints spread. People came by The Chiron Cafe to look at them more closely – locals, day-trippers, the odd coastal wanderer with salt on their skin. Stella framed three of the prints and hung them near the piano. Eloise offered to do a reading for each one, a series of "Tarot & Tannin" evenings where wine and mysticism danced freely. Even Rita warmed to the idea, grumbling but secretly pleased when people praised the likeness she'd captured. But it wasn't about art, not really. It was about presence. Memory. Continuity. Krissy felt it too. One afternoon, she found herself walking through the market alone, and it struck her how many people nodded in recognition now. She wasn't just "that colourful woman with the sketchook" She was Krissy. She was the one who drew the shoreline better than anyone had in years. The one who laughed too loud at Tom's jokes. The one who let Llew hold her hand in quiet moments and didn't always pull away. She was still herself – but anchored now, just enough to stay tethered through the tides.

One evening, the end of one month melting into the next, the group gathered again – this time for celebration. It was Stella's idea, of course. "Summer deserves a send off," she declared, "before the tourists make a mess of the rhythm." So they dragged mismatched chairs and fairy lights out to the green near the cliffs and set up a makeshift long table. There were jars of home-made lemonade and platters of bread and olives. Stella had brought a guitar. Eloise twirled in a flowing skirt, Albert grumbled about the lighting, and even Rita allowed herself a smile when Eve and Geraint performed an awkward dance between bites. Krissy sat at the edge of it all, sketchbook open on her lap. Not drawing, just watching. Absorbing. It struck her, then, how rare this kind of evening was. Not because of the weather or the food, but because of the ease. The quiet knowledge that these people, this town, would still be here in the morning.

Llew sat beside her, legs stretched out in front of him, fingers brushing against hers in the grass. "You've changed," he said.

"I've stayed," she replied.

"Same thing, maybe." They didn't speak for a while. The fireflies blinked lazily, the air full of night sounds. Then Krissy turned to him, a glint of mischief in her eye.

"You still have that list?" she asked. Llew reached into his coat and pulled out a folded piece of paper. The ink was smudged in places, the edges soft from wear. Krissy took it, smoothing it on her lap. Santorini. Dubrovnik. The Faroe Islands. She recognized the handwriting from the sketchbook and the postcard. Violet, apparent in all the sharp loops and confident slashes. There were doodles in the margins. Little boats. Compass roses. One star circled several times. "I don't need to go to all of them," she said. "But maybe one. One to start."

"Which one?"

She smiled. "Whichever one doesn't feel like an escape."

Ashcliffe had changed with the season, as seaside towns always do. The air was warmer, the children louder, and the sky lingered longer at twilight. But the pulse of it – steady, grounded, familiar – remained the same. On the wall above the bar in The Saltwater Siren, the community board now bore a line of Krissy's prints, carefully pinned beside handwritten notes and the occasional lost-and-found notice. One night, after the venue had emptied and the lights dimmed, Stella found Krissy alone at the bar. "Got another sketch in you?" she asked, pouring two mugs of cider.

"Always," Krissy said. She pulled out her pencil, fingers smudged with charcoal, and began to draw – not the past, not even the present, but something forward-facing: a girl at sea, yes – but also a home on the cliff, fire in the window, and someone waiting for her to come back to them. She paused, tilted her head, then added a second figure – hair tangled in the wind, hands outstretched – not to pull the girl back, but to welcome her home. And somewhere, just beyond the edge of the page, the tide kept rising and falling. Not erasing. Not undoing. Just shaping the shore, again and again, as it always had.

13

CHAPTER THIRTEEN: STORMLIGHT

The rain in Ashcliffe wasn't the cheerful, drumming kind. It was a grey, persistent drizzle that seemed to seep into everything – the slate roofs of the cottages, the worn leather of the chairs at The Chiron Café, and Krissy's bones. It matched her mood perfectly. Above the café, in what had once been Eloise's flat – now a slightly cluttered haven for forgotten things – she sat sketching on a scarred wooden table. The light was the kind that bled through grey, a diluted silver barely illuminating the sketchpad. She was working on a familiar subject: the lighthouse at the edge of town, its beam usually cutting a bright swathe across the turbulent sea. Today, though, it felt turned inward, as if straining to find its way back to itself in the gloom. It wasn't a particularly good sketch. The lines were hesitant, unsure. Like her. Krissy hadn't really thought about sketching for a while. It was just... happening. A compulsion, perhaps. Or maybe a desperate attempt to capture something she couldn't quite articulate – the feeling of being adrift, even when anchored. "Still chasing ghosts," she murmured to herself, her voice barely audible above the rain.

It felt ridiculous, almost cliché, to call it that. But Violet... Violet had been a ghost in many ways. A sudden departure, a flash of vibrant colour and then – gone. And now, a postcard: You saw me, once. That mattered. It wasn't exactly a declaration of regret, but it was enough to leave her feeling like she'd just stepped out from under a particularly damp cloud. Krissy folded up the lighthouse sketch, carefully creasing the paper. It felt small and vulnerable in her hand. She'd been sketching for nearly an hour, and hadn't really seen anything, not truly. Just drifted around the edges of things. It was a familiar pattern, wasn't it? The leaving. Always the first to pack, to move, to disappear when things started to feel... settled. She shifted in her chair, pulling her cardigan tighter around her. It hadn't been that long since she and Rita and Tom had been sharing plans for their next adventure – a weekend camping trip, maybe. A proper escape from Ashcliffe's grey embrace. Now? Now it felt like a lifetime ago. They were still her people, of course. Her chosen family. But the way they looked at her now was different – tinged with a little bit of wistfulness, a touch of "what if." They'd been so sure she'd be up for another trip. And she had been. Until... well, until Llew. It felt odd to say it out loud, like naming a long-lost pet. It wasn't about him, not really. Not yet. It was about acknowledging something that had been quietly shifting within her for days: the possibility that maybe, just maybe, she didn't need to run any more. She glanced out the window at the rain, a little less restless now. The clouds were thickening, gathering like sheep in a field. A storm was brewing – but not necessarily one of chaos and destruction. Sometimes, storms cleared the way for something new. Without another thought, she grabbed her worn canvas bag and headed down to The Archive.

The rain had intensified into a proper downpour by the time Krissy knocked on Llewelyn's door. It soaked through her cardigan in seconds, plastering the fabric to her skin and leaving damp trails down her arms. She hadn't even noticed until she was standing there, feeling like a slightly soggy, slightly lost creature. Llew's flat – above The Archive, a space that always seemed to hold the scent of old paper and forgotten stories – felt warm and welcoming despite the storm raging outside. It wasn't grand or decorated, just comfortably lived-in, filled with books stacked high on shelves and tables, and the quiet hum of knowledge. He was surprised, but not startled, when she knocked. He'd been absorbed in sketching at his desk, a pencil held loosely in his hand, as if still capturing the moment. He opened the door without hesitation, letting her in before he could even think to ask what she wanted. "You're soaked," he observed simply, stating the obvious with a small smile. Krissy shrugged, pulling the damp cardigan tighter around herself. "I know. It felt... right to be." The words came out softer than she expected, almost whispered. She hadn't consciously planned them; they had just tumbled out of her, carrying a surprising weight of meaning.

He handed her a thick, well-worn towel – one with a faint scent of beeswax and old books – without saying anything else. It was a small gesture, but it felt significant in the quiet space between them. Silence hummed. It wasn't an uncomfortable silence, not like the ones they'd shared before, filled with awkwardness or unspoken questions. This was different – deeper, richer, layered with something that hadn't been there before. It felt expectant. After drying her hair as best she could, Krissy hung up the towel on a hook by the door and stepped further into the flat, letting the warmth of the room envelop her. She noticed small details she hadn't seen before – a collection of antique maps pinned to one wall, a shelf overflowing with volumes on folklore and local history, a half-finished model boat sitting on the table. It was clear he loved this place, that it was more than just a flat; it was an extension of himself. "I didn't really have a plan," she said finally, breaking the silence. "Just... wanted to be here." He nodded, returning his attention to his sketchpad for a moment before turning back to her. "It's a good place for that." He gestured around the room with a quick movement of his pencil. "Ashcliffe has a way of drawing you in. Like it wants you to stay."

"I'm starting to think I might just be here for the long haul," she admitted, a small smile playing on her lips.

He leaned back against the door frame, watching her for a moment. There was something about him – a quiet observation, a gentle understanding – that always made her feel seen, even when she struggled to see herself clearly. "It's funny," he said quietly, "how little it takes sometimes. Just... being there." He paused, then added, almost as an afterthought, "Do you want some tea?"

Krissy took a step closer, drawn in by the warmth and the quiet intensity of his gaze. "Yes," she replied, her voice barely above a whisper. "That would be nice." As he moved towards the kettle, Krissy glanced around the room again – at the books, the maps, the sketches, the small details that made up Llewelyn's world. She felt a sense of... recognition, perhaps. Like she was finally starting to see something familiar in this place, in him. It wasn't a sudden revelation, not a dramatic 'aha!' moment. It was more like a slow dawn, the grey clouds parting just enough to reveal a sliver of light.

She noticed a small, framed photograph on his desk – a picture of him as a young man, grinning broadly. Beside him stood a girl with bright, mischievous eyes and a cascade of Welsh curls –Violet. For a moment, she felt a pang of something – not quite sadness, not quite regret – just awareness. A reminder that he too had known the feeling of being swept away by something, of chasing a dream that hadn't quite worked out. He returned with two mugs – Earl Grey and, as she'd noticed, honey – and handed one to her. "So," he said, settling into his armchair, "what are you sketching now?"

Krissy held up the sketch of the lighthouse, turning it slightly so he could see it. "Just thinking," she replied, taking a sip of tea. "About light."

The rain continued its steady percussion against the windows of Llew's kitchen/living space, a comforting rhythm to the quiet conversation unfolding within. It was a small room with mismatched chairs and a table that looked like it had seen a lot of stories told around it. The scent of Earl Grey mingled with the lingering aroma of woodsmoke, creating a cosy haven from the storm outside. "I miss you," Krissy said simply, almost as an observation. It wasn't a dramatic declaration, just a statement of fact – a feeling that had been building within her since she'd stepped into his flat. A long pause followed, broken only by the rain and the gentle gurgle of the kettle. Llew took a slow sip of his tea, his gaze fixed on the swirling steam rising from his mug. Finally, he turned to look at her, his expression thoughtful. "I miss you too," he replied, his voice soft. It wasn't overflowing with emotion: it was honest, quiet, and perfectly suited to him.

"I don't know how to not be scared," Krissy admitted, the words tumbling out before she could stop them. "Of... of getting close. Of letting people in. Of losing them again." It wasn't a new feeling, not exactly. It was a familiar ache, a shadow that had followed her around for as long as she could remember. But with Llewelyn, it felt different – sharper, more immediate. He reached across the table and gently covered her hand with his, his touch light and warm. "Let's be scared together," he said, his thumb brushing against her skin.

It wasn't a grand solution, not a promise of easy answers. It was simply an invitation – to share the burden, to face the unknown side by side. A brief flashback flickered through Krissy's mind – that night with Llew, huddled beneath a blanket, watching the waves crash against the shore. The feeling of being completely present, utterly comfortable in each other's company – a rare and precious thing. It was a memory that always felt imbued with a subtle magic, like something held just out of reach. "It's about... not knowing," she continued, "I've spent so long learning how to disappear, I never stopped to imagine what staying might look like." The words hung in the air, reflecting her own anxieties and uncertainties. Llewelyn nodded slowly, as if understanding something deep within her. "It looks like this," he said, gesturing around the room with a small smile. "Tea. Rain. You knocking."

"It's funny," he said, a hint of a smile in his voice, "how much of our lives has been built around absence. People leaving, choices avoided... always looking forward to the next thing." He paused, taking another sip of tea. "Like Violet." Krissy felt a subtle tightening in her chest – a ghost of echoed emotion. She understood the lingering ache of abandonment. "It feels like... we've both been building walls," she said softly. "To protect ourselves."

"And sometimes," Llewelyn replied, "the best protection is letting someone in to help you tear them down." The rain intensified for a moment, drumming against the windows with a little more force. It felt as if the weather itself was echoing their conversation – a mixture of turbulence and promise. Krissy took his hand in hers, her fingers intertwining with his. "It's just... scary," she said again, letting the truthiness of it sink in. "Like everything could change."

"Everything already has," he pointed out gently. "And maybe that's not such a bad thing." He leaned forward slightly, bringing his gaze to meet hers. "Maybe," he whispered, "it's just the beginning of something new."

The rain continued its steady rhythm, now punctuated by the occasional flash of lightning illuminating the small kitchen with a brief, electric glow. The silence between them had shifted, deepening slightly, less about unspoken anxieties and more about a quiet acceptance of something – or someone – just beyond reach. Llew's phone buzzed on the table, shattering the spell. He glanced down at the screen, his expression unreadable for a moment. A single text message appeared: "I'm sorry. I understand now." It was from Violet. Krissy felt it immediately – a subtle shift in the air, a ripple of something both poignant and final. She didn't say anything, didn't ask who it was from. There was no need. They both knew. She continued to watch him, observing the almost imperceptible tightening around his eyes, the slight clench of his jaw. It wasn't anger or sadness she saw, just recognition. Acknowledgment of a closed chapter. Llew read the text twice, then slowly pocketed his phone. He didn't respond to it, didn't even glance at it again. It was a small gesture, but loaded with meaning – a deliberate choice for presence.

"She... she sent that," he said finally, his voice low and gravelly.

"It's okay," Krissy replied softly, squeezing his hand briefly. "Violet's chapter has ended."

He nodded, returning her gaze. It wasn't a comfortable look – not exactly – but it was honest. Acknowledging the past without letting it consume them. Krissy noticed how the light from the window caught the dust motes dancing in the air, creating tiny shimmering constellations within the room. It felt symbolic, somehow – like fragments of past lives and experiences, settling into a new pattern. Like the rain washing away the old to make way for something fresh. Krissy leaned closer. In that small, rain-streaked kitchen, surrounded by the remnants of stories and secrets, she felt a sense of possibility. A feeling that maybe, just maybe, they were finally starting to build something real – something sturdy enough to weather the storms. The phone buzzed again, but this time Llew didn't even flinch.

The rain had eased to a gentle drizzle by now, the wind whispering through the gaps in the window frames. The kitchen felt smaller, cosier, as if shrinking to contain them. They'd shifted from the rickety chairs at the table to the worn floral couch, its cushions smelling faintly of something indefinably Llew – a blend of sea air, old paper, and a hint of beeswax. Krissy reached into her bag and pulled out the sketch she'd drawn earlier – the lighthouse. It was simple, just charcoal on paper, but it held a quiet strength. She handed it to him, watching his fingers brush against hers for a moment. "Looks like it's looking inward," Llewelyn observed, tilting his head slightly as he studied the drawing. He traced the outline of the lighthouse with his thumb, his gaze lost in the details. "Like it's searching for something within itself."

"Maybe we all are," Krissy replied softly, her voice barely above a whisper. He turned the sketch over, examining it from the back. "It's steady," he said, pointing to the beam of light. "Even with the storm."

"Exactly," she agreed. "That's what I like about it."

Without a word, she leaned on his shoulder. He didn't move – not at all. It was as if he'd been waiting for her to do that, as if he'd known exactly where she would end up gravitating. It wasn't an awkward or forced lean; it felt natural, instinctive. A long silence descended, filled only by the soft patter of rain and the low hum of the refrigerator in the kitchen. A silence built on familiarity, on shared glances and unspoken understandings. Krissy felt the warmth radiating from his body, the gentle rhythm of his breathing. She relaxed against him, letting herself sink into the comfort of his presence. It wasn't about needing to say anything, or to fill the space with words. It was simply being together. Slowly, almost imperceptibly, she curled up against him, her legs wrapping around his. He didn't adjust, didn't shift to make room. He just held her gently, a solid anchor in the quiet of the room.

It wasn't sexual, not in any overt way. It was something more fundamental – a physical manifestation of trust, slowly being rebuilt, one small moment at a time. Like pebbles settling on a beach after a storm, each touch, each shared glance, adding to a foundation that felt both solid and new. She brought her hand up and rested it lightly on his arm, feeling the rough texture of his wool jumper. He didn't pull away. It was a small gesture, almost insignificant, but it spoke volumes. Krissy closed her eyes for a moment, letting herself be completely present in that space – the rain, the couch, Llew. She thought about Violet, and how she'd always been searching for that same sense of shelter, that feeling of being truly seen and accepted. And suddenly, it didn't feel like such a distant memory any more.

This isn't about fireworks, she realized, letting the thought drift through her mind. It's not about grand gestures or dramatic declarations. It was about the quiet comfort of knowing you were safe, that someone had your back, even if they weren't saying anything. It was about shelter – a refuge from the storms both inside and outside themselves. A place to simply be, without judgment, without expectation, just... together. Llew shifted slightly, his hand tightening almost imperceptibly around her arm. It was subtle, intimate. Like he'd felt her shift and instinctively reached out to hold her a little closer. She opened her eyes and looked at him. He didn't smile or say anything, just held her gaze for a moment – a simple, honest connection that spoke of shared history and burgeoning hope. "It's good," she whispered, more to herself than to him. "Just... good." He nodded silently. Krissy curled up against him on the couch. She felt a small smile play at the corner of her lips. It was a simple, contented feeling – like finally finding your way home after a long journey. The scent of tea mingled with the dampness of the rain and the comforting aroma of Llew's presence. It was a perfect combination – a small, beautiful picture of their new reality in Ashcliffe-on-Sea. They stayed like that for a long time – simply being, wrapped in each other's warmth, until the light outside began to fade and the rain softened to a gentle whisper.

The rain had almost entirely stopped by now, leaving a damp sheen on the slate roofs and a clean scent in the air. The kitchen light cast a warm glow over the room. They'd decided on Welsh rarebit for dinner – a simple, comforting dish that felt perfectly suited to the evening. It was routine, rather than obvious romance. The quiet rhythm of chopping vegetables, the sizzle of cheese melting in the pan, the familiar clink of cutlery – it was the kind of small, everyday ritual that spoke volumes about their growing connection. "You're really good at this," Krissy commented, watching Llew expertly layer cheddar on the toast. He shrugged, not looking up from his task. "My grandmother used to make it. Said it was perfect for a grey evening." They worked in comfortable silence, punctuated by the scrape of a knife on a cutting board. Filled with a quiet understanding, a shared knowledge that they didn't need to fill every space with words.

This is better than nice, Krissy thought, watching him. This is what permanence might feel like — glowing, gentle, kind. Not always exciting or thrilling, but consistently good. Like a well-worn cardigan or a favourite mug – comfortable and familiar in the best possible way. The radio was playing softly – a little bit of folk, something with a melancholic beauty that suited the mood. It wasn't overpowering, just enough to fill the space without demanding attention. Krissy turned to grab the plates from the cupboard and noticed Llew watching her.

He didn't smile, not exactly, but his eyes held a warmth that made her feel seen. And then she heard it – a small, genuine laugh. He'd caught her grinning at something silly, something she'd said to herself while buttering the toast. "Your smile is everything, you know," he observed, his voice low and amused as he placed a plate of rarebit in front of her.

"I bet you say that to all the girls," she replied, returning his smile. "Or is it just the ones you're preparing to burn with cheese?" He chuckled, a warm, rumbling sound that seemed to vibrate through the room. "Maybe it's just you. Aren't you lucky?" The Welsh rarebit warm and cheesy on their plates, Krissy took a bite and closed her eyes for a moment – savouring the simple pleasure of good food and good company. "You were really funny earlier," Llewelyn said suddenly, breaking the quiet.

"What was I doing?" she asked, tilting her head.

"When you were talking to that snail on the windowsill."

Krissy laughed again – a little louder this time. "It looked lonely."

He nodded, his eyes crinkling at the corners. "They always do." He watched her laugh and it was the most alive he'd seen her. It wasn't a boisterous, attention-grabbing laugh – it was like seeing a small piece of sunshine break through the clouds.

"I think," Krissy said softly, reaching across the table to touch his hand, "that I'm starting to like this place. And even Eve couldn't get me to love The Archive downstairs. But this place? It's very much you." He squeezed her hand gently, and she felt a familiar warmth spread through her chest. They stayed there for a while after they finished eating, simply sitting at the table, listening to the rain patter on the roof and the music playing softly in the background. It was as if all the important things had already been said, all the important connections made – not in bursts of conversation, but in those quiet, unspoken moments between them.

The rain had finally relinquished its grip on Ashcliffe-on-Sea, pulling back like a retreating tide. The slate roofs glistened with the last of its sheen, reflecting. Outside, it was as though the world itself was taking a deep breath after a long, restless night. The rain had stopped, and now the air smelled powerfully of sea and clean stone – a scent that felt uniquely Ashcliffe-ian. Krissy stood at the open window, leaning her forehead against the cool glass. She wasn't looking out at anything in particular, just absorbing the feeling of it all – the dampness, the stillness, the returning light. The wind was still present, but it was gentler now, a playful whisper compared to the howling gale that had buffeted the town earlier. Llew had been sitting thoughtfully on the sofa, but he soon quietly joined Krissy at the window. They stood side-by-side, watching. The rain hadn't completely cleared the bay – just enough to reveal the distant outline of the lighthouse. Its beam was sweeping across the water, a rhythmic pulse of light that sliced through the lingering mist. It moved, steadily and reliably, then came back again, settling into its place like an old friend returning home. "Stormlight," Krissy murmured, her voice barely audible above the sound of the wind. "That's what they call it, right?" Llew nodded, his gaze fixed on the lighthouse. "Yeah."

"It comes back," she continued, turning slightly to face him, "even after the dark." He met her eyes then, his own holding a depth of something that wasn't always easy for him to articulate. "Like us."

The words were simple, almost understated, but they carried a weight of meaning. It was just... truth. A quiet acknowledgement of the journey they'd taken together – the storms they'd weathered, the doubts they'd faced, and the slow, steady process of building something strong and lasting. She took his hand, a simple, grounding connection. His fingers were rough with work, calloused. Hers were softer, marked by ink and the occasional smudge of watercolour. They fit together perfectly, a quiet testament to connection. The lighthouse beam continued its steady sweep across the bay, a symbol of hope and resilience in the face of uncertainty. Krissy squeezed his hand lightly, feeling the warmth of his skin against hers. It was enough. "It's... beautiful," she said, her voice slightly catching in her throat. "All that light."

Llew nodded again, his eyes still on the lighthouse. "It is." He didn't need to say anything more. He didn't need to reassure her or declare his feelings. She understood. The wind picked up a little, rustling the leaves of the trees that lined the street and sending a fresh burst of sea air into the room. But it felt less threatening now, more like a welcome embrace. She released his hand for a moment, turning back to look out at the bay. The last of the clouds were beginning to break apart, revealing patches of blue sky – hints of the sunshine that would surely return tomorrow. He watched her, quietly content.

Later that night, after she'd walked back to Eloise's old flat, Krissy returned to her sketchbook. She drew for a long time, capturing the scene she'd been watching earlier: a small fishing boat bobbing gently in the water, the sturdy silhouette of the lighthouse against the darkening sky, and two figures standing side-by-side, watching the storm pass. Beneath the sketch, she wrote a single word: "We stayed."

14

CHAPTER FOURTEEN: MARKED BY MORNING

A quiet, storm-dampened Ashcliffe held its breath as dusk descended. Rain had relinquished a little of its grip, leaving the streets gleaming with puddles that reflected the muted grey of the sky like scattered silver coins. The Saltwater Siren's lights cast a warm, amber glow on the wet cobblestones, and the scent of brine and damp wool hung in the air. The Chiron Café was shuttered, its cheerful clutter replaced by a sense of quiet waiting – a feeling that something, just beneath the surface, was about to shift. Krissy walked back from Eve and Geraint's cottage, her boots splashing through familiar alleys slick with rain. She wasn't rushing – not yet – but neither was she dawdling. There was a decision already made, settled deep within her like a newly-polished stone. It wasn't an explosion of certainty, more like the quiet confidence of knowing which way to turn after a long, dark road. She reflected briefly on the sketch she'd left behind – a marionette untethered and dancing across Eve and Geraint's hallway table. It felt right. A little bit fragile, perhaps, but undeniably right. Like letting go of something she didn't even realize was holding her back. It felt like she was finally ready to risk being seen and to see others in return.

The rain had begun to pick up again as she approached Llew's flat above The Archive. No need for knocking this time. She simply walked in, the door swinging shut behind her with a soft click that seemed to punctuate the silence. A crooked smile played on her lips – a little shy, a little self-aware. The energy between them was charged, frantic. No small talk this time. The rain pattered against the windows, and for a moment, they simply existed in the space between. "Hello," he said – his voice low and comfortable, as if he'd been expecting her. She returned it with a smile. He gestured to a small table by the window, overlooking the rain-slicked village. "Please," he said. She took that as all the invitation she needed. She moved towards him slowly, drawn like a flame-hungry, urgent moth. He didn't step aside, or offer any resistance. Just an open space –waiting for her. He offered her tea, she shook her head. He raised an eyebrow, she stepped into him.

Her kiss was deliberate. Not testing, not shy – just certain. Her hands curled into the front of his shirt and she kissed him like she'd made up her mind an hour ago and every second since had only sharpened the edge. He answered immediately, heat rising between them like breath on glass. His hands found her hips, broad and warm, gripping not possessively but reverently – like he was learning her shape with his palms, not laying claim. They stumbled back against the bookshelf. A few spines creaked under the weight, and something fell – neither of them looked to see what. Krissy's fingers were already in his hair, tugging just enough to make him groan against her mouth. That sound unlocked something feral in her. She tugged at his shirt. He helped. No ceremony. Just skin meeting skin. His hands trembled – not with nerves, but restraint – as she kissed down his neck, her breath hot where the storm had chilled him. He bent his head, resting it briefly against hers, and whispered, "You sure?"

She answered by taking off her t-shirt, slow but without hesitation, the fabric catching on her elbows before it joined the growing scatter of clothes around their feet. The lamplight traced the ink curling along her shoulder blade, stark against damp, freckled skin. Llew's breath hitched. He didn't reach for her – not yet. Krissy stepped back, straddled the reading chair behind her like it was always hers to claim. She didn't need to say 'come here' – he was already moving. He dropped to his knees before her, hands resting lightly on her thighs like a question. She guided him with one hand in his hair, the other tracing the line of his jaw. Her voice was low, steady. "Don't overthink it this time," she said.

"I won't," he replied, looking up like a man about to kneel at more than just an altar.

She drew him to her. Mouths crashed again – open, eager. His fingers left ink-smudged prints on her hips from the pen he'd been using earlier, forgotten now on the floor. She pulled his belt open. He groaned into her collarbone. It was messy, gorgeous, real. This wasn't discovery. This was recognition. He reached for her again, and this time there was no gentleness in the way he kissed her. His mouth opened over hers, hands rougher now as they slid up her sides and around her back. She arched into it, into him, nails already dragging lines across his shoulder blades. He hissed at the contact – and smiled against her mouth. "Oh," she said, that wicked grin curling across her face. "You like that."

"Keep talking," he murmured, dragging his teeth along the line of her jaw, "see what happens."

She laughed – a bright, breathless sound – and rolled her hips against him where he knelt, still fully clothed from the waist down. "What, gonna put me in my place?"

His hands gripped her thighs tighter. "Do you want me to?"

Her only answer was a sharp tug on his hair and a kiss that was all teeth. That did it.

Llew grabbed her wrists, not hard but definite, and pinned them to the arms of the chair. His gaze was dark, hungry. "Stay there." She tested it – of course she did. Twisted one wrist, just enough to make him push it back down, harder this time. Her pupils blew wide with delight. "Good girl," he said softly. Krissy flushed instantly, from her neck to her stomach, skin glowing in the lamplight. Her breath hitched, and this time, she didn't try to move. He released one of her wrists, stood, and pulled off his shirt in one smooth motion – his chest inked, lean, the kind of strength you didn't always notice until it was pressing you into something solid. Her eyes tracked every motion, lips parted. He reached for the old scarf coiled beside the chair – her own scarf, the one she always wrapped around her like armour when she wasn't sure she could stay.

She froze for half a second. Then her grin returned – slower this time. "What are you going to do with that?"

"Show you what happens when you come in here thinking you're in charge." He stepped close. Her breath shuddered as he tied one wrist, then the other, not tight enough to hurt, just enough to hold her – just enough to say, you chose this. Her scarf. Her surrender. The weight of that made her exhale like she'd been holding the decision in her lungs for months. He climbed onto the chair, straddling her legs, mouth hovering just above hers. "You can stop me any time," he murmured.

She shook her head. "Don't you dare."

That was all the confirmation he needed. His mouth moved down her neck, biting gently, then rougher. One hand slipped under the waistband of her trousers, and she gasped, hips jerking. He didn't give her what she wanted – not yet. Just slow, measured teasing. She tried to wriggle closer. "No way," he said, pulling back just enough to deny her friction. "I tied you up for a reason, Krissy."

"And here I thought you were just feeling a type of way," she shot back. He rewarded her with a sharp bite to her collarbone and a hand sliding lower, finally giving in to her need with maddening precision. She swore – loud, honest, beautiful – and arched hard enough to make the chair creak beneath them.

He untied her wrists slowly, deliberately, but didn't let her go. Just guided her arms around his shoulders and lifted her in one effortless movement – her legs wrapped around his waist, lips against his throat.

He walked them across the room, dodging books and papers, until her back hit the bookshelf with a soft thud. "No way," she whispered, laughing breathlessly. "Are we really gonna do this where you shelve your first editions?" He smiled, wicked and close. "You'll be the only story anyone remembers in here." He kissed her hard then, biting her bottom lip and drinking the way she moaned into his mouth. Her fingers fumbled at his belt, impatient, frantic. He let her win that round, tugging his trousers just low enough so she could slide against him — the heat between them unbearable. Her nails scraped down his back and caught on the edge of his spine, where his oldest tattoo lived — a sea serpent winding into runes. He groaned at the contact. "Do that again." She did. With intention this time. Her nails left jagged little lines over inked skin, and the scrape of it — her claiming him — made him curse and press her harder against the shelf. Her breath hitched, her smile was pure challenge.

"I want you to mark me too," she said, voice low, hoarse.

"You already are." He lifted her higher, pressed himself into her with one powerful thrust, and her head knocked lightly against a row of hardcovers. She didn't care. She was laughing and gasping and saying his name like it tasted dangerous. The rhythm built fast — urgent, ragged. His hands held her like a dare, like he wasn't sure if he wanted to hold her still or let her ruin them both. Her scarf slipped from her wrist and hung down beside them, brushing the floor like a remnant of who she used to be. He gripped her jaw, tilting her face up. "Look at me." She did. Eyes wide, mouth slack. She wasn't teasing now. She was all in, raw and electric. "I've got you," he said. "You feel that?"

She nodded. Then shook her head. "No — say it again."

He thrust deeper, slower this time, grinding her into the wood. "I've got you."

And again. "Say it, Llew."

"I've got you, Krissy."

She came undone then — hard and loud, fingernails digging half-moons into his shoulders. He held her through it, kissed the corner of her mouth while she trembled and swore into his skin. Still moving. Still his. When her legs stopped shaking, she whispered, "Your turn." He didn't wait. Set her down on trembling legs, turned her around and bent her over the old reading table. One hand on her hip, the other tangling in her hair. Her laughter was pure delight. "Oh," she said, breathless. "You're gonna wreck me, aren't you?"

"No," he said. "I'm going to make you beg." He didn't rush. Dragged it out — deep, rhythmic, calculated. Every time she got close to clawing control back, he changed pace. Bit her shoulder. Licked down her spine. Pulled her scarf around her throat—not tight, just present. Her body writhed beneath him. "Please," she whispered.

"What was that?"

"Llew – please."

"Good girl," he growled, and finally let go — of himself, of her, of everything. They collapsed in a tangle of limbs and heat, still half-naked, still pulsing. Krissy's laugh was wrecked and elated.

"Okay," she said, breath catching in her throat. "Yeah. That was..."

He kissed her temple. "Still breathing?"

"Just barely." They were on the floor now, skin sticking slightly to the hardwood, surrounded by a trail of clothes and smudged sketches. Her thigh bore the inked print of his palm. His back was streaked with lines and her fingerprints like graphite ghosts. The whole room smelled like sex and ink and something sweeter — something like surrender.

She curled into his chest without a second thought, one arm draped lazily across his stomach. He was still catching his breath when she whispered, quieter now, real: "I didn't know it could feel like that."

He ran a hand down her spine, slow and grounding. "Like what?"

"Like I'm not disappearing afterward."

He paused, then pressed his lips against her hairline. "You're not."

Silence settled again, warm and honest.

Then, a whisper, just above her ear — almost reverent:

"Still here."

Her smile was slow, tired. Full. "Still want to be."

They cleaned up slowly, the silence comfortable now – not the quiet of anticipation, but the quiet of shared space. There was no rush to untangle, no need to separate limbs still humming with warmth. Their knees brushed as they reached for a fallen shirt, hands laced together beneath the quilt, legs curled into a tangled knot that felt utterly natural. Krissy's thumb traced the jagged line of the scar on Llew's shoulder – a pale white ribbon against tanned skin – and he didn't pull away. "It's... deeper," she murmured, almost to herself. "More defined." He shifted slightly, bringing his hand up to cup her cheek. "Been through something," he said, his voice low and gravelly. "Like you."

"It doesn't feel like me any more," she said, pulling her thumb away, "Not completely. I think I'm ready to sketch something new." She looked down at the scattered clothes around them – a chaotic tapestry of their shared intimacy – a blank canvas for whatever came next.

He brewed her tea this time, a precise ritual he seemed to have adopted since... well, since everything shifted. He used the small kettle from the shelf, filling it with water and setting it on the stove with the carefulness of someone measuring up ingredients for a delicate recipe. She accepted the steaming mug – warmed by his touch – without a word, simply letting him fuss over her. They settled onto the floor, backs against the bed, legs tangled beneath a hand-stitched quilt – a patchwork of faded florals and muted greens that smelled faintly of lavender. It wasn't grand or ornate; it was just... them. No longer lovers in the abstract, poised on the edge of something, but partners in presence—simply sharing the space between them, letting the quiet settle around them like dust motes dancing in a sunbeam. "The bookshelf," Krissy said, breaking the silence, "Is a terrible headboard."

He chuckled, a low rumble in his chest. "I'll build you a better one. Something with more... substance. Maybe carved from oak."

She smiled – a slow, genuine smile that reached her eyes – like he'd offered her a lighthouse. It wasn't about grand gestures or extravagant promises; it was the small, comforting certainty of his presence, his attention. The rain started again, light and persistent, tapping against the windows in a gentle rhythm. The light faded to greys and muted blues as dusk deepened, painting the room in shades of quiet melancholy. It felt appropriate – a perfect backdrop for their shared stillness. Krissy watched the curve of Llew's jaw as he drifted off, his breathing deepening into a slow, regular rhythm. He was handsome, even asleep – the lines around his eyes softened, his dark hair falling across his forehead. She let herself relax fully – for the first time in months, maybe longer – shedding the layers of vigilance and guardedness she'd worn like armour. She shifted slightly, her hand instinctively finding its way to his chest, resting lightly on his heart. It felt significant. He wasn't loud or demonstrative; he communicated through touch, through shared space, through the quiet language of their bodies. "The first time I saw you," she whispered, barely audible above the rain, "you stole something inside of me. Something I didn't know I still had." He murmured something unintelligible and continued to sleep.

She kissed his collarbone – a fleeting, light touch – and then curled closer, her head finding its comfortable place nestled against his chest. His hand instinctively found hers, drawing it up to rest on his hair, fingers threading through the strands like he was examining an intricate design. "That girl ran," she said, her voice soft and laced with a hint of nostalgia. "This one's tired of running." He murmured again, a soundless word – perhaps a memory – and then shifted slightly, pulling her closer until their bodies were nestled together, warmth radiating from him into her skin. She could feel the steady beat of his heart beneath her hand, a comforting anchor in the quiet darkness. The rain continued its gentle drumming, a lullaby to their shared stillness. Krissy watched the subtle movements of his face as he slept – the slight twitch of his nose, the way his lips occasionally curved into a small smile. She let herself be absorbed by these small details, noticing the way the lamplight caught on the faint lines around his eyes, the way the dark hair framed his face like a shadow.

She remembered the feeling of being constantly alert, always scanning for danger, always bracing herself for the next unexpected shift. It was exhausting – a constant state of readiness that had defined her life for so long. But here, in this quiet space with him, it felt... possible to let go. He shifted again, turning slightly towards her, and she instinctively tightened her grip on his hair. She felt the warmth of his skin through the quilt, the steady rhythm of his breathing. It was a simple comfort – the feeling of being held, of being safe – and it was more profound than she'd realized. "You remind me of a winter storm," he murmured, his voice thick with sleep. "Beautiful and fierce."

She smiled, letting herself drift into the quiet rhythm of his breath. "And you," she replied, tilting her head up to rest it against his chest, "Are like the slow thaw after." He tightened his hand on hers, a gentle pressure that spoke volumes. She let herself sink deeper into the comfort of his arms, feeling the tension slowly bleed away from her muscles. "This is enough," she whispered, barely audible, her fingers stilling on his heart. "Just this." He didn't answer – not immediately. He simply held her tighter, a silent affirmation of their shared stillness, and continued to watch her, as if measuring the depth of her contentment with just one glance. Then, very softly, he murmured again, "Still here."

The next morning broke with pale sunlight through sea-salted glass, filtering into the room in soft, diffused beams. It was as if the night had bled away slowly, leaving behind only traces of warmth and shadow. Krissy woke first, her body still heavy with sleep, a pleasant weight against Llew's chest. She watched the room – the faint marks on the floor where they'd tangled, the strip of scarf carelessly tossed aside, her sketchbook closed on the chair as if it had simply been waiting for her to open it again. It doesn't feel like aftermath. It felt like arrival – a quiet settling into something new and undeniably good. There was no jarring rush, no immediate need to assess or plan. No lingering anxiety about what might come next. She just was, suspended in the quiet of the morning light. Her internal monologue was gentle, almost detached. She didn't panic – not at the thought of leaving, not at the memories that might surface. She felt exceptionally still. Central – as if she'd always been there, waiting for this moment. Maybe even loved – but more importantly, enough. Acknowledged. Not chased, not chased away; simply accepted, in all her complicated, running glory. A small, tentative feeling of self-worth bloomed within her – a quiet confidence that she hadn't realized she'd lost somewhere along the way. It wasn't a triumphant declaration, just a subtle shift in perspective – a recognition of her own worthiness to be held, to be seen, to simply be.

Krissy traced the ink on her shoulder blade with a fingertip – a ghost of his touch, a reminder of last night's intensity. It felt... right. Like she'd been missing a piece of herself and last night she'd finally found it. A small smile touched her lips. She remembered the feeling of always being on the move, of running from something – or perhaps running to something she couldn't quite name. But now... now it felt like she could stop. She glanced down at her hands – still faintly dusted with ink, still carrying the subtle scent of him. They weren't hands that screamed 'fighter,' not any more. These were hands that knew how to hold – and how to be held. Llew stirred then, a slow, deliberate movement. He opened one eye, dark and heavy-lidded, and looked down at her. A warm, slow smile spread across his face. Just a warm, slow smile and the words: "Good morning, Krissy."

Her reply is simple, honest, and perfectly measured. "Still here." It's not a grand statement, not a sweeping promise. It's just a declaration of her own quiet contentment, of her willingness to stay, to be, to simply be with him. The stillness after the storm, marked by morning. A feeling of peace settled over the room as she watched Llew's smile deepen, knowing that for now, for this moment, everything felt exactly right. She shifted slightly, drawing him closer, and nestled her cheek against his pillow. He didn't move to push her away, didn't need to. The rain had stopped completely now, and a single ray of sunlight made the room dance like it had a confetti of tiny, shimmering stars. Krissy closed her eyes, content, "Still here," she agreed.

PART THREE: SAFE HARBOUR

15

CHAPTER FIFTEEN: THE LIGHTHOUSE PARTY

The lighthouse stood sentinel over Ashcliffe-on-Sea, its beam already hinting at the golden hour to come. It was transformed – not dramatically, but with a comforting, communal energy that perfectly captured the town's spirit. The clifftop had been draped in bunting, strung between weathered cottages and sturdy lampposts, while lanterns of all sizes cast a warm glow on the makeshift stage built from reclaimed wood. The air smelled of salt, sea air, and Mrs. Prior's freshly baked Victoria sponge – a heady combination that drew people in like tides. This was a joint effort, a testament to Ashcliffe's ability to pull together, even after all its storms. The Town Council, spearheaded by the ever-efficient Councillor Davies, had provided the logistical backbone; Rita and Tom's Chiron Café were supplying the refreshments – iced tea flowing freely alongside fish cakes and sandwiches; and, of course, The Saltwater Siren, with Stella, Eloise, and Albert at its helm, was providing the soundtrack and a touch of bohemian magic.

Albert, a man built like a sturdy oak, wrestled with the final cables of the lighting rig. His work boots crunched on the gravel as he muttered to himself, "If this thing shorts, it's your mic getting fried, not mine." He wiped a smudge of grease from his cheek with the back of his rolled-up sleeve – a practical, focused presence amidst the flurry of activity. He was a constant reassurance; a man who made complicated things look simple, and a man who could fix anything with a bit of wire and patience. Stella, her hair a wild halo, strummed a chord on her guitar, testing levels as she sang softly to herself – a melodic thread weaving through the growing buzz. Her voice was like the sea itself, both powerful and soothing, carrying with it a hint of melancholy and a promise of joy. She moved with an instinctive grace, pulling people in with her magnetic presence. Eloise, shimmering with glitter that clung to her cheeks like captured starlight, meticulously arranged her "fortune for a fiver" booth. Tarot cards were laid out on indigo cloth, interspersed with sea-worn crystals – smooth pebbles and iridescent shells collected from the beach. She looked up periodically, offering gentle smiles to those who passed by, as if waiting for a particularly auspicious sign.

Councillor Davies, resplendent in a slightly too-bright green tweed jacket, navigated the crowd with practised ease. He scanned the faces of the attendees selfie-ing, checking his watch frequently and nodding politely to anyone who caught his eye. "Excellent turnout," he murmured to the press photographer, "Certainly demonstrating the Council's commitment to community engagement." Mrs. Prior, a woman whose smile was as warm as her cakes, presided over the cake table – her Victoria sponge halfway gone. "Just a few left, dear," she announced cheerfully to anyone who passed, offering a generous slice with a dab of clotted cream. A good-natured argument flared between Mr. Linden and Mr. Jones regarding traffic cones and crowd flow. "They need to be closer to the stage!" Mr. Linden insisted, gesturing dramatically. "People won't see anything!" Mr. Jones countered, adjusting his spectacles. "And they'll block the exit! It's a delicate balance."

Rita and Tom moved as one, a well-oiled machine behind The Chiron Café cart. Rita, sharp and efficient, barked out orders in between handing out iced tea, while Tom, quiet and steady, expertly sliced sandwiches with an expert hand. Their movements were fluid, unspoken teamwork – a testament to years spent together. Then, just as the last of the lanterns were being lit, Krissy arrived. She stepped through the gathering crowd with salt-wind confidence, her boots crunching on the gravel, and a purpose in her stride. She was dressed simply – faded jeans, a cropped jumper – but there was an undeniable spark about her, as if she'd just emerged from a storm herself. She scanned the scene, taking it all in – the laughter, the light, the feeling of something quietly settling into place. It felt right.

Krissy found Llew helping Albert test the floodlights, a scene that felt both wonderfully ordinary and subtly charged. He was crouched by one of the towering lamps, his hands covered in grease and grime, a tool-belt strapped around his waist – which looked both impressively practical and incredibly sexy. He was meticulously adjusting a wire with a small screwdriver, his brow furrowed in concentration. "About time," Albert grunted, not looking up from his work. "This whole thing needs to be blinding by nine." Rita walked by, carrying a tray laden with pasties, and paused for a moment, observing the scene with a knowing smile. "That one's a keeper," she commented slyly, glancing at Llew. Krissy, who had been watching them from across the field, threaded her hand into Llew's, a small, almost unconscious movement. Her eyes sparkled – a sudden flash of warmth and something a little more – a quiet declaration. "He's mine, actually," she said, her voice low and steady. Tom, passing by with a tray piled high with warm pasties, stopped for a beat and offered a small, knowing smirk. "Took you long enough."

"I was busy sketching," Krissy replied, pulling her hand up to rest against his forearm. Eve, radiating warmth and carrying a large glass of lemonade, waddled up towards them, her belly prominent beneath a flowing linen dress. She looked at Krissy, a brief, radiant smile gracing her lips, and nodded – a simple, approving gesture that spoke volumes without needing words. She was glowing with the promise of new life, a quiet anchor in the gathering excitement. "Everything looks lovely,"

Eve said, handing Krissy a glass of lemonade. "Albert's done a wonderful job."

"He has," Krissy agreed, taking a sip. "It's...perfect." Llew simply nodded, returning her gaze to his work on the floodlight. He didn't need to say anything; his presence was enough.

Albert flipped a switch and bathed the field in golden light. The sky deepened into a rich indigo, and the lanterns seemed to glow even brighter. It was as if the sun itself had decided to join the party. "There," Albert declared, stepping back to admire his work. "Now we're ready for dancing." A collective murmur of approval rippled through the crowd. People began to move – couples swaying gently, children chasing each other across the grass. The sound of laughter mixed with the distant crash of waves and the strains of Stella's guitar, creating a perfect soundtrack to the evening. Krissy looked at Llew, his face illuminated by the golden light, and a genuine smile spread across her face. Contentment. A feeling that she had finally found her place in this little corner of the world, with this particular man, under this particular sky.

Rita, observing them from across the field, offered another knowing glance to Tom before heading back to the café. "See?" she said quietly. "I told you." Tom simply grinned and continued distributing pasties, his eyes twinkling with amusement. He knew – as everyone else seemed to – that something special was brewing in Ashcliffe-on-Sea. As the first notes of Stella's song drifted across the field, Krissy leaned a little closer to Llew, letting the golden light illuminate their faces. The light had softened further now, painting the sky in shades of lavender and rose. At the edge of the cliffs, overlooking the restless sea, Violet watched. She was a solitary figure – half-shadow, half-moonlight – pulled into herself beneath a hooded sweatshirt. Her sketchbook lay open in her lap, and her hand moved across the paper with quick, angry strokes, capturing the drama of the waves crashing below.

She wasn't sketching the beauty of the scene, she was sketching its turmoil. The jagged rocks, the churning water, the feeling of something vast and powerful just beneath the surface – all translated onto the page in a flurry of dark lines. It was as if she were trying to capture the very essence of Ashcliffe itself – its beauty and its sorrow. Eloise, walking from her brightly decorated tent (filled with tarot cards and crystals), caught sight of Violet across the field. She faltered for just a moment – recognition flickering in her eyes like a candle in the wind – before it passed, dismissed as a trick of the light or a familiar face. Eloise continued on her way, arranging another deck of cards, seemingly oblivious. Meanwhile, Geraint stood at the cider station, carefully pouring himself a glass. He was observing Violet with quiet intensity. She was an easy sight to spot – even from across the field – and he recognized her immediately. It was like seeing a ghost – someone familiar but distant, a memory brought vividly back to life. He mused, almost frozen, watching her. Recognition flickered in his eyes, followed by a brief flash of something akin to pain. He knew her story – the sudden departure, the lingering ache. But he didn't know what to do with it. Should he approach? Offer a word? Or simply let her be, a quiet observer of the evening's revelry?

He shifted his weight from one foot to the other, taking a sip of cider – the tartness doing little to cut through the stillness in his mind. He caught Eloise's eye for a moment, and she offered a small, encouraging nod – a silent question that he didn't quite have an answer to. Violet continued to sketch, oblivious to the gaze of the townspeople. She seemed lost in her own world, wrestling with something deep within herself. It was as if she were trying to capture not just the scene before her, but also the emotions swirling beneath—the ghosts of the past, the uncertainties of the future. A gust of wind swept across the cliffs, ruffling Violet's hair and scattering a few pencils lines from her sketch. She didn't bother to gather them up. It was as if she were deliberately letting go – releasing what no longer served her. Geraint took another sip of cider, his gaze fixed on Violet. He felt a pull towards her

– a quiet connection that he couldn't quite place. He wondered if she was running from something, or simply seeking refuge in the solitude of Ashcliffe's wild edges.

As the last sliver of sun dipped below the horizon, casting long shadows across the field, Violet finally closed her sketchbook and turned to leave. She moved with a quiet grace, disappearing into the gathering dusk – a fleeting glimpse of a familiar face, leaving behind a lingering sense of melancholy and unanswered questions. She was a reminder that even in a town brimming with stories and connections, some people remained just a little bit outside – marked by their own unique brand of sorrow and resilience. The lighthouse beams began to turn, rhythmic and reassuring like a giant, watchful eye. Stella stepped barefoot onto the stage – her guitar nestled beneath her arm – and began to play. Her set was brief, just a few lowing melodies and whispered vocals – her voice low and aching, perfectly capturing the mood of the evening. It was as if she were inviting everyone to share in her quiet sorrow, her gentle hope.

Then, with a graceful nod to Albert, she passed the mic to Councillor Davies, who took over with ease. "Right then," he boomed, beaming at the crowd. "Let's see if we can raise some money for – well, for whatever it is we're raising money for!" His jokes only half-landed – a familiar Ashcliffe quirk – but the crowd chuckled politely anyway. The auction had begun, and it was a delightfully eclectic collection of local treasures and experiences. Eloise had donated a couples' tarot reading – "For when you need to know if you're still compatible after a glass or two," she'd said with a wink. Next up was a free month of the beverage of our choice' from The Chiron Café, courtesy of Rita and Tom, followed by a private acoustic set by Stella at a location of the winner's choice. The bidding for Stella's set was fierce – fuelled by both affection and desire. Then came Mr. Linden and Mr. Jones's offering: a historic lighthouse tour with a sea-shanty serenade. "We'll even let you steer," Mr. Linden promised, his face flushed with enthusiasm.

The crowd buzzed with activity, bidding on everything from Mrs. Prior's famous plum jam to Albert and Tom's promise of fixing anyone's broken boat – for free. As the evening progressed, and the bids climbed higher, a sense of shared purpose filled the air – a feeling that even this small town could achieve something remarkable when it worked together. Then, just as everyone thought they had seen it all, Albert stepped forward with a final surprise item. He lifted a simple wooden board from behind him and mounted an anonymous sketch on it. It was breathtakingly raw. A girl standing barefoot in the wind, her hair whipping around her face. But it wasn't just her appearance that captivated – it was the feeling she evoked: a storm swirling inside her. Literally inside her. Her ribs were open, as if exposed to the elements, and lightning stitched into her heart – a jagged bolt of raw emotion. A hush fell over the crowd. It felt... intimate somehow, as if they were peering directly into someone's soul.

Krissy recognized it instantly – a gasp escaping her lips. So did Llew. He shifted slightly, his eyes fixed on the sketch, a familiar ache settling in his chest. Geraint stared at it for a long, long time. His usually-bright gaze was clouded with recognition and something else...a deep, unspoken sadness. He didn't say anything, didn't move, simply lost in the memory of – what? "Violet," someone whispered from the edge of the crowd. No one spoke for a moment. Then, another whispered, "It's... it's her." The silence stretched, punctuated only by the sound of crashing waves and Stella's soft guitar chords. The golden light of the lighthouse seemed to intensify, bathing the scene in an almost ethereal glow. It was as if the very soul of Ashcliffe – its beauty, its sorrow, its secrets – was captured on that single sketch. Finally, Eloise broke the silence, a knowing smile playing on her lips. "I heard she liked to capture moments," she said quietly. And there it was: the final revelation, hanging in the air like the salty sea breeze. The girl in the sketch – a ghost from Ashcliffe's past – a reminder that even in the most unexpected places, and at the edges of our memories, we can find traces of ourselves and those we've loved and lost.

The auction continued in a muted hum, the earlier excitement tempered by the revelation of the sketch. Krissy leaned into Llewelyn, her breath warm against his ear. "It's her," she whispered, barely audible above the sound of the sea. "Has to be," he replied, his voice low and gravelly. He hadn't moved from his spot in front of the stage, still lost in the image. Eve, who had been watching with a thoughtful frown, murmured, "That's not just a drawing. That's an exorcism." She gestured towards the sketch with a delicate finger. "It's like she's laying her soul bare." Geraint was completely still now, frozen as if carved from stone. His jaw clenched – a subtle but telling sign of the internal struggle he was clearly experiencing. He hadn't spoken since the sketch was revealed and seemed unable to break free from its gaze. Krissy shifted, a sense of urgency pulling her forward. She moved toward the front of the crowd, gently drawing Llew with her, until they were standing just beside him. "I know it," she whispered again, her eyes searching his. "It's Violet."

He didn't say anything at first. He simply nodded slowly, his expression unreadable. Then, almost imperceptibly, a muscle ticked in his jaw. "Do you...do you remember?" she asked softly. His gaze flickered to the sketch, then back to her. "Fragments," he said finally, his voice rough with emotion. "Fleeting glimpses. Like trying to hold water in your hands." He looked at the girl in the sketch – a young woman with haunted eyes and a hint of defiance. "She was... incandescent."

"Like a firework," Krissy echoed, remembering Violet's description of herself. A hand slipped into hers. It was Eve – her face pale but her grip firm. She raised an eyebrow slightly – a silent question, a wordless offer of support. "She was beautiful," she murmured, her voice soft with memory. "And... complicated."

Geraint finally moved, taking a slow step forward. He stared at the sketch for another long moment, as if trying to pull something back from the edge of his memory. It felt as though he were reaching across time and space to touch Violet herself. Something about her drew him in – like a magnetic force. "She always did have a way with charcoal," Krissy observed quietly, breaking the spell. Llew took a deep breath and finally spoke, his voice tinged with a sadness that seemed to stretch back decades. "She liked to capture moments," he said quietly. "Like this one." He turned to Krissy, his gaze locking onto hers. For the first time since the sketch was revealed, there was something undeniable in his eyes – a mix of recognition, pain, and perhaps hope. As if on cue, Violet took a step forward – just enough to be seen. She stood framed by the light of the lighthouse, her face partially hidden by shadow, but withstanding the gaze of everyone in Ashcliffe. A small, almost wistful smile played on her lips. "Hello," she said, her voice soft and low – as if she'd been waiting a long time to be seen again. "It's good to be recognised."

The silence after the sketch was revealed hung heavy in the air. Then, Councillor Davies, ever the pragmatist, broke it with a casual gesture. "Right then," he boomed, raising his hand. "I'll start at fifty." He glanced around at the faces in the crowd – seemingly oblivious to the emotional weight of the item up for auction. Krissy watched him, a quiet intensity in her eyes. Then, without hesitation, she raised her own hand – a small movement, almost imperceptible, but unwavering. It was a subtle declaration – a signal that she wanted this. The bids began slowly, steadily rising. A local collector, a retired fisherman with twinkling eyes, offered seventy. Then, a stranger – an artist Krissy recognized from a recent exhibition in London – jumped in with a hundred. The crowd murmured, sensing the growing interest. Krissy didn't flinch. She simply observed, her gaze fixed on the sketch and then on Violet, who was still watching . When it reached two hundred, she doubled the amount – a decisive move that immediately silenced the competition. A ripple of murmurs swept through the crowd. "She's serious," someone whispered. "That's a good price."

No one countered. The bidding war had begun – and Krissy was clearly determined to win. She raised her hand again, meeting the gaze of the London artist – a silent acknowledgement of their shared appreciation for the sketch. The bids climbed higher. Finally, she won. It was a quiet victory, marked only by her steady hand and the satisfied murmur of the crowd. Stella, who had been watching with a thoughtful expression, stepped forward and, with a note of reverence, said: "Sold – to the one who knows the storm best." Krissy accepted the sketch from Albert – collecting it like it was something sacred – as if holding a fragment of a lost memory. She turned slowly, her eyes meeting Violet's for just a moment. There was recognition in Violet's gaze – and perhaps a hint of gratitude. Krissy held the sketch close to her chest, feeling its weight – both physical and emotional. It was more than just a drawing, it was a piece of herself – a reminder of her own tangled history, her own capacity for both joy and sorrow.

As she turned back toward the crowd, a small smile played on her lips. The rain had stopped, and the last rays of golden light bathed Ashcliffe-on-Sea in a warm glow. It felt like a fitting end to a remarkable evening – a night where old wounds were laid bare, new connections were forged, and a little piece of the past was finally brought into the light. As the party wound down, a sharp sea breeze swept across Ashcliffe, carrying with it the scent of salt and damp earth. The laughter and music faded into a gentle hum, replaced by the rhythmic crash of waves against the cliffs. Krissy, feeling restless and slightly detached, found Violet standing at the cliff's edge, sketchbook closed in her lap. She was silhouetted against the darkening sky – a solitary figure wrapped in shadow. Krissy approached slowly, drawn to her like a moth to a flame. "You still draw like you bleed it out," Krissy observed quietly, her voice barely audible above the sound of the sea. Violet turned, her face partially obscured by shadow. "Guess I'm still bleeding." Her tone was simple, devoid of artifice and yet filled with a quiet sadness.

A quiet tension settled between them, thick and palpable like the mist rising from the water. It wasn't angry confrontation, nor a joyful reunion – simply two people standing on the edge of something, something they hadn't quite figured out. "Was it meant for me?"

Krissy asked, her voice laced with curiosity and a hint of vulnerability. Violet turned again, studying Krissy for a moment. "Wasn't meant for anyone. But you'd know if it was." Her gaze held a flicker of something – recognition? A shared secret? They stood in silence for a long moment, the only sound the ceaseless rhythm of the waves and the distant cries of gulls. The wind whipped around them, tugging at their hair and clothes – a tangible reminder of the wildness of Ashcliffe and its secrets. Finally, Krissy took a step forward and offered the sketch to Violet. It wasn't a dramatic gesture – just a simple extension of her hand. But it was loaded with meaning. Violet didn't take it immediately. She simply looked at it for a moment – as if assessing its worth, or perhaps searching for something within it. Then, she hesitated – and Krissy realized that Violet wasn't accepting the sketch.

It was uncertain. Did she keep it? Was it a small act of defiance? Or merely another subtle gesture in their ongoing dance of recognition and avoidance? Krissy didn't push. She simply stood beside her, watching as Violet turned back to face the sea. The last of the light faded, and Ashcliffe was plunged into darkness – illuminated only by the glow of the lighthouse beam. Krissy felt a strange sense of peace – a feeling that she had finally confronted something, or perhaps someone, that had been lingering in her life for far too long. She started to leave, but paused for just a moment turning back to face Violet one last time. And then, she was gone – disappearing into the shadows, leaving Violet alone on the cliff's edge, with nothing but the sea and the stars above.

Music lingered. A reprise of Stella's song, soft and achingly beautiful, drifted from a speaker as the last of the guests began to depart. It felt like a perfect soundtrack to the evening – bittersweet and hopeful all at once. Krissy rejoined Llew near by the stage, slipping the sketch into her bag without a word – a small, almost unconscious gesture that spoke volumes. She leaned into him then, resting her head on his shoulder for just a moment, a quiet acknowledgement of their shared connection. Across the field, Eve sat beside Geraint, rubbing her belly contentedly. He stared out at the water, lost in thought – his gaze distant and preoccupied. It was as if he were watching something – or someone – across the horizon. Rita danced with Tom, grinning sternly as she twirled him around. They moved as one—a comfortable rhythm of shared laughter and easy companionship. Albert switched off the last generator with a sigh – a small puff of smoke rising into the night air. "That's that," he muttered to himself, his voice laced with satisfaction. "Another storm weathered." Eloise watched the stars from atop the hilltop, pulling tarot cards in the dark, a quiet ritual under the vast expanse of the night sky. She seemed lost in thought, as if reading the future in the patterns of light and shadow.

The crowd thinned out, leaving behind a sense of peacefulness and quiet reflection. The last few lanterns flickered and died, casting long shadows across the field. Finally, the lighthouse beam swept across the sea—a brilliant arc of light that cut through the darkness. It felt like a benediction – a final blessing on Ashcliffe-on-Sea and all who called it home. Krissy turned to face Llew, hand in his. They stood together, watching the horizon, the sea stretching out before them like an endless possibility. Something was turning – something subtle, almost imperceptible. A shift in the air, a change in the light, a feeling that Ashcliffe had settled into its own rhythm once more. Something was coming – not necessarily defined or certain, but promising – a sense of hope and renewal after the storm. It felt like the beginning of something new.

16

CHAPTER SIXTEEN: ALMOST BROKEN

The rain in Ashcliffe was a soft, persistent grey that blurred the edges of town. Inside The Saltwater Siren, it was a comfortable kind of chaos – Stella adjusting fairy lights, Eloise shuffling tarot cards with a thoughtful frown, Albert coaxing life back into a slightly temperamental microphone. It was a typical morning, full of quiet industry and the comforting scent of saltwater and old wood, but this morning, something felt fragile. Krissy settled onto a worn velvet stool by the window, pulling out her sketchbook and charcoal. She'd been sketching Llew for the past few minutes – trying to capture the way he seemed lost in thought, his brow furrowed slightly as he stared out at the sea. He was a study in quiet strength, she realised, a man built of weathered stone and unspoken stories. Today, though, there was a subtle shift in him, a quietness that wasn't entirely comfortable. She noticed he was meticulously polishing an old silver compass – its face etched with intricate nautical designs. It caught the light just so, flashing briefly with a glint of silver. It was beautiful, and familiar – she'd seen it before, tucked away in his satchel. A small detail, almost insignificant, but one that sparked a flicker of recognition.

"Lost again?" she asked, her charcoal gliding across the paper. He glanced up, a brief flash of something – vulnerability? – crossing his features. "Just remembering," he said simply, returning to his polishing. "It belonged to my grandmother, once upon a time." The compass seemed to hum with unspoken history – journeys taken, and perhaps not always happily completed. Krissy felt it then, a gentle fracture in Llew's carefully constructed calm. It was as if a small piece of him – something precious – had almost broken free. She wondered what secrets that little compass held, and whether, for Llew, they were about to be revealed. The rain had eased to a gentle drizzle as Krissy and Llewe settled into the worn armchairs by the window at The Saltwater Siren. Steam curled from their mugs of tea and the rhythmic lapping of waves against the harbour wall provided a soothing backdrop. There was an easy intimacy between them now. They'd built it slowly, brick by brick, with stolen glances, murmured conversations, and the quiet satisfaction of simply being near each other.

"I got offered a job in Cardiff," Llew said, his voice barely above a whisper, as if afraid to disturb the peace. He didn't look at her, instead focusing on swirling the last bit of sugar into his tea. "A position at the Archive." Krissy continued to sketch – idly capturing the way the light caught in his grey-blue eyes – and for a moment, it felt as if he hadn't spoken at all. Then, slowly, she lowered her charcoal.

"Of course you're leaving," she said, her voice surprisingly flat. It wasn't an explosion of anger or a torrent of questions; rather, a slow, creeping disbelief began to spread through her, accompanied by a dull ache in her chest. "After everything." It felt like hearing about someone else – a distant acquaintance moving away, a colleague transferring departments. She was almost detached, as if observing the event from afar, rather than feeling it herself. "Of course you're leaving," she repeated, letting the words hang in the air between them. "Just...of course."

Llew finally looked up then, his expression guarded. "It's a good job," he said quickly, almost defensively. "And my mum – she could really use me being around more. It's not exactly a hardship." He offered a brief, somewhat vague explanation – needing to be closer to his mother, the job was a good fit – but it felt like a carefully constructed shield, designed to deflect any further probing. Krissy set down her sketchbook, the charcoal leaving a smudge on her fingers. "Just...how long?" she asked, trying to keep her voice even. "A few months," he replied, avoiding her gaze again. He picked up his mug and took a small sip of tea. "Maybe six. It depends on how quickly they need me."

"And what about...us?" The question hung in the air, tentative and slightly fragile.

He hesitated for a moment – a brief flicker of something that might have been regret crossing his face – before saying, "We'll see." It wasn't a promise, not really. It felt more like an acknowledgement, a simple statement of fact. "It just feels sudden," Krissy said softly, watching him. "Like you were just starting to let yourself feel something again." He finally met her eyes then, and for a moment, she thought she saw a glimpse of the vulnerability he usually kept so carefully hidden. But it was gone in an instant, replaced by that familiar, slightly distant expression. "Sometimes," he said simply, "you just have to move on."

Krissy felt a small, sharp pang of something – not exactly anger, but perhaps disappointment, or maybe even a touch of resentment. She'd been starting to believe – truly believe – that Ashcliffe, and perhaps she herself, was beginning to feel like home. Now, suddenly, he was going to leave again. "Of course," she murmured, turning back to the window. Outside, the sea continued its relentless rhythm, a constant reminder of change and movement – and of Llew's quiet determination to keep moving on. "Just...of course."

Krissy's initial reaction, a simple, almost detached, "Just...of course," had acted as a small pebble dropped into a still pond. It triggered a chain reaction, drawing Llew out of his carefully constructed silence and into a conversation that threatened to unravel the fragile peace they'd found. "Why now?" she asked, her voice softer this time, but no less insistent. "After everything. After the lighthouse party? Didn't it feel like a commitment to you too?" She turned from the window, fixing him with a searching gaze. He shifted slightly in his armchair, pulling at the sleeve of his woollen jumper. "It felt...good," he admitted quietly. "Like a nice thing. A bit of warmth."

"A bit of warmth?" Krissy repeated, raising an eyebrow. "You were smiling. You actually seemed to enjoy it."

"Well, yes," he conceded, a hint of defensiveness creeping into his voice. "It was pleasant."

"Pleasant," she echoed, letting the word hang in the air. "But not enough to stop you from packing your bags and heading back to Cardiff?"

He took a sip of tea, avoiding her eyes. "I just... it's a good job, Krissy. It's stable."

"And I'm not?" she challenged gently. "Is that what this is about? Are you afraid of something settling down here for you?"

He hesitated again, his gaze flickering over the sketchpad on her lap. "It's not just me," he said finally, a little reluctantly. "It's...it's Violet." The mention of her name seemed to hang heavy in the room, triggering a subtle shift in Krissy's mood. "Violet?" she prompted softly.

"She...she left," he said simply, almost as if it were still a painful memory to articulate. "Just...vanished. One day, she was there, and the next..." He trailed off, searching for the right words. Krissy noticed a fragility beneath his usual stoicism. It made her feel closer to him, of course – as if she'd glimpsed something deeper within, but it also sparked a little anxiety, a feeling that she might be about to uncover something he wasn't quite ready to face. "You never really talked about what happened," she observed quietly. "Just that she 'left.'"

He sighed, running a hand through his hair. "It was...complicated. She just...felt like she needed to be somewhere else. Like she needed to run."

A quick flashback snippet flickered through his mind – Llew at Cardiff Central Station, watching Violet disappear through the throngs of people, rain lashing down around them. The image was sharp and poignant: a young woman melting into the crowd. He'd been standing there, frozen, feeling utterly abandoned. "Do you feel as if it was it something you did?" Krissy asked softly, the question hanging between them like mist. He looked up then, his eyes holding a trace of sadness and perhaps even guilt. "I don't know," he admitted quietly. "Maybe I wasn't...enough. Maybe she just needed to be on the move again. To keep running."

"And you think that's what you need now?" Krissy asked, her voice laced with a hint of understanding and something akin to sadness.

"I don't want to," he said quickly, as if fearing she'd misunderstood. "But...it's just...it's how I've always done things. It's what feels safe." He shifted again. "Like it or not, I keep getting pulled back to Cardiff. It's like a current – you can fight it, but eventually, you get dragged under."

Krissy considered his words for a moment, watching the rain streak down the windowpane. "So," she said slowly, "it's not about you. It's about...Violet? About needing to escape something?"

He nodded almost imperceptibly. "Maybe it's both."

A silence fell between them, a comfortable one this time, but still laden with unspoken emotions. Krissy reached out and gently took his hand, her thumb tracing circles on the back of his. He didn't pull away. "Well," she said finally, her voice soft but firm. "Then let's see if we can find a way to weather this current together." He squeezed her hand briefly, then looked out at the sea, his expression unreadable. The rain continued to fall on Ashcliffe – a steady, persistent rhythm that seemed to mirror the unfolding layers of history and hurt between them. It wasn't a solution, not yet, but it was a start – a simple sentence spoken in a room full of unspoken words, promising perhaps, just perhaps, that they would find their way through the storm together.

The rain continued its steady rhythm over Ashcliffe as Llew wrestled with his decision, the unspoken weight of his impending departure hanging heavy in the air. Suddenly, the door to The Saltwater Siren swung open and Geraint strode in, a calming presence amidst the quiet tension. "Llew! Thought you might be brooding by the sea," he said, offering a warm smile. "Heard about Cardiff. Bit of a blow."

"Just...thinking," Llew mumbled, not looking up from his tea.

"Well," Geraint said thoughtfully, settling into a chair opposite him. "Family is built. Choose yours. And it's not always about distance – sometimes its about roots." Krissy watched them, noticing the way Geraint's gaze held a hint of understanding, of knowing that this wasn't just about Llew leaving – it was about something deeper.

Stella, ever observant, noticed Krissy's quiet sadness and the slight tremor in her hand as she stirred her tea. "You okay?" she asked softly, her voice laced with genuine concern. "You look a bit like you've lost your favourite scarf."

Krissy managed a weak smile. "Just...thinking about it," she said, gesturing vaguely towards Llew. "He's a good one," Stella continued, tilting her head. "Quietly good. And he makes a mean cup of tea." Rita, as if summoned by the unspoken emotions, popped up behind them with a steaming mug of tea and a characteristic grunt. "Don't let him run off like that," she declared bluntly, placing the mug in front of Llew. "He needs you."

"Thanks, Rita," he said dryly, taking a sip. "Always to the point."

"That's what you get," Rita replied with a shrug. "And don't let his past drag him away from now". She paused, studying Krissy for a moment. "You two have something good going on here. Don't lose that." Krissy realized then – this wasn't just about Llew leaving Ashcliffe; it was about the place itself, about the small community they were starting to build together. It felt fragile and vulnerable, like one of the café's chipped teacups – beautiful but easily broken. The memories of Ashcliffe – the annual village fete, Mrs. Prior's jams, Mr. Jones complaining about the paper – all seemed to echo around her now, a reminder of the connections they had forged. "It's not just him," she murmured, more to herself than anyone else. "It's... Ashcliffe. It feels like... like we're finally starting to feel settled here." Llew looked up then, his gaze meeting hers for a moment. "It does," he said quietly. "It's a quiet place. A good place." Krissy realized that his simple statement held so much more than just sentiment – it was about security, about belonging. And the thought of him leaving, of disrupting that feeling, felt... unsettling.

She took a sip of her tea, trying to gather her thoughts. "It's just," she said finally, "it feels like...like we're starting to build something here. Something real." Geraint nodded in agreement. "Ashcliffe has a way of doing that," he said. "Of holding onto you. Of reminding you where you belong." A small group was gathered outside The Saltwater Siren, chatting and laughing – a comforting group of familiar faces. It felt like everyone in town knew – or at least suspected – what was happening. Ashcliffe wasn't just a place, it was a repository of memories, of stories – and of people. Krissy looked around at the rain-soaked streets, at the quaint cottages huddled together against the wind, and suddenly, Llew's decision felt even more significant. It wasn't just about him and his past, it was about their future – about whether they would stay in Ashcliffe or allow themselves to be swept away by the current. She looked back at Llew, a question lingering in her eyes. He offered only a small, hesitant smile, as if bracing himself for something. The echo of Violet's laughter – faint but distinct – seemed to hang in the air, a reminder that even in the quietest of places, the past could always come calling.

Later, the rain had softened to a gentle drizzle and a grey light filtered through the windows of The Chiron Cafe, casting long shadows across the worn wooden floor. Krissy was alone again, sketching quietly in the corner near the window – her favourite spot. She'd been capturing Llew's face for over an hour, trying to capture the quiet intensity she found so captivating. He'd left a few minutes ago, heading towards the harbour. She continued to sketch, lost in the rhythm of charcoal on paper – a familiar comfort amidst the uncertainty swirling within her. He was her favourite face, really – a comfortable blend of quiet strength and hidden vulnerability. She wasn't sure what she was feeling exactly – a mix of anticipation, anxiety, and something akin to bittersweet acceptance. It wasn't just that she feared he'd leave Ashcliffe; she realized she was starting to fear letting go of the possibility of them – of the fragile connection they were building.. "Almost broken," she murmured to herself, a small smile playing on her lips. The phrase felt apt – like a delicate vase that had been nudged slightly askew, threatening to shatter.

She added a subtle detail to the sketch – a small, broken compass needle, pointing tentatively towards Cardiff. It was almost invisible at first glance, but it was there – a quiet visual representation of his decision, of the duality between his past and his future. He'd choose stability, perhaps, or maybe he'd simply need to keep running for a while longer. Krissy tilted her head back, studying her work. It wasn't a perfect likeness, but it captured something – the depth in his eyes, the slight furrow of his brow, the hint of sadness that she couldn't quite shake off. She added a tiny detail to Llew's face – a faint smile, almost as if he was recalling a happy memory. She knew, instinctively, that this sketch wouldn't be just a drawing, it would be a reminder – a tangible symbol of their complicated dance. It represented his strength and his vulnerability, his past and his present, all captured in a single charcoal stroke. As she put down her sketchbook, she felt a sense of quiet acceptance settle over her. Perhaps, she thought, the best thing to do was simply to keep sketching – to capture the moments as they unfolded, to hold onto them until she could figure out what came next. And maybe, just maybe, if she kept capturing Ashcliffe too – its beauty, its quirks, its echoes of the past – then a part of it would come with her, wherever he went.

The next morning dawned grey and damp, clinging to Ashcliffe like a second skin. Krissy found Llew sitting outside The Chiron Café, meticulously polishing the silver compass – his ritual. He looked older than yesterday, more worn, as if the weight of his decision was already settling on his shoulders. She joined him, pulling up a weathered stool.

"Still shining?" she asked quietly, gesturing to the compass. He offered her a small smile. "Trying to," he said, his voice low. "It belonged to my grandmother. Said it always pointed you towards where you needed to be." He paused, studying the face of the compass. "Sometimes, I wonder if it's lying to me."

"Maybe it just needs a little more polishing," Krissy replied, offering him a small smile in return. She noticed he hadn't touched his tea, and that he was staring out at the sea – as if searching for something. "I spoke to Geraint," she said after a moment. "He says don't worry about it too much. That Cardiff might need you for now, but that Ashcliffe will always have a place in your heart." "He's right, of course," Llew said, his gaze distant. "But it's not just about duty, is it? It's about wanting to stay." He turned to her then, and for a brief moment, she thought she saw something – vulnerability, hope – flicker in his eyes.

"It's about wanting to," she confirmed softly. "And I think you might be surprised at how much you like it here." She gestured around at the rain-slicked streets, the quaint cottages, the comforting bustle of The Chiron Café. He chuckled, a low rumble in his chest. "You've certainly sold me on it." He closed his eyes for a moment, as if savouring the thought. "So," he said finally, opening his eyes and returning her gaze, "when do I start?" Before she could answer, Rita burst out of the café, brandishing a steaming mug. "Llew! You're looking like you've spent the night wrestling with a grumpy seal!"

"Just polishing my memories," he said, accepting the mug with a grin. "Thanks, Rita." As Llew settled back into his routine, Krissy felt a surge of...something – relief? Hope? – mingled with a touch of sadness. He was starting to feel like himself again, the quiet strength returning to his demeanour. But she also knew that this feeling might be fleeting, that he would inevitably start pulling away as soon as he got settled in Cardiff. If he got settled in Cardiff.

17

CHAPTER SEVENTEEN:
THE CHOICE

Rain, as always in Ashcliffe, was a generous painter this morning, splashing grey across the slate roofs and the edges of the harbour. Inside The Saltwater Siren, a comforting warmth battled with the dampness outside – a mix of woodsmoke from Albert's impromptu fire and the lingering scent of Stella's lavender tea. Krissy, perched on a worn velvet stool by the window, was lost in capturing the scene: the rhythmic churn of the waves against the breakwater, the muted colours of the cottages huddled together like worried sheep, and Llew, pacing restlessly near the stage as if searching for an answer within its shadowed depths. He'd been restless all morning, a quiet tremor beneath his usual calm. Stella watched him from behind the bar, her hands expertly polishing a tankard – a silent question in her eyes. He was a sturdy oak, Llew, but today he seemed poised on the edge of being blown over.

"You didn't decide yet," she finally said, tilting her head and offering him a warm smile. "Because it matters what you want." Llew stopped pacing, turning to face her. The rain seemed to momentarily intensify as if mirroring his own internal storm. "It does," he admitted, running a hand through his already-dishevelled hair. "It always has.

And this time...it feels bigger." He gestured vaguely towards the sea, as if seeking reassurance from its vastness.

"About Cardiff?" Stella prompted gently.

He nodded, resuming his pacing, slower now, more deliberate. "They offered me a senior position – – proper archival work, in the main office. A real chance to... settle." He paused, choosing his words carefully. "To finally stop feeling like I'm drifting from coffee shop to coffee shop. To actually use what I studied at university all those years ago." Krissy continued sketching, adding a delicate wash of blue to capture the way the light caught on Llew's face – a face that held both strength and a hint of vulnerability. She knew 'settling' wasn't always a good thing for him, it often meant burying something.

"And what about Ashcliffe?" she asked, not looking up from her sketchpad. "What about... us?" He stopped again, turning to face her fully this time. "That's the tricky part," he confessed, his voice low. "It's not just me deciding. It's... my mother. She wants me back in Cardiff. Says I need roots. And she doesn't make it easy." A silence fell between them, punctuated only by the rhythmic drumming of the rain and the occasional cry of a seagull. Then, Llew lifted his hand, offering her a small, worn compass – his grandmother's. "She said this always points to where you belong," he explained quietly. "But lately... I think it's pointing back to Cardiff." Krissy took the compass, turning it over in her fingers. It was beautiful, intricately carved, and felt strangely weighty with history. "Well," she said, a small smile playing on her lips, "Maybe your grandmother is wrong." She held up her sketch – a slightly blurred image of Llew, captured mid-stride, his face etched with contemplation. "Or maybe," she added softly, "she just hasn't seen you yet." He stepped closer, taking the sketch from her hand and studying it intently. "You see me," he murmured, his voice thick with emotion. "Really see me."

The rain outside had softened to a gentle drizzle by mid-morning, painting the cobblestones of Ashcliffe in shimmering puddles. Krissy, feeling a sudden, almost desperate need for perspective, impulsively headed to The Archive – a place she'd previously viewed as slightly dusty and melancholic but now felt held a potential key to understanding not just Ashcliffe's past, but perhaps her own. The Archive was exactly as she remembered: cool and dimly lit, filled with the scent of aging paper and leather-bound books. Eve, her hair pulled back in a practical braid, was meticulously digitizing an old photograph – a black and white image of Emily Thornton looking remarkably young and vibrant, standing on the cliffs overlooking the sea. "Still wrestling with the echoes," Krissy observed, leaning casually against a shelf overflowing with journals. Eve glanced up, offering a small smile. "Always. This place is full of them. It's like everyone leaves a little piece of themselves behind."

Krissy paused, considering her words. "Do you ever feel like you're just carrying on someone else's story?" she asked, gesturing to the photograph. Eve nodded slowly, adjusting the focus on the screen. "All the time. Especially Emily's. She built this place – a legacy of knowledge and memories. I try to do it justice. But sometimes it feels like I'm just archiving her life, not living my own." Krissy spent the next hour browsing through the digitized records, absorbing snippets of Ashcliffe's history: shipwrecks and smuggling rings, lost loves and forgotten promises. She found an entry detailing Emily Thornton's own restless spirit, her desire to break free from the constraints of her small-town life – a feeling remarkably familiar.

After bidding Eve a fond farewell, Krissy returned to The Chiron Cafe to find Llew still pacing, now staring out to sea. He seemed lost in thought, wrestling with his decision. "It's funny," he said quietly, turning back to her. "My mother keeps saying I need to settle down, that I should embrace 'stability'. Like it's some kind of virtue."

"Maybe she just wants you to be happy," Krissy offered, gently.

"Happiness isn't always about staying put," he replied, a hint of melancholy in his voice. "Sometimes it's about choosing where to go." He held up the compass again. "This has always pointed me back to Cardiff, but maybe it's time to let it point somewhere else." He took a step towards her and then hesitated, looking at her with an intensity that made her breath catch. "Do you think I'm running away?" he asked, his voice barely above a whisper.

Krissy reached out and touched his hand – a simple gesture that felt charged with significance. "Maybe," she said softly, "you're just choosing your own story." The sound of rain continued to fall, but now it sounded less like a mournful lament and more like a gentle encouragement – a reminder that sometimes, the greatest choices are the ones that lead you toward the unknown. Outside, Llewelyn glanced out at the sea. He turned back to her with a faint smile. "Well? What about your story?"

Krissy didn't know. All she did know was that now that Llew was a main character in her story, she couldn't let him go. Not easily, anyway. She just didn't want to.

The rain had eased to a persistent drizzle by mid-afternoon, leaving the cobblestones of Ashcliffe slick and reflecting the warm glow spilling from the windows of The Chiron Café. It was exactly the sort of day that called for tea, a bit of gossip, and perhaps a touch of melancholic observation – the perfect setting for a gathering of Ashcliffe's residents. The café was humming with activity, a microcosm of the town itself: Mrs. Prior bustled about with trays of scones, Mr. Jones grumbled about the price of kippers, and children chased each other through the tables. Llew stood near the counter, nursing a lukewarm coffee – an almost permanent fixture at The Chiron Café, seemingly content to observe the ebb and flow of life around him. Krissy joined him. "He's dithering like a lost sheep," Rita declared, wiping down the counter with efficiency. "Shoulder-shrugging and fidgeting. Doesn't seem to know whether he wants to be happy or miserable."

Tom nodded in agreement, his gaze thoughtful. "Llew's always been good at feeling things... and then letting them weigh him down." He glanced at Krissy, a subtle question in his eyes – acknowledging her own current state of anxious contemplation.

"It's just... it feels like he's carrying on someone else's story," Krissy murmured, swirling the tea in her cup. "Like he's trying to fit into a role that doesn't quite belong to him."

Rita snorted. "Well, maybe he should choose his own story then!" The door swung open and Geraint and Eve arrived, laden with flyers advertising the upcoming fundraising event for the lighthouse – a vital project for Ashcliffe's struggling economy. The party they'd held near the lighthouse made the Town Council realise exactly how much work the lighthouse itself needed. "We need volunteers!" Geraint announced, beaming. "The lighthouse is hauling in, and it's up to us to keep it shining."

"And we need people to man the stalls," Eve added, handing out sign-up sheets. "Every little bit helps." Councillor Davies fretted over his sheet. "It's vital, you know," he said to Llew, his brow furrowed. "Ashcliffe relies on these things. On its community."

"It does," Tom murmured quietly, observing Llew's thoughtful expression. Llew offered a small smile. "Just trying to figure out where I fit in," he admitted. As they were discussing volunteer slots, Stella and Albert emerged, their faces radiating quiet observation. Stella subtly gestured towards Llewelyn with her hand – a silent question of support, or perhaps a gentle reminder of the emotions he'd been trying to suppress. Albert simply nodded, his expression a mixture of concern and understanding.

Krissy turned to Llew. "It's not just about you," she said softly. "It's about what Ashcliffe needs."

He met her gaze, a hint of vulnerability in his eyes. "I know," he replied. "And maybe it's time for me to finally figure out what that is." He paused, then added with a small smile: "Do you think I should go?" Krissy didn't answer immediately. She looked around the bustling café – at Rita and Tom, at Geraint and Eve, at Stella and Albert, at Mrs. Prior and Mr. Jones – at all of Ashcliffe's residents, each holding their own piece of the town's story. Finally, she simply said: "Let's just see."

The rain had finally ceased by late afternoon, leaving Ashcliffe washed and gleaming under a bruised purple sky. Krissy found herself drawn to the small, slightly cluttered flat above The Chiron Café – her temporary haven, her sketchpad, and now, the locus of a growing understanding. She was sketching again – yet another charcoal study of Llewelyn's face, capturing not just his features but also the quiet intensity she'd noticed in him. She heard footsteps approach. Llew stood in the doorway, leaning against the frame – his gaze thoughtful, observant. He stepped into the room and closed the door behind him, gently shutting out the sounds of the café. "Do you know what you want?" he asked, his voice soft.

"I think... I think I'm starting to," she replied, her gaze meeting his. "But it feels like everyone else has a map. And me? I've just been wandering." He moved closer, and for a moment, they stood in silence – the only sound the gentle ticking of an old grandfather clock.

"You're not just worried about losing me, are you?" he asked softly, tilting her chin up with his finger. "You're worried about Ashcliffe. About leaving."

Krissy hesitated, then nodded slowly. "It feels like if I stay, it's me trapping myself. Like I'll always be looking out the window waiting to leave."

"And if you go?" he prompted gently. "What do you think will happen then?"

"I don't know," she confessed, her voice barely a whisper. "Maybe I'll just keep running." He reached out and took her hand, his touch warm and reassuring.

"What do you truly want?" Llewelyn asked, his eyes searching hers. "Do you want to build a life here? To put down roots?" Krissy looked out the window at the rain-washed streets of Ashcliffe – at the familiar shapes of the houses, the curve of the breakwater, the glow of The Saltwater Siren's windows. "I don't know if I want to build," she said slowly. "But I think I want to feel like I belong. Not just here, but somewhere. To stop feeling like a ghost."

"And what about being brave?" he challenged gently. "Are you brave enough to stay? Brave enough to let yourself be seen?"

"Maybe," she replied, her voice gaining strength. "Maybe if I let myself be seen, it won't feel so scary."

He squeezed her hand. "It doesn't have to," he said quietly. "And maybe you don't need to do it alone."

The sound of the door opening startled them – it was Rita, carrying two mugs of tea and a plate of biscuits. "Thought you might need this," she said with a wry smile. "You two look like you've been wrestling with the world." As Llew turned to thank her, Krissy caught his eye – a promise held in that brief moment. He stepped back towards her, pulling her into a gentle embrace. "Then don't," he murmured against her hair, his voice laced with reassurance and something more – perhaps a hint of challenge. "Don't you leave, and neither will I." And as she nestled closer to him, surrounded by the familiar comforts of Eloise's old flat, Krissy felt a sense of quiet certainty – that despite all her running, maybe, just maybe, she had finally found her way home.

The rain had eased to a soft drizzle by late afternoon, painting the cliff side in shades of grey and silver. Llew and Krissy walked along the path, their boots splashing through puddles – mirroring the emotional currents swirling within them. It wasn't a boisterous walk, it was a quiet communion, punctuated only by the rhythmic crash of waves against the rocks and the occasional cry of a gull. The air was cool and damp, carrying the scent of salt and seaweed – a familiar fragrance to Ashcliffe. They walked in comfortable silence for a while, each lost in their own thoughts, before Krissy spoke – her voice barely audible above the sound of the sea. "It's not about whether I want to stay," she said softly, turning to face him. "It's about whether Ashcliffe needs me to."

Llew stopped and turned to face her, his gaze searching hers. "And do you think it does?" he asked, a hint of hope in his voice. Krissy took a deep breath, letting the rain dampen her hair – feeling more exposed than ever before. "I think... I think it might," she replied, offering a small smile. "It needs people who are willing to put down roots." He stepped closer and took her hand, his fingers intertwining with hers. "And maybe," he said, squeezing her hand gently, "it needs you to be brave enough to stay." They continued their walk, the rain falling steadily around them – washing away the last vestiges of doubt. Llew reached down and picked up a small, smooth stone from the beach – its surface worn by years of tumbling in the tide. He turned to Krissy and offered it to her. "Here," he said simply, handing her the stone. "A little something to hold onto." It was a quiet gesture - simple and profound – a symbol of resilience, of weathering storms together. The stone felt warm in her hand, grounding her amidst the swirling emotions tormenting her. They looked out at the sea together – vast and endless.

"Thank you," she whispered, clutching the stone tightly in her hand.

"Anytime," he replied. As they turned to walk back towards town, the rain seemed to lighten slightly – as if acknowledging their decision. They didn't speak, but there was a comfortable understanding between them – a shared knowledge that whatever the future held, they would face it together. Finally, they stopped at the edge of the path and looked back at the sea one last time. It stretched out before them – grey and shimmering in the rain – a symbol of both mystery and possibility.

The rain continued its gentle rhythm over Ashcliffe as Llew and Krissy walked back towards town, the stone a warm weight in Krissy's hand. It felt like a small anchor, tethering her to this place, to him. The shared glance at the sea – that final, quiet acknowledgement – settled something deep within her. "It's funny," Krissy said quietly, breaking the comfortable silence, "how much simpler things feel now."

Llew nodded, his gaze fixed on the path ahead. "Sometimes," he replied thoughtfully, "it's not about making a big decision. It's just... letting go of the ones that don't serve you any more." They reached The

Chiron Café and, to their delight, Rita was already bustling behind the counter, wiping down surfaces with her usual brisk efficiency. "Well, look who it is," she announced, barely glancing up. "Took you long enough. Thought you were off gallivanting again."

"Just contemplating," Llewelyn said, offering a wry smile. "And I decided against it."

Rita raised an eyebrow, a hint of amusement in her eyes. "Good. Ashcliffe needs all the good men it can get."

The warmth of the café, the familiar chatter of locals catching up on their news, and Rita's blunt observations were comforting – small anchors in themselves. As they settled into a corner, Krissy noticed Llew had a nautical chart spread across the table – a detail she hadn't seen before.

"What are you looking at?" she asked.

"Just... old charts of the coastline," he said vaguely, tracing his finger along the jagged edges of the breakwater. "Trying to figure out where it all fits." He didn't elaborate, but Krissy sensed a deeper significance. It felt like he was trying to map out not just Ashcliffe's geography, but their own futures.

Later that evening, after helping unload some of Stella and Albert's equipment from the Saltwater Siren, Krissy found herself drawn back to The Archive. It wasn't a conscious decision – she felt a pull, a resonance with the quiet space and the weight of forgotten stories. Eve greeted her warmly at the door. "Still haunted?" she asked, a gentle smile playing on her lips. "Don't worry, ghosts are not as fussy as they used to be." Krissy chuckled, browsing through the shelves filled with local history books and documents. She found herself drawn to a section detailing Ashcliffe's early days – its struggles with the sea, its reliance on fishing, and the stories of those who had built it. She picked up a faded photograph of Louisa Thornton as a young woman, standing proudly on the cliffs overlooking the sea – the same view Llew often gazed upon. Suddenly, she noticed a small, handwritten note tucked inside the back cover of a local history book – a detail she hadn't seen before. It was from Llewelyn himself, written in his characteristic neat script: "To Evie – May your roots run deep here." A warm feeling spread through her – a confirmation that he too felt connected to Ashcliffe's past.

The next morning dawned bright and clear, the rain having finally retreated completely. The sun cast a golden glow over Ashcliffe, illuminating the slate roofs and sparkling harbour. Krissy found Llew already at the lighthouse, his silhouette outlined against the rising sun. She joined him without hesitation. "Thought you might want to see it again," he said, turning as she approached – a small smile gracing his face. "It's good up here." They climbed the winding staircase to the top of the lighthouse, passing through rooms filled with antique equipment and nautical charts. The view from the lantern room was breathtaking – Ashcliffe spread out below them like a miniature world, framed by the vast expanse of the sea. "It's been lonely," Llewelyn admitted quietly, gazing out at the horizon. "But it's good to know someone is watching." Krissy nodded, understanding dawning on her. He wasn't just guarding the light – he was guarding Ashcliffe, its memories, and perhaps even their future together. She looked down at the stone in her hand, the one he'd given her, the one she'd been keeping in her pocket as a tangible reminder of his choice, of his decision to stay.

"So," he said finally, turning to face her, "What do you think?"

Krissy smiled, clutching the stone in her hand. "I think," she said, her voice filled with certainty, "that Ashcliffe might just be home after all." And then, leaning in, she kissed him – a slow, sweet kiss that spoke of shared stories, quiet hopes, and a future finally taking shape. As the sun began to set over Ashcliffe, casting a golden glow across the town, it felt like a new chapter was beginning – a chapter where they would both be written together, side by side, in the heart of this beautiful, windswept little seaside town.

18

CHAPTER EIGHTEEN: WRECK ME GENTLY

The rain had eased to a persistent drizzle by mid-morning, clinging to the slate roofs of Ashcliffe like a lingering kiss. Inside The Chiron Cafe, a warmth had settled – not quite sunny, but certainly promising. The scent of salt, woodsmoke, and strong tea mingled in the air, and the room buzzed with the low hum of conversation from the preparations for the evening's fundraising party to fix the lighthouse. Krissy had been sketching there all day, at her favourite window seat. But now, she waved to Llew and Rita and went upstairs to Eloise's old flat. There, she continued to sketch, her charcoal dancing across the paper, capturing the curve of Llew's jaw as he straightened a stack of napkins. It wasn't a grand portrait – just a quiet study, trying to capture the way light caught in his dark eyes when he was lost in thought. She felt it then – that familiar flutter beneath her ribs, a subtle reminder of the delicious tension that always seemed to simmer between them. It was a comfortable feeling now, not frantic or anxious, but like a well-worn blanket – familiar and reassuring. She'd been wrestling with a small, persistent worry all morning: whether Ashcliffe, and Llew, were truly solid enough to hold her, or if she'd just be another tide pulling out to sea.

"Lost in thought?" His voice was low, a gravelly rumble that seemed to vibrate through the room. He'd been leaning against the flat's doorway, watching her with an unreadable expression for goodness knows how long now. Krissy glanced up, a smile tilting at the corner of her lips. "Just trying to capture your brooding." She gestured to the sketch with her charcoal. He pushed off the door frame and came around to sit beside her on the worn velvet armchair. "You've got the brooding down pat," he said, taking in the drawing. His hand brushed hers as he tilted it slightly for a better view. "It's almost... intimidating."

"Only if you let it be," she replied, letting her fingers linger on his.

His thumb began tracing circles on her knuckles. "I've been thinking about you," he said simply. "About Ashcliffe."

"Have you now?" she asked, a blush rising to her cheeks.

"Yeah," he replied, and that was it – no grand declarations, just a quiet acknowledgement of the pull they both felt. He shifted closer still, until their knees were almost touching. "It's like... being here with you," he murmured, his voice rough with feeling.

"It's like being tangled in your hair," she teased, nudging him gently with her elbow.

He chuckled, a deep rumble that seemed to shake his chest. "You try to wreck me."

She tilted her head back, meeting his gaze. "Is that a bad thing?"

"Not if you're good at it," he said, and then, almost before she could react, he was pulling her closer. He didn't say anything – just wrapped his arms around her, drawing her in until there was no space between them. The rain outside intensified for a moment, drumming a steady rhythm against the windowpanes – a quiet storm mirroring the one gathering within her. She leaned into him, breathing in the scent of salt and something uniquely Llew – old books, polished wood, and a hint of that earthy, comforting smell he always had.

"What's this about?" she murmured into his shoulder. He shifted slightly, pulling back just enough to look at her. "The job offer," he said, gesturing vaguely with his hand. "Cardiff. It's... serious." A brief flashback flickered – her mother's stern face, urging him to accept, to take advantage of an opportunity to secure his future. "My mother wanted me to. Said it was time I stopped drifting."

Krissy felt a pang of something – not jealousy, exactly, but a quiet vulnerability. She knew how much the call of Cardiff meant to him, how deeply rooted he was in his family history. "And?" she prompted softly. It was why he'd come to Ashcliffe, wasn't it? To see the newest member of his family properly welcomed into the world.

"And...," he said, stepping back and looking at her with an intensity that made her breath catch. "It would mean being away for a while." He reached out, his hand finding hers and holding it firmly. He didn't pull away, didn't let go. "I suppose I just wanted to know... if you'd miss me."She met his gaze, letting the question sink in. "More than words," she admitted, her voice a little breathless. "But... that doesn't mean I want you to go."

A slow smile spread across his face. "Good. Let's not stand around thinking about it, then," he murmured, tilting his head. Before she could say anything, he gathered her into his arms, lifting her slightly off the ground. His grip tightened, a comfortable pressure against her back. "You know what you want," he said, his voice low and close to her ear. "Don't give it to me without a fight." He didn't kiss her – not yet. He just held her there for a long moment, letting her feel the warmth of his body against hers, letting the quiet anticipation build. Then, he lowered her gently to the floor and stepped back, giving her space. "You can start," he said, a hint of challenge in his eyes.

Krissy took a deep breath, letting herself relax into the feeling of being wanted, of being desired. She smiled – a slow, deliberate smile that promised resistance and delight in equal measure. "You're on," she replied, stepping forward to meet him. And as they finally kissed – a messy, passionate tangle of limbs and longing – it felt less like an invitation and more like a promise: a pledge to weather whatever storms came their way, together.

The kiss deepened, a slow burn that started tentative and blossomed with a delicious urgency. Krissy hadn't planned it – hadn't even consciously decided to fight back – but as his lips settled on hers, she instinctively twisted one wrist, just enough to create a little space, a tiny barrier. He didn't pull away, didn't break the connection, but he adjusted slightly, his hand sliding further up her arm, anchoring him to her. "You're awfully sure about that," she murmured into his mouth, finally breaking the kiss. Her breath came in little puffs, a mix of anticipation and lingering heat. He chuckled, a low rumble in his chest. "I like being sure," he said, pulling back just enough to look at her, his eyes dark and intense. He ran a thumb over her lower lip, tasting the faint sweetness of her skin. "Especially when it comes to you." She tilted her head, studying him. "Maybe because you tend to surprise me?" he continued, stepping closer until they were practically chest-to-chest.

He reached for the silk scarf knotted loosely around her neck – one of her many, this particular one a little memento from the lighthouse gift shop – and gently tightened it, pulling it just a bit higher. "Like this," he murmured, his fingers brushing against her skin. "Don't try to control me with scarves," she teased, feeling a thrill of both amusement and something deeper – a recognition that he was enjoying the little dance they were doing. "It's a cliché." He grinned, a flash of white teeth against his tanned skin. "Maybe," he admitted. "But clichés are often true." He shifted, stepping around her until he was behind her. She could feel the warmth radiating from him, smell the salt and sea air clinging to his clothes. "What's next?" she asked, turning slightly to face him, giving him a glimpse of her shoulder. He didn't answer with words. Instead, he reached out, his fingers tracing the line of her collarbone before gently curving around one of her wrists and bringing it up behind her neck. It wasn't forceful – just a soft, deliberate movement. Her breath caught in her throat.

"Letting go is always an option," she whispered, her eyes widening slightly as he began to tie the silk scarf around her wrists, securing them together. The pressure was light at first, a gentle restraint, but it steadily increased, not tight or constricting, just... holding. "You're good at this," she observed, her voice barely audible. "Making me feel like I'm trapped."

He leaned down, his breath warm against the back of her neck. "It's a useful skill," he murmured, and then, with a slow, deliberate movement, he tightened the knot slightly further. "Especially when you need to be reminded who's in charge." She closed her eyes for a moment, letting the silk scarf glide against her skin – the cool smoothness of the silk a welcome contrast to the heat rising within her. She could feel the subtle pressure on her wrists, the awareness of being contained, but it wasn't uncomfortable. It was... stimulating. A delicious shiver ran down her spine. "Is that what you want?" she asked, opening her eyes and meeting his gaze. He didn't say anything – just continued to look at her, his eyes dark with desire. He lowered his head slightly, bringing his forehead close to hers. The scent of him was intoxicating – a heady blend of sea, woodsmoke, and something uniquely Llew. "I want everything," he murmured, and then, with another gentle tug on the scarf, he pulled her a little closer until she could feel the warmth of his chest against her back. She could hear the steady rhythm of his breath, feel the strength in his arms holding her.

Her fingers instinctively curled around the silk of the scarf, tightening it slightly as if to anchor herself. "Don't," she whispered, a hint of challenge in her voice. He didn't heed her warning. He lowered his head further, kissing the pulse point on her wrist – a slow, deliberate kiss that sent sparks of heat racing up her arm. Then, with a soft smile, he tightened the knot just a fraction more, and she knew – absolutely knew – that she was thoroughly, deliciously captive. He continued to kiss her neck, slowly, deliberately, as if measuring out each drop of sensation. Then, he shifted his hand, sliding it down to cup the back of her head, tilting her face up slightly so she could look into his eyes. The bite on her collarbone was deeper now, a delicious pressure that made her shiver. "It's... nice," she breathed, trying – and failing – to sound as this was something she was used to. Inside, she was a swirling vortex of sensations: the silk against her skin, the warmth of him, the gentle restraint of the tie, and, of course, him. He didn't speak, simply continued to kiss her, his lips hard and sure. He lowered his head further, tasting the corner of her mouth, then slowly slid one hand down her thigh, fingers tracing the curve of her hip. It wasn't a demanding move – just an invitation, a suggestion.

He's so good at this, she thought, letting herself sink deeper into him. Like he knows exactly where to touch, how to make you want more. There was something inherently exhilarating about his control, a feeling of safety nestled within the little bit of tension. It reminded her of that first evening, when he'd simply been there – solid and quiet – as she'd shivered on the rocks, watching the storm roll in. He deepened the pressure of his hand on her hip, then slowly began to slide one wrist up, loosening the knot on the scarf just a fraction. She felt a shiver run down her spine, a delicious anticipation building within her. "You're taking your time," she murmured, her voice husky with pleasure. He chuckled softly, and then, with a fluid motion, he brought his hand up to her face, gently stroking the curve of her cheekbone. "Why rush?" he whispered, his breath warm against her skin. "There's plenty of time to savour everything."

He kissed the sensitive skin at the base of her throat – a slow, deliberate exploration that made her moan softly. She tightened her fingers around the silk of the scarf, pulling it just slightly, as if asking for more. Let's go faster, she thought, but didn't say. He responded to her subtle cue, easing his hand from her cheek and sliding down to her waist. His fingers brushed against the soft fabric, and a delicious heat spread through her as he gently began to slide it down, just a few inches at a time. "Mmm," she breathed, letting out a small shiver. It wasn't just the physical sensation – it was the knowledge that he was in control, that he was choosing this moment, this pace. It was intoxicating. A memory flickered – him holding her hand as they walked along the beach at dusk, his thumb tracing circles on her palm with a quiet confidence. He paused for a moment, letting his fingers linger against her skin before continuing to slide the waistband down. He wasn't rough or forceful – just smooth and sure. Then, he leaned back slightly, giving her a glimpse of his lips. "What do you want?" he murmured, his eyes dark with desire.

She met his gaze, letting him see the yearning in her eyes. "More," she whispered, tilting her head ever so slightly to the side – a small, subtle invitation. A little pull on his hand, just barely noticeable, as if asking him to move faster.

He didn't hesitate. He tightened his grip on her waist, pulling her closer until their bodies were pressed together. The scent of sea and him filled her senses. He lowered his head again, kissing her with a passion that matched her own – a deep, consuming kiss that stole her breath away. His hand continued to slide down her thigh, and she let out a small moan, a sound of pure pleasure. Her fingers tightened on the scarf, and she shifted slightly, bringing her hip up against his. "You're beautiful," he murmured against her lips, and then, with another deliberate movement, he tightened the knot on the scarf just a little bit – securing her, but not restricting her. He continued to kiss her, slowly, sensually, exploring every inch of her skin. The touch was light at first, then grew deeper, more insistent. She arched into him, wanting to be closer, wanting to feel everything he was feeling. It wasn't about domination; it was about connection, about savouring each moment together. "Yes," she breathed, letting out a longer, more contented moan. "Definitely more."

He deepened the kiss, pulling her flush against him, feeling the rise and fall of her chest beneath his hand. The silk scarf felt like a tangible promise – a quiet declaration of their intentions. He tasted the salt on her skin. The sweat, the memory of the sea's kisses. "Tell me," he murmured into her mouth, his voice low and rumbling. "What's making you want more?" She didn't answer with words, not immediately. Instead, she shifted slightly, bringing her knee up to rest against his, a small, possessive gesture. He responded by sliding one hand further down, fingers curling around the curve of her thigh, deepening the sensation. It's not just him, she thought, letting herself be fully absorbed in the moment. It's the way he does everything – so quietly, so confidently, like he knows exactly what you want before you do. It was a comforting feeling, this sense of being understood, of being taken care of. He tightened his grip on her leg just slightly, a subtle pressure that sent another shiver through her. "Is it the control?" he whispered, as if reading her mind. She nodded almost imperceptibly, letting him feel the slight tension in her thigh beneath his hand. A tiny moan escaped her lips – this time, a little louder, a little more deliberate. "Or is it," he continued, tilting her face up slightly so she could look into his eyes, "the feeling of being held?" She met his gaze, and for a moment, she was lost in the dark depths of his eyes. He wasn't demanding; he was simply offering – an invitation to surrender completely.

"Both," she admitted, her voice barely above a whisper.

He chuckled softly, murmured "You're such a tease." Let him tease me more, she thought, letting out a sigh that mingled with his. She tightened her grip on the scarf again, pulling it just slightly, as if to say, Go on. He responded immediately, sliding his hand up her thigh, fingers tracing the line of her hip and buttock. He paused for a moment, letting his fingertips brush against the sensitive skin, then continued, smoothing out any wrinkles in the fabric. It was intimate, almost reverent. "Like this?" he murmured, tilting her face up slightly so she could look at him. She nodded again, unable to speak, lost in the delicious sensation of his touch. She felt a flush rise to her cheeks, and she shifted slightly, trying to catch his eye. He brought his hand back down, sliding it further down her thigh until he was running his fingers along the curve of her hip. He tightened his grip slightly, pulling her closer until her body was pressed firmly against his. Then, with a slow, deliberate movement, he began to slide the waistband down completely, revealing her lower hips. "Mmm," she breathed.

He leaned down, kissing the curve of her hip – a soft, lingering kiss that sent shivers running down her spine. Then, with another gentle tug on the scarf, he pulled her closer still, and she knew that he was about to take her completely. "Ready?" he murmured into her ear, his breath warm against her skin. She closed her eyes for a moment, letting herself be swept away by the anticipation. "Always," she whispered back. He paused, just above her hip, his fingers lingering for a moment before continuing their ascent. He felt the slight tremor in her leg beneath his hand, a delicious invitation. "You're such a fighter," he murmured, tilting her face up slightly so she could look into his eyes. "But you let go easily too, don't you?" She met his gaze, and for a heartbeat, she felt a little bit of the wariness that still lingered within her – the remnants of past betrayals. But it was quickly overshadowed by the overwhelming desire that surged through her as he continued to kiss her.

He lowered his head again, deepening the kiss, sliding his hand further up her thigh until he reached her inner hip. Then, tilting her towards him, "Let me show you," he murmured, his fingers gently tracing the curve of her hip and thigh. "Just let me." It wasn't a forceful command; it was an invitation – a promise of pleasure. And she couldn't resist. She relaxed further into his embrace, allowing herself to sink into the sensation. He tightened his grip slightly on her leg, pulling her closer still, and then with a fluid motion, he brought her hand up and gently cupped her face in his hands. "Tell me what you want," he murmured, tilting her face up so she could look into his eyes. "Don't be shy." She met his gaze, letting herself be swept away by the intensity of his desire. "More... more now," she breathed, her voice slightly husky.

The air between them thickened, charged with a heat that felt like it had been building since the first breath they'd shared together. His fingers traced the curve of her hip as if memorizing every contour of her skin. She could feel his pulse beneath his touch, a rhythm that matched the frantic thrumming in her own chest. He tilted her face up again, his gaze devouring hers, and she didn't pull away. The world faded. No waves, no distant voices, just the scent of salt and his skin, the way his hand pressed into her thigh, grounding her, holding her. He shifted, moving closer, his body a warm, solid weight against hers. His lips brushed the curve of her jaw, then trailed down to her neck, lingering there as if testing the terrain. She arched into him, her breath shallow, her fingers tightening around the fabric of his shirt, desperate for something more. Still, he didn't rush. Instead, he slid his hand lower, pressing into the small of her back, his thumb brushing against the swell of her hip, and she let out a soft, wet sound – part moan, part surrender.

His fingers found the edge of her waistband again, this time sliding it down with a quiet precision that made her shiver. The silk fell away, leaving her bare, exposed, and utterly vulnerable. He didn't stop there. His hand moved to her thigh, tracing the line of her inner hip, and she gasped, her body reacting to the touch as if it were a memory burned into her bones. He leaned in, his lips brushing against her skin, and she arched higher, her legs wrapping around his waist, her thighs pressing against his hips. "I keep noticing the looks you give me when I've got my sleeves rolled up. Let me," he murmured, his voice low and urgent, "let me show you just how good I am with my hands." She trembled, her breath coming in short, ragged gasps as his hand moved higher, slipping between her legs, finding the warmth of her flesh. He didn't say anything more. He didn't need to. His fingers hovered there and she felt the weight of it – his desire, his control, the way he knew exactly how to touch her.

She pressed against him, her body alive with a need that burned through her, a fire that had been smouldering for hours now. He slid his hand, his fingers pressing into her, and she moaned, her legs trembling as she pulled him closer, her knees pressing against his ribs. "More," she whispered, her voice raw with need. His fingers moved, slow and sure, and she felt the heat of his touch spread through her, a fire that ignited every nerve ending. He pressed into her, his hand finding her, and she gasped, her body convulsing as the sensation surged through her – deep, hot, and absolutely unbearable in its intensity. He didn't pull away. He held her there, his fingers moving in slow, deliberate circles, his thumb pressing against her, and she arched into him, her legs wrapping around his waist, her thighs pressing against his ribs. The world faded, and all she could feel was the heat of his touch, the weight of his body, the way he held her as if she were the only thing in existence. Then, with a final, slow motion, he pulled her into him, his fingers finding her, and she came again – sudden, violent, and absolutely perfect. When she finally stilled, he lifted his head, his gaze heavy with desire, and she looked into his eyes – dark, deep, and entirely hers.

The aftermath was thick with the scent of salt and sweat, the air between them heavy with the remnants of their shared passion. He held her close, his fingers still pressed into her, his thumb tracing slow circles against her as if to remember every curve, every pulse, every breath she had given him. She didn't pull away. Her body trembled in his arms, her legs still wrapped around his waist, her thighs pressed tight against his ribs. The world had faded, leaving only the warmth of his touch, the weight of his body, and the way he held her as if she were something fragile, something he'd been desperate to protect all along. She blinked, her eyes fluttering open to meet his. His gaze was dark, intense. Full of the quiet understanding that had always lingered between them. She could see it in the way his fingers tightened slightly, the way his breath came slow and steady, as if he were trying to hold onto the moment like it might vanish if he let go.

She let out a soft, wet sound – part sigh, part moan – as if the words were too heavy to carry. She pressed her forehead against his, letting herself be held, let herself feel the weight of his body against hers. He wasn't just holding her in the physical sense; he was holding her in the way that made her feel safe, whole, and entirely his. For a long moment, they simply remained like that – tangled together, breathless, the air between them charged with something unspoken. Then, slowly, he pulled his hand away, his fingers still brushing against her, lingering just enough to leave her breathing unevenly. She didn't move, didn't try to pull away. "I've been waiting for this," he said again, his voice quieter now, almost reverent. "Waiting for you." She looked into his eyes, searching them for the truth buried there. The way he had always held himself, like he knew exactly what he was doing. Like he had been preparing for this moment all along. She had been too busy doubting herself to see it. To feel it.

"Then don't let me go," she whispered, her voice barely above a breath. "Don't ever let me go." He didn't answer immediately. Instead, he lifted his head slightly, his lips curling into something that looked like a smile. A small, knowing smile. One that made her heart stop for a moment. "Then I'll stay," he said finally, his voice low and steady. "I'll stay with you." She didn't know how to respond. She didn't need to. Because in that moment, she knew that this was more than just a physical connection. This was something deeper, something that had been building for far longer than either of them could remember. He pulled her closer, his fingers finding the curve of her hip again, and she let herself be held, let herself believe in the quiet promise he was making. All of it at once.

19

CHAPTER NINETEEN: WHAT WE KEEP

The rain had stopped, leaving Ashcliffe washed clean and shimmering in the late afternoon light. It was one of those moments where the grey seemed to have retreated, revealing the town's colours – the ochre of the sandstone cottages, the teal of the sea, the vibrant splashes of paint on Krissy's new gallery walls. A familiar rhythm settled over Ashcliffe: the gentle thrum of a fishing boat returning to harbour, its engine a low rumble against the cries of the seagulls overhead, and the comforting murmur of conversation drifting from The Chiron Café. Inside the small studio/gallery that she had just signed a lease on, nestled next door to the Archive, Krissy was lost in her work. Sunlight streamed through the window, illuminating dust motes dancing in the air and bathing her latest sketch in a warm glow. It was a simple scene – a weathered fisherman mending his nets on the harbour wall – but it felt imbued with something more than just observation. It captured the very soul of Ashcliffe. The studio itself was small, cosy, and perfectly her – a little chaotic, filled with half-finished canvases, paint tubes scattered across a worn table, and stacks of sketchbooks overflowing with ideas.

She'd been sketching for hours, almost without noticing, her hand moving instinctively to capture the light and shadow on the canvas. It was a quiet activity, one that allowed her to process the whirlwind of emotions – the lingering traces of Violet, the comfortable certainty of Llew's presence, and the slow-growing roots she felt taking hold in this windswept town. A robin landed on the windowsill, tilting its head as if offering a silent critique, before flitting off into the dappled light. Krissy smiled and continued to work, feeling, for the first time in a long while, that she was finally starting to find her place within Ashcliffe's quiet embrace.

Llew was behind the counter at The Chiron Café, greeting regulars with his easy charm and familiar smile. Heaps of books were still stacked on the shelves, and the aroma of Earl Grey and warm scones filled the air. There was something about him that felt different. More confident, more settled. He moved with a little less haste, his gaze lingering for a moment longer on each customer. Rita and Tom were laughing, a comfortable sadness in their eyes. "After tonight's dinner, we're hitting the road," Rita had declared, brandishing a crumpled map. "Van's sorted, unicorn hunting's on! We'll send you postcards – and maybe a glittery horn or two." Tom simply squeezed his shoulder, offering a silent promise to keep the café running smoothly in his absence. They were chasing something new, a little bit of freedom, and it felt like Ashcliffe was holding onto him with all its grey charm.

"Morning, Krissy," Llew greeted her warmly as she entered, a small smile gracing his lips. "Sketching already? Capturing the soul of Ashcliffe one brushstroke at a time, I see."

"Just trying to keep up," she replied, returning his smile. "It's hard to compete with your charm.

Rita bustled over from behind the counter, wiping down the surface. "He's stuck here like glue," she observed, grinning at Llewelyn. "Glad he is, though. We wouldn't want him gallivanting off to Cardiff again."

Tom nodded in agreement, pouring Krissy a cup of tea. "He's part of the furniture now," he said, with a wry smile.

Llew chuckled and handed her a biscuit. "Speaking of furniture," he said, glancing around the café, "I think I'll finally tackle that pile of books in the corner." Krissy watched him as he turned back to serve a customer, feeling a sense of contentment wash over her. The rain had stopped, and as she looked out at Ashcliffe from her new studio window, she realized that maybe, just maybe, she had been drifting for too long, too. And perhaps, like Llew, she'd finally found somewhere to put down roots.

The sounds of everyday life in Ashcliffe drifted – the clatter of cups at The Chiron Café, the distant bark of dogs, the gentle hum of conversation. It was a comforting soundtrack, a reminder that Llew and Krissy were settling into their own rhythm, and that Ashcliffe itself was quietly embracing them. Drawn by a feeling she couldn't quite place, Krissy wandered over to Eve's cottage – a charming, slightly overgrown little dwelling nestled amongst the trees at the edge of town. Inside, the cottage was awash in soft light and a flurry of activity. Eve and Geraint were meticulously preparing the nursery – a cosy room painted in a calming shade of blue, filled with adorable baby clothes, plush toys, and handmade mobiles. They moved with a quiet efficiency, a comfortable dance honed by weeks of anticipation. Geraint was noticeably more relaxed than he'd been recently – a hint of a smile playing on his lips as he carefully arranged a stack of soft blankets. He was embracing the chaos of it all, a welcome change from his former intensity. Eve, ever practical and thoughtful, was fussing over the details: ensuring the crib was perfectly level, checking that the changing table was within easy reach, and meticulously arranging the baby clothes in colour order.

"Do you think it's too much lilac?" she asked, holding up a tiny lavender onesie. Geraint glanced at it, then back at her. "Perfect," he said, his voice softer than usual. They exchanged a quick glance – a quiet acknowledgement of how much Ashcliffe had changed them.

The arrival of their baby was a tangible symbol of stability and love, a grounding force in the midst of all the town's secrets and stories. "I think it's lovely," Krissy said, stepping into the room and offering to help. "It feels... warm."

Eve smiled gratefully. "Thank you. It just felt right for here." She gestured around at the cottage. "Ashcliffe has a way of pulling you in, doesn't it? Making you feel like this is where you've always belonged." Geraint nodded, carefully hanging a mobile above the crib – a delicate arrangement of stars and moons. "It feels... settled," he said. "Like we're finally putting down roots."

Krissy helped them fold blankets, enjoying the simple pleasure of shared activity. As they worked together, a sense of peace settled over the room – a feeling that everything was falling into place. The nursery felt like more than just a space for a baby, it was a symbol of their new beginning and a testament to their love and commitment. "I keep thinking about Violet," Eve said quietly, running her hand over the soft fabric of a blanket. "Do you think she'll ever come back?" Geraint hesitated for a moment, then offered a thoughtful reply. "I don't know. But wherever she is, I hope she's happy." Krissy, who had been quietly observing them, felt a pang of empathy for the woman with the captivating smile and the lingering sadness. She wondered if Violet, too, was finding her way back to Ashcliffe – or perhaps, simply trying to escape it.

As evening approached, they moved the celebration to The Chiron Café, which had been transformed into a cosy haven for the occasion. Fairy lights twinkled amongst the bookshelves, casting a warm glow on the mismatched furniture and creating an inviting atmosphere. Llew and Krissy were bustling around, putting the final touches on the meal – a simple sourdough loaf, still warm from the oven, sat alongside a selection of local produce. The guests arrived in a steady stream: Albert, ever-reliable with his quiet observations; Eloise, radiating a gentle wisdom; Stella, her voice laced with both joy and a hint of melancholy; Rita, sharp as ever, scrutinizing everyone's food choices;

Tom, offering a silent nod of approval; Eve, heavily expectant; and finally, Geraint and Llewelyn. "It's brilliant, you two," Geraint said, settling into an armchair. "Thank you for hosting."

"Don't mention it," Llewelyn replied, already pouring wine. "Just glad to see everyone."

The conversation flowed easily from there – a warm, comfortable exchange of stories and reminiscences. Snippets of their early days in Ashcliffe were woven into the chatter: memories of a particularly fierce storm that had blown out all the street lights, the time they'd gotten hopelessly lost on the cliffs, and the hilarious mishaps that had cemented their friendship. "Remember when we tried to build that boat?" Albert chuckled, recalling a particularly disastrous attempt involving a leaky hull and a very grumpy fisherman. "We swore we'd conquer the sea – didn't get very far." "And then there was the time you convinced everyone that seals were nesting in the harbour," Stella added, laughing.

"You," Rita observed dryly, taking a sip of wine, "always with the stories. You've got a lifetime of them crammed into that head of yours."

"And you've got a lifetime of pointed observations," Llewelyn retorted, grinning. "It's what makes you, you."

A touch of melancholy hung in the air – a subtle acknowledgement that "before the baby" was a special time that wouldn't last forever. "It feels like just yesterday we were all causing chaos," Eloise said softly, gazing around at the group. "Now look at us."

"Time flies when you're having fun... or surviving," Geraint added with a wry smile.

"And now," Rita observed, her eyes twinkling, "we've got a tiny human almost here ready for us all to worry about. Love does that to you, doesn't it? Makes you realize how fleeting everything is." The conversation shifted as they reminisced about their individual lives – Llew's past with Violet, Krissy's nomadic journey through flats and houses, and the quiet contentment of their shared life in Ashcliffe.

"You know," Tom said quietly, breaking the silence, "Ashcliffe doesn't change you, it just shows you who you already are."

As the evening drew to a close, with plates cleared and glasses emptied, a sense of warmth and connection filled the room. It felt like a perfect, slightly chaotic family meal – a testament to the bonds forged over shared laughter, tears, and small dramas. Krissy caught Llew's eye across the table—a silent exchange of affection and reassurance. He squeezed her hand, his gaze filled with warmth. For now, surrounded by the people she loved in this little corner of the world, Krissy felt like she'd finally found home. It wasn't always easy, but it was hers.

A few months drifted by, marked by the quiet rhythm of daily life in Ashcliffe. The rain had long since ceased, replaced by a golden warmth that seemed to seep into everything—the sandstone cottages, the sea, and the hearts of its inhabitants. Llew found himself brewing coffee at The Chiron Café with a comfortable regularity, the familiar scent of roasted beans mingling with the aroma of Earl Grey and toast. He was going through the morning's post, sorting through the usual mix of bills, local newsletters, and postcards from afar, when his eye caught something tucked amongst the pile – a simple, cream-coloured postcard depicting a windswept coastline. He turned it over, revealing a single message written in Violet's elegant script: "I get it now." Llew smiled – a quiet, knowing smile that held a hint of both relief and understanding. It was a small thing, a fleeting moment, but it felt like a significant marker – a confirmation that Violet had finally come to terms with her past and perhaps, even found a measure of peace. He stared out the window at Ashcliffe, watching as Mrs. Prior wheeled out her famous jam tarts for the morning rush. The town was bustling with its usual charm – children laughing on their way to school, fishermen mending their nets by the harbour, and the gentle murmur of conversation drifting through the breeze.

The postcard felt like a small, tangible piece of the puzzle – a reminder that even after all the storms and silences, some connections endure. It suggested she'd not only seen him – but truly seen him –

and that her sudden departure hadn't been as simple or selfish as he'd once believed. He tucked the postcard into his pocket, a subtle weight of comfort against his thigh. He took a sip of the coffee he was brewing, the warmth spreading through him – a feeling that perhaps he'd finally found a place for himself in this little corner of the world, alongside the people he loved – and with a touch of Violet's memory to keep him grounded.

Time in Ashcliffe flowed with a gentle rhythm, a comfortable blend of familiar routines and unexpected delights. The days unfolded like the tide, marked by small shifts and quiet observations. Krissy found herself increasingly drawn to her new studio/gallery, nestled next door to the Archive. Sunlight streamed through the large windows, illuminating dust motes dancing in the air and bathing her latest sketches in a warm glow. She'd spend hours lost in her work, capturing the essence of Ashcliffe on canvas – the moody skies, the windswept cliffs, the faces of its inhabitants. The scent of oil paints mingled with the salty tang of the sea breeze that drifted in through the open door, creating a uniquely Ashcliffian atmosphere. Lately, she'd been working on a series of portraits. Depictions of the town's regulars – Mrs. Prior with her jars of jam, Mr. Jones grumbling about the paper, and, of course, Llew, his face etched with quiet contemplation. She caught glimpses of him often – reading by the fireplace in the evenings, a cup of tea steaming beside him, lost in the pages of a book.

At night, Krissy and Llew often dropped in to Eve and Geraint's cottage. It was filled with the soft glow of fairy lights and the comforting sounds of family life. Eve and Geraint were utterly devoted to their newborn son, Rhys – a tiny bundle of joy who spent his days cooing and gurgling. They could be found in the kitchen, cooing over him, joyful and sleepy, with a warmth that radiated throughout the cottage. One evening, Krissy found herself in The Chiron Cafe with Llew after he'd locked up. "Just keeping busy," he said, offering her a smile. "Trying to keep up with all this newness."

"It suits you," Krissy replied, leaning against the counter. "You always did like a good routine."

"He's growing fast," Llewelyn said suddenly, gesturing to his head with a smile. "Feels like just yesterday he was fitting in my pocket."

"And you're handling it remarkably well," Krissy observed, returning his gaze. He chuckled. Later, as she turned to leave, he added quietly, "Thank you for visiting."

Krissy smiled a genuine, heartfelt smile that reached her eyes. "Anytime," she said.

The sounds of Ashcliffe continued to weave their way into the fabric of her days – the rhythmic crash of waves against the harbour wall, the gentle patter of rain on the rooftops, the warmth of shared smiles. The regulars at The Chiron Café were always there to chat, laugh, and offer up a slice of gossip. Krissy was sitting by the window in her gallery, sketching with a focused intensity – the late afternoon light casting a warm glow on her face. It was one of those perfect Ashcliffe moments that was quiet, peaceful, and utterly beautiful. She was capturing the scene before her: Llew, sitting beside her, his arm casually draped around her shoulders. He'd approached quietly, as he often did, without saying a word – simply taking up space beside her, radiating a comfortable warmth. He looked at her for a moment and then said simply: "You're still my storm."

Krissy smiled – a quiet, knowing smile that held all the unspoken emotions of their shared journey.

"And you're my lighthouse," she replied, leaning slightly closer to him. A confirmation that despite their different paths and pasts, they had found something enduring in each other – a balance between chaos and calm, between intensity and peace.

He squeezed her hand gently, offering a reassuring smile. And for a moment, Krissy felt like all the questions and all the doubts simply melted away, replaced by a profound sense of belonging. The rain had long since stopped, and the sea glimmered under a cloudless sky. A fishing boat bobbed gently in the harbour, while children chased seagulls along the shore. The sounds of Ashcliffe filled the air: the clatter of cups at The Chron Café, the distant bark of dogs, the gentle hum of conversation. It was a scene of quiet contentment and enduring love, a testament to the small moments that make up a life well-lived. Life pulsed on in Ashcliffe – steady, reliable, and full of promise. A place where storms might come and go, but the light always found a way to shine through. And as Krissy looked out, she knew – with a simple certainty – that she was exactly where she belonged.

9 781068 293627